The Silver Stiletto

The Silver Stiletto

Roger S Nelson

The Silver Stiletto

iUniverse books may be ordered through booksellers or by contacting:

iUniverse
1663 Liberty Drive
Bloomington, IN 47403
www.iuniverse.com
1-800-Authors (1-800-288-4677)

ISBN: 978-1-4917-6011-6 (sc)
ISBN: 978-1-4917-6012-3 (e)

Library of Congress Control Number: 2015901763

Print information available on the last page.

iUniverse rev. date: 03/13/2015

Contents

Preface

I first wrote this story in 1996 after taking a bicycle trip on a route virtually identical to the one described in the story. Everything that happens to Jim happened to me—the weather, the problems, the flora and fauna, and the roads and places visited. From a biking/camping viewpoint, I am Jim, and every time I read this story, I relive my experience. However, I am not Jim. He and all the major characters are fictional.

Jim's route can be reconstructed from the story if one is so inclined. Like Jim, I did manage to spend a little less than two hundred dollars for the trip, mostly just for food, but I doubt I could do that today. Things have changed since then. Many people didn't have cell phones, and for those who did, the coverage in rural areas was nonexistent. Smartphones hadn't been invented yet, and GPS wasn't available. Gasoline was less than a dollar a gallon.

I am an avid bicycle rider, and in my heyday, I often rode five thousand miles a year or more. I trained hard and eventually, in 1994, qualified to ride in the Race Across America, although I never did it. Today, I ride only about two thousand miles a year. In 1996, when I wrote this story, I was burned out and hadn't ridden any miles at all until the day I took this trip. Trying something new—that is, self-supported touring—kept me in the sport.

1

The Impossible Dream

Jim put down his book. "That's it! I know what I gotta do," he said as he rammed his right fist into the palm of his left hand. He picked his book up and continued reading about King Arthur. His heart stirred as he imagined himself riding alongside the king. His horse reared, and he fell off while a warrior charged him with a sword. He barely had time to get his shield up before it came crashing down on him. He rolled over, sprang to his feet, and fought back. There were only two kinds of fighters on this field, the quick and the dead.

Jim turned the page in the book he was reading and stretched his lanky frame in his hammock, which he'd strung in the shade of two tall maple trees in his yard. Firecrackers left over from the Fourth of July occasionally banged and echoed in the neighborhood. At every bang, his little white dog, Booty, huddled under the hammock closer to him. The noise didn't seem to bother Duffy, Jim's black Scottie, who lay out in the sun chewing a rawhide bone. The temperature was just right for cutoff jeans, a T-shirt, and bare feet. An occasional bee droned by, but there had been a dry spell so that the nasty bugs, especially the mosquitoes, were not bothering anyone this time of day. This was Michigan's summer weather at its best.

While Jim's eyes darted from line to line, he was oblivious to the smell of fresh-cut grass and the noise of his neighbor's lawn mower. He didn't notice when the mower stopped, nor did he hear the leaves rustling in the treetops or the squirrel that chattered and hopped from limb to limb. A siren whining as an ambulance headed for nearby Sparrow Hospital went unheard as did the penetrating sound of a train as it blew its whistle and rumbled down one of the many rails in Lansing. All Jim heard were hoofs beating on the moor, swords banging against shields, and men yelling as he and King Arthur fought off Saxon invaders.

Jim didn't notice when his neighbor, Dave Campbell, stopped mowing, picked up a handful of grass clippings, and crept up behind the hammock. Dave was a big man, originally from Texas, and was wearing his cowboy hats and boots, as usual. Duffy and Booty came up to Dave, wagging their tails. Jim was so engrossed in his book that he didn't even notice Dave coming up behind him and when Dave dumped the clipping on Jim's book, he was so startled he almost fell out of the hammock. Dave stood there grinning.

Jim sat up. "Oh, Dave!" He took a deep breath. "You got me that time!" he said, chuckling. "What's up?"

"I'm fixing to build a porch swing. What gives with you?"

"I'm reading about King Arthur. I was just thinking of the adventure Arthur had. His ideals about law and order rocked England. In fact, they spread through Europe and even to America later."

"Well, I was thinking about rocking my cares away here in America."

"King Arthur traveled all over England sitting on a horse's back."

"I'll sit on my swing and think of England," Dave said.

Jim had a faraway look in his eyes. "This author portrays King Arthur as a good singer. He could have been a bard."

Dave could see Jim wasn't paying any attention, but he continued the bantering. "I could sit on my swing and sing, but if anyone heard me, I'd be barred."

"King Arthur would swing his sword to establish justice and peace in England."

"A good porch swing will help establish peace and harmony in the soul."

"Think of it, Dave; he searched for the Holy Grail, and he almost found it."

"I've been searching for the right design for this swing, and I think I've found it."

"He slept in the woods at night."

"I lay awake last night wondering what kind of wood I should use—walnut, maple, ash, or oak?"

"He fought with evil knights."

"If I don't screen in my porch, I'll have to fight off evil mosquitoes at night."

"He lived close to the sounds of nature."

"Some swings I've seen squeak a lot. But mine won't. It has a sound design that will be quiet by nature."

"King Arthur had a purpose in life. I need a purpose, Dave."

"Jim, hold on."

"My job is so dull … I'm not really needed there, you know."

"Jim."

"I've no one to care for. It's lonely since Linda left."

"*Jim*," Dave scolded. "Have you been listening to me?"

"Sure, Dave, what you need is a porch swing."

"What?"

"I'm going to give you this book on King Arthur when I'm done with it. Then you can sit on your swing and read it." Jim held the book up. "See? It's good."

"A book?"

"Yeah, it'll inspire you. It inspired me. I want you to read it."

"Inspire me?"

"Well, this book got me thinking. Reading about King Arthur traveling all over England and all the different things that happened to him, well, I want some adventure, too."

"What are you talking about?"

"Adventure. This book has inspired me go on an adventure."

"It did? Where to? What?"

"Here. In Michigan. We live in a vacationer's paradise in the summer. Good roads. Good weather. Lots of beaches. People come from all over the country to vacation in Michigan. Why should I go somewhere else?"

"Any particular place in Michigan?"

"Ironwood. It's about as far away from here as you can get in Michigan."

"Ironwood?"

"It's in the western UP," Jim said, using the local term for the Upper Peninsula of Michigan. "Near Wisconsin."

"Sounds expensive. What did you do, win the lottery?"

"I have plenty of money for a little trip. I'm only going to spend two hundred or even less for the whole two-week trip."

"Really?" Dave sounded doubtful. "What are you going to do, sleep in your car every night? It doesn't sound like much of a vacation to me. How far is Ironwood, anyway?"

"The state map lists it as 535 miles from Lansing, but I'll be taking some back roads and maybe even making some side trips. I'm guessing around twelve hundred miles, round-trip."

"And you think you can go that far and stay that long for only two hundred dollars?" Dave asked.

"Sure. We can both have a vacation. Well, you retirees are on vacation all the time. Maybe you should try a little work! I know. While you're building your swing, keep your eye on my lawn for me. Cut it if it gets too long, though with this dry spell, I don't see it growing much. I'll pay you when I get back. You can use my hammock until your swing is built. Read about King Arthur. He might inspire you, too. In the meantime, I'll have my own little adventure."

"A two-week trip, for two hundred dollars?" Dave sounded doubtful.

"Yup."

"Impossible! You're dreaming!"

"No, I'm serious."

"And you're not sleeping in your car?"

"Of course not!"

"So you're going to cook your own meals?"

"No way! I don't cook. Maybe King Arthur killed game for food on his trips and cooked it over campfires, or maybe he carried enough food on his horse to get him from place to place. It doesn't matter. I'm eating out. That's what the two hundred is for."

"Really! You think you can go on a two-week vacation for two hundred dollars or less—all the way to Ironwood—and eat out the whole time? Gas has gone up to over a dollar a gallon now. Hmm."

Dave did some calculations in his head. "If you get thirty miles per gallon, you're going to spend about forty dollars just for gas. That leaves, what? A little over ten dollars a day for food and lodging. You can't get a room in a motel for that. You must be camping. You're going to come back even skinnier than you are now. I bet you can't do it."

"A bet? All right, if I spend less than two hundred dollars, you mow my lawn, watch my house, and take care of my dogs for *free* while I'm gone."

"And if I win?"

"Then I'll mow your lawn for free for the rest of the summer. At least once a week through September."

"And you won't stay with friends?"

"Nope. I don't know anyone in the UP. Besides, I'm going up there to be by myself, to get away from it all. Even if I did know someone up there, I wouldn't stay with them. I want to be alone for a while."

"How will I know you're in Ironwood?"

"If you want, I'll call you collect when I get there. Then you can check your phone bill. Or you could just take my word for it. This is just a friendly bet, isn't it?" Jim laughed.

"Well, yes, I'll take your word for it. How will I know you spent two hundred or less?"

"I'll start out with two hundred cash. Whatever I come back with is how much I didn't spend. If I have to use a credit card or withdraw money during the trip, I lose the bet."

"And how will I know you didn't use your money card."

"I'll give you my word. You did agree this is a friendly bet? We can trust one another, can't we?"

"Sure. So when are you leaving?"

"The last Saturday in July, the twenty-seventh."

"All right. Let's get this straight. You're going on a two-week vacation. That's fourteen days and fourteen nights, for only two hundred dollars. And you're eating out every day, buying all your own food, not getting handouts from friends or relatives. And you're camping all fourteen nights, not staying with friends. Is that right? You're covering all your own expenses?"

"Yeah, what's so hard about that? I'm going to have a great time without spending a lot," Jim said.

"I still don't think you can do it."

"So have we got a bet?" Jim asked.

"I believe we do," Dave said, extending his hand. "Shake?"

Jim stood up and grasped Dave's hand. The bet was made.

"You know, Jim, when I go on vacation, I figure it costs almost a hundred dollars per day. And you're going to do this for a hundred per week. I just don't see how you can do it," Dave said, shaking his head. "This is like an impossible dream. You're not King Arthur. You're Don Quixote, the man from La Mancha. You're imagining things."

"Well, Dave, there are two things in life you need to know to be successful."

"Yeah? And what are they?"

"The first one is 'Don't tell people everything you know.'"

"Okay. What's the second one?"

"See ya." Jim turned and walked into the house, chuckling to himself.

2
I Can't Stop Loving You

The next day, a Sunday afternoon, Jim put his sander down and took off his safety glasses. He needed a break and saw Dave get home from church, so he went next door to see him. Maybe they'd play a game of chess. Dave's house was similar to his own, two stories, wood frame, and clapboard, high ceilings, rich woodwork inside, and a fireplace in the living room. Dave, a retired oil man, lived in his house by himself since his wife died from cancer five years ago. He didn't have any children, and being lonely, became friends with Jim. Woodworking was his hobby, his house was restored and beautiful inside, but Jim was new in his house, and it needed tons of work. Dave's house was a dark blue with light-yellow shutters, University of Michigan colors. Jim's house was white with green shutters, Michigan State University colors. There was a friendly rivalry between the two.

Dave was wearing his usual white hat, blue jeans, and cowboy boots when he let Jim in. Jim was wearing a Detroit Tigers ball cap and running shoes. They both had on green, short-sleeve, cotton shirts.

"I see you got the memo," Jim said.

"What memo?"

"The one that said to wear your green shirt if you're a Michigan State fan. Are you finally converting? Coming to your senses?" Jim teased.

"I didn't see that memo. I got up early this morning and dressed in the dark. I thought I was putting on my University of Michigan shirt. Can't tell green from blue in the dark. I didn't even know I had a green shirt. I'll make sure this one goes in the rag bin."

"And here I imagined your tastes were improving. How's your chess game? Is that improving?"

"I hope so!" Dave laughed. "Let's play a game of chess. I have a new strategy I want to try on you. If I lose, I'll blame it on this shirt!"

They set up a board on Dave's kitchen table and played a couple of games. After half an hour, they each won a game in rapid play.

"You know what?" Dave said. "We play too fast. I don't really have time to think out my moves the way I'd like to. Let's play another game where we each make one move a day."

Jim frowned. "A move a day? It'll take forever! You think that's going to help you beat me?"

"Well, maybe. I'm serious, Jim. Would you do it for me? There are postal tournaments that take months to play. However, we don't have to take that long. I'll tell you what. You make a move on Monday, Wednesday, and Friday. I'll make a move on Tuesday, Thursday, and Saturday. We'll have Sunday off. We could have a game well started by the time you leave for vacation. We can finish it when you get back."

"All right, Dave." Jim rolled his eyes. "I'll do it for you. Except, we take a break from the game while I'm gone for two weeks. We can continue when I get back."

"Okay."

"Today is Sunday, the eighth, so we start tomorrow. Since it's Monday, it'll be my turn to move, and since it's the first move of the game, that makes me white. But I already know my move. Pawn to king four. I always do that. So what's the point? Do you want me to get out some chess books and study up so that I might be tempted to move pawn to queen four?"

"The point is, by taking time, you can look up moves in books or consult with friends and get help. You learn that way. Since both of us are allowed to do this, it's still a fair game."

"But that's only three moves a week. We'll only have finished nine moves when I go on my trip, just barely into the game. It'll take months to finish the game."

"True, but it's still faster than postal chess. At least we won't have to wait for the postal service to deliver the next move. Besides, you'll have something to look forward to when you get back from losing your bet."

"Well, I don't really want to spend all my time studying a chess game. If you're going to study that hard, I'll probably lose. I just like to relax and have fun. I'm not that serious about the game."

"Let's just try it for one game. Maybe you'll change your mind. Besides, we can still play speed chess. Or I could invite a couple of friends over and we can play double chess. Ever do that?"

"No. What's double chess?"

"It's partners. You and your partner take opposite colors and sit on separate boards. When your partner takes one of his opponent's pieces, which is the same color as your men, and sets it on the table, instead of making a normal move, you can pick up a captured piece and put it on your board anywhere you want. Of course, you play the game on the clock, like speed chess. It's exciting and can get kind of loud at times—not like your serious tournament game."

"On the clock?"

"Yes. In speed chess (and in tournament chess, for that matter), there is a double-faced clock. The minute hand is set five minutes before the twelve on each side. White makes a move and then presses his button, which starts black's clock. When black moves, he presses his button, which starts white's clock, and so forth. As the minute hand moves toward the twelve, it raises a little flag. When the minute hand reaches the twelve, the flag drops. Game over. Whosever flag drops first loses. It keeps the game moving. Of course, the game can end sooner if one of you checkmates. They use a clock in tournament chess, too, but instead of five minutes, they usually get two hours to make forty moves."

"I think I like the five-minute game better," Jim said. "I can just see myself playing one of those tournament games, which would take all evening and then some. I'd probably lose for my effort and all I'd get out of it would be a headache. What a time waster."

"Would you like to try some speed chess now?"

"Not with a clock. I'll play a fast game or two, but then I have to get back to work on my house. I've been stripping and sanding some woodwork."

They set up the board. Jim chose white, and he made his usual pawn-to-king-four move.

"Have you heard from Linda at all, Jim?"

Jim didn't know it, but Dave's *new* strategy in chess was to distract his opponent.

"No, I haven't." Jim thought about Linda Fenton—tall, five-foot ten inches, with lovely shoulder-length dark tresses with a little curl in them. She was thin, maybe not quite skinny enough to be a model, but curvy, and she always dressed nicely, usually in hose and heels (two or three inches), usually pumps, so she looked rather tall, sort of intimidating to some men. Once he got used to it, Jim liked her height, even though in her heels, she was taller than his own six feet. Linda made her face up perfectly, her dark eyes captivating. Since Linda worked at a cosmetics counter in the J. C. Penney store at the Meridian Mall, she had access to all the cosmetics she needed, and she knew how to use them. She was right there for all the good clothes sales and used her employee discount. Like a lot of women, she enjoyed being pretty, and she was more than just adept at it; she had a natural talent for it. It wasn't just her makeup; it was how she dressed, her poise and grace, and how she moved. She was like a princess. Had she gone to charm school? She looked like an angel even when dressed in jeans and tennies. She could probably even wear jeans and tennies to a high school prom and fit right in.

"Checkmate," Dave said.

Jim came back to reality. He'd been playing the game but his mind was on Linda.

"Huh? Darn it, Dave. How'd you do that?"

"Keep your mind on the game, Jim, if you want to win."

"I guess I better go on home. I can't concentrate tonight. Besides, I need to get started on that woodwork."

"It's Linda, isn't it?"

"You should know. I'll see you later."

Jim walked back to his house, slowly, sadly, thinking of Linda. Why did Linda leave? He didn't think it was another man. He remembered the night in February when she walked out on him. She had seemed upset about something from the moment she walked in the door, white hose, red pumps, red dress, face made up like an angel. Those dark eyes were captivating, hypnotizing. He had been painting, and the house smelled like latex. He had light-blue smudges on his clothes, and the drop cloth was over the hardwood floor in the small bedroom. There was no furniture in the room, and it echoed when she asked what he thought he was doing.

"I wanted wallpaper in this room," she said. "Didn't we discuss this at Home Depot? I thought we were going to get the light-lavender paper with the lilacs on it."

They'd been having more and more arguments about the house, which colors and styles to use. The thing was Jim didn't care about the colors and styles. He was doing it for her, what she wanted, and then after he put it up, it seemed like she changed her mind. Was she doing this to him on purpose? If so, why? When had they ever talked about the lavender paper with the lilacs?

He remembered her slim, sexy legs turning on those red heels and stalking out, the door slamming behind her. He cried out to stop her, but she wouldn't listen; she just kept walking. He tried to phone her, but she wouldn't answer her phone or return his messages. She wouldn't answer or open her door for him at her house. He tried to visit her at work, but she wouldn't talk to him. She even threatened to call store security on him. What could he do? He wasn't a stalker. He respected her. He loved her. She shut him out. He remembered the saying, "If you find something you love, let it go. If it returns, it's yours. If it doesn't return, it never was." He let her go. He had to. She hadn't returned.

For the next three weeks, Jim went over to Dave's house each evening, and they made their moves. On Friday, July 26, Jim went over and made his ninth move in the game. They were just starting the middle of the game now, and it looked fairly equal. "This game is boring, Dave. It's just a standard opening that we could've made in less than ten seconds of speed chess, and it's taken us three weeks to get here. Not only that, one of us is going to have to blunder for the other to win. The game is too equal."

"You always say that. And then you do something really stupid, like giving up your queen … trying to parley it into a win."

"I got an idea for you, Dave; why don't you try a king sacrifice? See if that works." Jim grinned.

"That's what I like about you, Jim. You may not play a good game, but you sure talk a good game." Dave chuckled.

"Yeah, well, I play good, too. I always say, 'Good playing beats good talking every time.'"

"So how come you're one of the best talkers?"

"Who? Me?"

"Yeah. Whenever you're moaning and groaning the loudest, I know I better watch out. You're up to something. Trouble is—even when I know you're up to something, I still don't see it. You just can't trust a chess player."

"I know. I learned that from you."

Jim and Dave often bantered, and it was as much fun as actually playing the game. In fact, for them, it was part of the game. If one were keeping score, one would see that Jim and Dave were about equal players, and they didn't play it quietly.

"Tomorrow, you leave on your vacation. Are you ready?" Dave asked.

"Not yet. Come over to my house for a while. I can use your help or at least your company."

They walked next door to Jim's house, and in the breezeway between the house and the garage, there was a red Schwinn bicycle. When Jim bought the house, there was no breezeway, so he had added it and made it wide enough so that he could store his bikes in it and also use it for a workshop. The garage had two bays for cars, but one hadn't been used yet, since Linda never moved in with him. The other bay held his black Escort. Jim kept the garage clean and neat. "Hold the bike for me while I put this rack on it," Jim said.

"Taking the old bike on your vacation? I don't see a bike rack on your car. Where is it? I'll help you put it on your car," Dave said.

"Who said anything about taking a car?"

"Let me guess. You're going to ride your bicycle?" Dave said, joking.

"Yup." Jim wasn't joking.

Dave blinked. He pushed his white hat up and scratched his head. When he realized Jim was serious, he let out a low whistle. "Come on, Jim. I haven't seen you on a bike all summer. In fact, I didn't even know you had a bike until tonight. Twelve hundred miles? Are you sure you're ready for this?"

"I've done a whole lot of biking in the past, and I really do know what I'm doing. It's true; I haven't ridden this year with moving into a new house and all. However, I think I can make up for a lack of training because of my experience. Experience really does count for a lot, you know." *Dave might be right,* Jim thought, but he wasn't going to admit it.

"That's an awful long way. You'd have to average almost a hundred miles a day. If the weather's bad or you get strong headwinds, it could be quite a challenge. And you're only spending two hundred dollars? I still don't see how you can manage."

Jim got a dreamy look in his eyes. "That's the whole point of this trip. I want a challenge. In fact, I need a challenge. But I am going to make it. Think about it. This is 1996. Michigan is celebrating the one-hundredth anniversary of the automobile this year. Only one hundred years ago, there were few paved roads and no interstates. There were no cars. Everyone went on foot or by horse. That's the way King Arthur won England. That's the way George Washington fought the British. Even our own Civil War was fought on horseback and foot. Along comes Henry Ford, and the whole world changes. Now the only exercise we get is pushing harder on the accelerator. Our only challenge in life is to go faster than the speed limit without getting caught. King Arthur rode a horse, but I don't have a horse, so I'm using my bike. My England is Michigan. And I'm not just going on a vacation. A vacation is going to the beach and sitting around doing nothing. I'm going on an adventure. If there was no challenge, no risk, there wouldn't be any adventure."

"But aren't you worried about getting hit by a car?"

"Not really. I'll ride sensibly and carefully, so there should be no problem. Automobile drivers have a very good reason not to hit you; it messes up their grill and screws up their day. And a person can't stop living just because something might happen. I'm taking the back roads in the LP," Jim said, using the local term for Lower Peninsula, "so there shouldn't be too much traffic. In the UP, I'll be taking US 2, which has a nice wide shoulder to ride on. It's part of the adventure. King Arthur had evil knights. I dodge traffic. King Arthur ate in inns or taverns along the way or hunted and cooked out. I'll have to dodge mosquitoes and maybe a few cars and eat in restaurants or get sandwiches from little stores along the way. I think I've got it pretty easy compared to him."

"So you're doing this to fulfill some sort of fantasy about King Arthur. Is that it?"

"Sort of. Or a fantasy about crossing to the old west in a wagon train. Or maybe even about crossing the galaxy in a starship. It's about going new places and facing problems on your own, taking charge. It's about adventure. It's about doing something rather than sitting around hoping nothing bad happens to you. It's about living, not just existing."

As Jim continued working on his bike, Dave held the bike steady. After the rack was attached, Jim took a bicycle generator, bolted it to the back of his bicycle, and adjusted it. Then he bolted a light to the front of his bike and ran a wire to the generator. "I used to use batteries for the light," Jim said, "but they don't last long. Besides, once when I was hooking one up, I accidentally got the wires reversed and everything went black."

"Went black?"

"I know you're not an electrician, but think about it. When you get the wires hooked up right, the light comes on and you can see. Right? So what do you think happens if you got the wires reversed? It sucks all the light right out of the area. You can't see a thing. The really wild thing is that after the battery sucks up enough light and can't hold it anymore, it explodes, like a little hand grenade. You've heard of batteries exploding before, haven't you? It's really dangerous to use batteries. That's why I use a generator now."

"Oooookay."

"Generators are a lot safer. If you do reverse the wires, you can still pedal backward and get light. At least you can see where you've been that way."

"I think I better go home and get my hip boots. It's getting a little deep around here." Dave couldn't help smiling.

"No, wait. I'll be done in a few minutes."

Jim fastened a red blinking light to the rack on the back of the bike.

"You're not really thinking about riding after dark, Jim?" Dave sounded worried.

"Depends on the weather, Dave. If it's real hot during the day, I might ride at night some when it's cooler. Or if it rains a lot during the day, I may ride more at night to catch up on lost mileage. You can never tell about Michigan weather. If there's a full moon and the weather is nice, I may just ride at night for the fun of it. Between three and five in the morning, there is hardly any traffic. It's so quiet and peaceful. In the past, I've done some of my best riding at night. But … well … actually, no, I probably won't ride at night. I just want to be prepared in case I can't find a place to camp before dark."

Then Jim fastened some bags, called panniers, to the sides of the bike's rack. Finally, he was satisfied that the bike was set up properly. He got out the tire pump and put 110 pounds per square inch in the tires. Jim told Dave, "The tires are supposed to have a hundred psi in them, but I always put in extra. If I hit a stone, there is less chance of getting a flat from a pinch-out. Besides, they lose some pressure during the trip. And now that the lights are set up, the tires are pumped up, and everything else is adjusted, I'm ready to start loading my gear. Obviously, I'm traveling light."

"So what are you taking?"

"I don't have enough room to take along any food. But I'll take a couple of spare tires; tubes; a patch kit; a few tools; a little flashlight; an insulated sleeping pad since the ground is cold in Michigan, even in the middle of summer; a small tent in case it rains, and some mosquito netting in case I want to sleep in the open. It may get down to forty degrees at night, or maybe even down to thirty in the UP, you never can tell, so I'll take a wool blanket. A couple of changes of clothes and my personal stuff, you know, a toothbrush and that sort of thing. I don't think I'll need my razor. It will be nice to go for a couple of weeks without shaving. And a map." When he was done, both panniers were full. He used bungee cords to strap the blanket, tent, and ground pad on the top. The bike looked really loaded.

Jim stepped back and thought for a moment. "Come in the house with me for a minute, Dave. I want to clean out my refrigerator so I don't have any spoiled food when I get back."

They went into the house and into the kitchen. "Nice job in the kitchen, Jim. You've been busy."

"Thanks. It was a hassle. Linda wanted it blue, but then she wanted it green, and she kept changing the cabinets she wanted. Finally, after she left me, I just picked out these oak cabinets, since they were on sale, and painted the kitchen this bright yellow. It reminds me of sunshine. A kitchen should be a warm, happy place, and the yellow seems to do that for me. It's really the only room in the house that I'm finished remodeling. It's also the most expensive and hardest room to remodel. I guess I saved the easy stuff for last." Jim opened the fridge, took out a half-full quart of milk, and gave it to Dave. Then he took out a hot dog and a bun and put them in a baggie. He gave the rest of the hot dogs and buns to Dave. "I'll have the hot dog for breakfast. It only takes a minute to nuke it in the microwave, and I'm not much for cooking. I usually eat out. Sometimes I wish I had someone to cook for me. I don't think there's anything else in here that will spoil while I'm gone. My fridge is usually pretty empty."

Jim went to a large desk in the living room and took out some keys. Dave noted that the living and dining room had bare hardwood floors that were in various stages of deconstruction. The living room had a nice fireplace, and there was a sofa and coffee table in front of it. The dining room didn't have any furniture. Jim gave a key to Dave. "This key is for the house. Keep it locked up. Bring the mail in the house and set it on the table in the kitchen. I've stopped the newspaper for two weeks, but if one comes anyway, bring it in with the mail. Here's where I keep the dog food. Make sure Booty and Duffy have enough food and water. The weather is nice this time of year so you can leave them out most of the time. I put the lights on timers so it will look like I'm home. I don't really expect any trouble, but I do appreciate you keeping an eye on things for me."

"So you're really going through with this then?" Dave said, shaking his head. "What if your bike breaks down? What if you find out you can't ride fast enough to make the trip in two weeks?"

"Dave," Jim interrupted, "there are hundreds of what-ifs. I've already asked myself, 'What is the worst that can happen to me?' I take longer than two weeks? I don't make it? It costs more than two hundred? I lose the bet? I suppose the worst that could happen is an accident. But that could happen even if I stayed home. There's no adventure if I stay home worrying about something that might happen. Besides, I've thought this out thoroughly, and I'm prepared for anything. I'm sure I can do it. Don't worry about me; I'm an adult. I'm almost thirty years old. I might lose the bet, but I can certainly take care of myself. So don't try to talk me out of it now. If I have any serious problems or a change in my schedule, I'll call."

"Suppose something serious goes wrong with your bike. Suppose your fork breaks or a wheel comes off. Are you going to ride on one wheel? I can just see you doing a wheelie across the state. Ha."

"I didn't think of that, but it sounds like fun," Jim said and laughed. "Actually, I have a phone number for a bicycle company to call if I need to order parts. I'll just have the parts and tools, if I need them, shipped overnight to general delivery in whatever town I'm in. Or if the town has a bike shop, I can have them fix it. If I'm in the boonies, I might have to hitchhike or walk to a town."

"Will the post office do that?"

"I've heard of other people doing it, so I think so, but I probably won't get to find out. If something expensive breaks on my bike, I'll probably lose the bet. But it's not likely that I'll have any problems other than a flat tire. I take good care of my bike."

"But what if you have a really serious problem? For example, a gorgeous chick asks you out to dinner. Are you going to turn her down? If you don't, you lose the bet, you know." Dave chuckled.

Jim sighed. He was used to Dave hinting around about getting a girlfriend. He broke out laughing, "Me? Oh sure! I turn down gorgeous chicks all the time. Movie stars. Models. Sometimes several in the same day. After all, I'm the confirmed bachelor, right?" Jim hid his pain well. He knew Dave was just teasing him, even if it did hurt.

Jim had been engaged when he moved next door last November. The Christmas season had been good, but shortly after New Year's, the pointless arguments had started. It was in February, right after Valentine's Day, that Linda had left him, and although Jim put on a good front, he was bitter. Bitter and hurt. He really didn't want to have anything to do with women, although he enjoyed watching them, looking at them. Part of the reason for this trip was to recover from the breakup, to move on with his life. And yet he had mixed feelings about the breakup. Part of him felt relief, since they had argued over the silliest things. He really had loved Linda, but it had become harder and harder to keep the relationship going until it had finally failed. He remembered the arguments. *Marriage is not easy,* he thought. *There would always be disagreements. But it shouldn't be so hard to love someone. It just shouldn't be so hard. The one you marry should be easy to love. Maybe it could even be love at first sight—or at least seem that way. I'm certainly not going to get into another relationship. At least not right away. Especially with old wounds to heal. Will I ever trust a woman again?*

"Can't you find someone to go with you?" Dave asked, interrupting his thoughts. "It would be a lot safer if there were someone with you."

"Not this late in the game. It would be nice to ride with someone, but not many people want to rough it like I do or go as fast and as far as I do—or can get two weeks off work. Besides, I really do want to be by myself this time. I need to be alone for a while."

"Okay, hermit. You win. Enjoy yourself in the UP. This is the right time of year, and the people who live up there are sure it's *God's country.* I guess that's because it's so beautiful. Have a good time, and don't worry about things here; I'll take care of them." But Dave was obviously still worried about him; there were so many things that could go wrong.

"Well, I guess that's about it, Dave. Looks like I'm ready. I better turn in; I'm planning on getting an early start tomorrow."

Dave thought a moment. "By the way, Jim, what towns are you going through?"

Jim got out a Michigan map. "Here's the route to the bridge." A red line drawn on the map showed Jim's route from Lansing to Mackinaw City. "I go through a lot of small towns—Shepherdsville, Bannister, Sickles, Gordonville, Sanford, Edenville, St. Helen, Lewiston, Atlanta, Onaway, Cheboygan, and Mackinaw City. I'll probably be in Cheboygan by Monday. Tuesday at the latest. The rest of the towns are all on US 2. I've used this route before, and it's a good one. The US 2 part will be new, but I don't expect any problems."

"Well, good luck, Jim."

After Dave left, it was deathly silent in the house, and Jim felt lonely, but he was so used to it, he barely noticed. He turned the radio on to break the silence. A country station was playing heartbreak music. He didn't need that. He turned to PBS and got some Italian opera. Nope. A soft rock station was playing love songs. Nope. And oldies station was playing something that fit his mood, "The Lion Sleeps Tonight." He left that station on and turned the volume down. Then he went to the living room and lay down on the love seat, one leg dangling to the floor, to read the last chapter in volume 2 of the Pendragon series of books about King Arthur. He wanted to finish it before he left on his trip. Volume 3 was already packed. Booty followed him into the living room and rubbed her white fur against his leg as she lay down on the floor beside him. He rubbed his foot against her back. Booty rolled over so she could have her stomach rubbed. Duffy was in the kitchen, eating. Having a couple of dogs took away some of the loneliness.

He glanced at the empty fireplace, a symbol of his empty life, and sighed. No flame there. No passion in his life either. There weren't any ashes either. His life was as empty as the fireplace. He was depressed. He sensed that he was falling apart, that he was on the edge of a complete breakdown. Instinctively, he knew this adventure was just the therapy he needed. Somehow, he knew getting away from it all for a couple of weeks would restore him. He would set his own goals at his own time and enjoy the peace and quiet of nature. Reassess his life. No phones. No bills. No boss. He would be on his own, facing or not facing the challenges as he chose and as nature dealt. He would have time to think. Maybe he would make some major changes in his life when he got back. Things just could not go on the way they were.

He remembered some of the arguments he had had with Linda. "You always get your own way. You never do what I want. You don't love me. Sometimes I think you like your bicycle-sports-computer-house-whatever better than me." He had tried to talk with her about their problems, but talking only seemed to make things worse. He just couldn't understand her. How could two people fall in love and then end up fighting all the time? It didn't make sense. There was no reason for it. Yet the harder he tried, the worse it got. Finally, Linda left him. And now he was stuck with this big house and no one to share it with. What did he do wrong? Would he ever figure it out? "I Can't Stop Loving You," was now playing on the radio. How did that get on there? That was not on the play list for the oldies station, was it? Was his radio playing tricks on him? It was a sad song that expressed exactly how he felt about Linda. *I can't stop loving you,* he thought. *I've lost you. I guess this trip is about grieving for you as much as anything. It's almost like you're dead. Our relationship is dead.*

Jim had a hard time concentrating on his book but somehow managed to stumble through and finish it anyway. He kept going over things in his mind. *Did I pack everything I need? What will I need to buy along the way? What if I meet a bear in the UP? Is there anything else I need to take care of at home before I go?* He finally fell into restless sleep thinking about the adventure he would start in the morning and the way his life was going. *Oh well,* he thought, *so what if a bear does find me? I'd stand and fight him, find a big stick or something. And if I lost, well, life just doesn't seem to matter all that much anyway. Something's got to change.* This trip was not just about winning a bet. It was about getting his life back.

3
On Top of the World

Dang, Jim thought, *I not only fell asleep on the sofa, but I slept in, too. I must have really been tired last night. I gotta get going.* He laughed to himself. Duffy had replaced Booty during the night, and Jim reached down to scratch his coarse black fur. Jim got up, showered, and changed into a yellow T-shirt and black shorts. He got out two pairs of white socks, one with blue letters advertising NIKE and the other with red letters. On a whim, he made them into two unmatched pairs and put one of them on, red letters on his right foot, blue on his left. *Maybe it'll bring me good luck,* he thought. *Linda would probably have had a fit about me wearing mismatched socks, but she's not around; I'll do as I please. Besides, who will even notice?* He put the other pair in his pannier.

He started to roll the bike out of the breezeway, but found the front tire was flat. He sighed. *Here I am running late, and I already have a flat. I sure hope this isn't a sign as to how my trip will go.*

Until he laid the bike down to fix the flat, he didn't realize how heavy it was all loaded down; with all the weight on the back, it almost did a wheelie by itself. He was glad it was the front tire that was flat. It was easier to take off the bike because he didn't have to mess around getting the chain off the gears. He flipped the quick release, took the wheel off, and then took the tube out and blew it up to about twice its normal size using the little pump that mounted on the frame. He heard a faint hissing sound and located a pinhole in the tube. He patched the tube and then searched the tire for a piece of glass, a cut, anything that could account for the pinhole.

Aha. *There she is,* he thought, comparing the sliver of glass to a woman and the inner tube to a man. *Women are always trying to puncture the male ego. Are there any women who might act like the patch, not the glass? Women have no idea what pressure men are under, and an ego that can't hold air is useless. Maybe too big an ego is bad, but too small an ego is just as bad. Both men and women need a reasonably good self-image.* He put the tube and tire back on the rim, pumped it up, slipped the wheel back onto the fork, and gave it a spin to see that everything looked okay. *If I ever find a woman who's like a patch, rather than glass, well …*

Duffy was barking to go outside, so he got up and let him out. *Where's Booty?* He found her sleeping under the bed, so he got her up and put her out also.

His stomach growled. *Breakfast,* he thought. *I need to eat.* He took the hot dog out of the fridge and nuked it. While it was heating, he opened the front door and saw the paper lying on the steps. Darn. They were supposed to stop it. He picked it up, sat down at the kitchen table, and read the sports section while he ate. The Detroit Tigers were having a terrible year. Again. More and more losses. No surprise there.

After eating, he felt a lot better. He took some Gatorade out of the fridge, went to the sink, and poured it into his Camelbak, a skinny, black, insulated backpack with a plastic bladder and sipping tube. *Maybe it's a good thing I had a flat,* he thought. *I was in such a hurry I was ready to tear outta here without eating, and I almost forgot my Camelbak.*

Then he went back to the breezeway, rechecked his gear and bike, and decided that everything was ready to go. The two hundred dollars was in his wallet and the map on the bike. *Might as well get started,* he thought. *I'm already running late.*

He put his helmet and gloves back on and started to roll the bike out of the breezeway again when the phone rang. *Now what?* he thought. *I hope it's not some salesman. Am I ever going to get out of here?*

It was his neighbor, Dave. "Jim. I'm really glad you're still home. I thought you might have left already. I hate to bother you again, but my niece stopped over yesterday and left me some homemade chocolate-chip cookies. I can't eat all of these, and I was wondering if you'd take some on your trip with you."

"Sure, if this won't count against my bet."

"You haven't actually started your trip yet, so they can't really count against you."

"I'll be right over."

As Jim opened the gate to go next door, Booty squeezed through and took off running. "Get back here, Booty!" Jim yelled. Booty kept running. "Dumb dog," Jim grumbled under his breath. "Even the dog is trying to keep me from leaving."

Dave was on his back porch where he handed Jim a small package of cookies. "These are really good; I hope you enjoy them. I figure with all the biking you're gonna be doing, you'll burn them off in no time. All they're gonna do here is settle around my waist."

Dave's porch had a good roof over it and plenty of room for the swing he was building, but it wasn't screened in. Not yet. Dave showed him his latest woodworking project. "All finished but the varnish. The all-time perfect porch swing. Most swings just have four chains, one on each corner. This one has eight chains, two on each corner, arranged so the swing won't rock side to side, only front and back. In addition, I put the top hooks into roller bearings so it won't squeak or creak. It just needs to be finished, and I have to get some cushions made for it."

Jim sat in it. "This is quiet. And comfortable. I like it." They sat and talked for a few minutes until Jim realized how late it was getting. "Dave, the paper came today. I thought I'd canceled it. If it comes tomorrow and Monday, would you call them and try to cancel it for me? Otherwise, I'd appreciate it if you'd collect them for me while I'm gone. I have to get going if I'm going to win our bet, but first I have catch that dumb mutt of mine. He escaped again."

Jim walked around the block calling, "Booty! Booty!" No answer. Finally, he came back home, and there was Booty inside his fence. "Now, how did you find your way back in there?" he muttered, shaking his head.

As he started to walk back to his yard, something glittered in the grass by the sidewalk. He stooped to pick it up. It was a small silver shoe. A stiletto. Maybe it had come off a charm bracelet or an earring. He wondered how it had gotten there and who had dropped it. Linda? Probably not. She hadn't been around for weeks. Besides, if she'd worn something like that, he thought he would have noticed. It was kind of cute, like Cinderella's slipper, only not glass. It looked like real silver. It was heavy like real silver, too. Maybe it would bring him good luck. He'd attach it to his bike or key chain or something. He didn't know why he would want a charm. He didn't have anyone to give it to, and he didn't think he needed it, but it just looked too nice to throw out. *Maybe someone will come looking for it,* he thought. He was pretty sure someone had lost it recently; otherwise, he would have noticed it before then.

Jim looked down at the shoe in his hand. Somehow, he felt attached to it. It was a nice-looking shoe, a pump with a stiletto heel. He wondered what sort of woman would wear a shoe like it. *Lots of women would enjoy wearing one like it,* he thought. Linda would. But this shoe didn't make him think of Linda. In his mind, he saw another person, someone he didn't know, someone with light-brown hair, bleached by the sun, a pretty girl with perfect teeth in a pretty smile, apple-red lips, and dark-brown eyes, someone who made him feel at ease and happy. He could picture her walking barefoot on a beach in black biker shorts and a purple top, the wind gently blowing her hair. She turned and looked right at him with her dark doe eyes, and his heart melted, his hurt and heartache gone. It was as if she were a real person.

The telephone ringing brought him out of his reverie. *Dang! Is everyone conspiring to keep me home? Should I just let it ring?* He had a feeling that he should answer it. *Oh, why not? I'm already running late. It'll only take a minute. I'll be lucky to hit the road by noon, the way things are going. So much for my early start.*

"Hello. Jim Sanders here."

"Loretta here, I'm so glad I caught you. I thought you might be out today."

"Loretta? Loretta Lindsey? From Los Angeles?

"The very one. Only I'm in Lansing today."

"Hey, it's really good to hear from you," Jim said genuinely. "How is my favorite cousin today?"

Loretta was a year younger than he was. They had grown up together in the Detroit area and were good friends. Ten years ago, Loretta had moved out to Los Angeles with her mother, but the friendship had endured.

"What are you doing in Lansing?" he asked.

"I'm fine. I'm in Lansing on business, and I thought I'd surprise you. Would you like to go for lunch? I know a real good restaurant."

Jim didn't answer right away.

"Hello? Jim? Are you there?"

"Yes, I'm here, Loretta. I was just thinking. I'd love to go to lunch with you, but I was just getting ready to leave on my vacation. Well, it's almost lunchtime, and I'd have to eat somewhere anyway. Is it someplace close by?"

"I'm at the Freewheel. Do you know where that is?" Loretta asked.

"Sure do."

"Good. I'll wait for you here."

Jim slipped some slacks on over his bike shorts and drove over. Ten minutes later, he was at the Freewheel, a restaurant with a bicycle theme. There were bike racks out front, and Jim often found some of his biking friends eating there. He quickly spotted Loretta's blond hair and went toward her. She was wearing white sandals with a low heel and a light-blue business suit with small gold hoop earrings. "It's so good to see you, and you look great," he said. "I really miss you now that you're in LA."

She stood, and they gave each other a heartfelt hug.

"Thanks. I stay in shape biking and running. The weather out there is perfect for it. You look pretty good yourself."

They sat at a table, and when the waitress came, Loretta ordered a salad and a tuna sandwich. Jim decided to get a personal pizza.

"Are you dating anyone?" Loretta asked.

"No." Jim smiled at her. "I'm holding out for someone like you. How about you?"

"I've seen a few guys, but nothing serious. I'm just too busy with my career to get very involved, but I don't mind. I like being independent, and sales are booming now. Maybe when I get to be as old as you are, I'll feel more like settling down," she said, emphasizing the *old* with a grin.

"Just call me over the hill," Jim groaned, as he thought about turning thirty.

"Actually, Jim, I came to see you with a purpose in mind. I know you're going on vacation now, but when you get back, would you consider coming to LA and working for my company? I know of your abilities, and I'm sure I can get you a good position in sales. I know you don't have any experience in this, but we also value honesty and dependability highly and I know I can count on you for that."

"Selling women's clothing? Come on, Loretta. I'm an analyst. I work with computers and data, not clothing."

"The company wants to open a line of sportswear. I'm not talking about being a salesman; I'm talking putting you in charge. You would coordinate the buying and selling. I know you have good taste. In fact, I think you could do the women's line if you wanted. Who better to know what looks good on a woman than a man? You could be my assistant if you wanted. I would certainly appreciate your abilities. You probably won't make as much money as you are now, at least not at first, but if the line grows …"

"Well, I—"

"No need to give an answer now. Think about it over your vacation. The company will help you with your moving expenses. I'm sure it will be a job you'll enjoy. Do you like your current job? Let me know when you get back. In the meantime, what's your new house like? I hear it's an old farmhouse. Does it need a lot of fixing?"

"It's not really a farmhouse, but it does need lots of fixing," Jim said. "I've already done the furnace, central air, electrical, insulation, and plumbing. There's tons of painting and decorating left to do. Are you offering to help?"

"No, but I'd like to see it."

"Okay, but I would like to hear more about this job offer. Are there other options? I mean, do I have to go to LA, or could I do it from here? Do I have to be a buyer? I think I might rather be a store manager or work in inventory control. You know I'm a whiz with computers."

"The company is growing. There will be other options available. Basically, the company emphasizes ability rather than experience. We believe that experience doesn't always count. A person who works at a job for twenty years has twenty years' experience, but that doesn't mean that he did a good job or that he's honest. He might have done a poor or mediocre job for those twenty years. Why should we hire him over someone who has no experience but good ability? A person with ability, properly motivated and trained, can often do just as well or better than someone with just experience and education. We won't lock you into a job just because that's what you've always done. When something opens up, anyone in the company has an opportunity to get that job, and we try to promote from within. We test people for their abilities and also train them. Of course, you'll be tested, but I don't think there's any problem there." She continued to talk about possibilities.

"You've convinced me, Loretta. I'll take the testing when I get back. I'm ready for a change. I really am, even if it means a cut in pay. I'm paid well on my current job, but I'm not given any responsibility. I'm given assignments, do them, and then can't get them approved or even looked at. It's not that they're rejected; my boss just doesn't look at them, and he won't give me the authority to go ahead with them on my own. He's too busy, and he won't delegate. It really makes me feel useless. Between that and Linda leaving me in February, well, I'll be honest with you, I'm just plain depressed. I'm leaving on this vacation today to get away from it all, to have some time to think things through. I'm going to make some changes in my life."

After lunch, Loretta followed Jim's black Escort in her rented red Caprice back to his house. He gave her the grand tour. It had a Michigan basement, one with a dirt floor and a ceiling so low they had to walk all hunched over, with a cistern. The cistern collected water from the eave troughs when it rained. In the old days, a hand pump pulled water from the cistern to the kitchen, and then later, an electric pump was installed. Today, the house had city water and the cistern wasn't used. "I'm thinking of disconnecting the eave troughs and knocking out the cistern," he said. "It just makes it too damp in the house."

The main floor had ten-foot ceilings. The walls were mostly bare. The woodwork had all been painted over in a yucky green, and Jim wanted to restore the wood finish. Some of the wood windows were painted shut. Some of them had no storms, and none of the windows had proper curtains or drapes. There was only one bath, and it only had an old-fashioned claw-footed tub with a tubular frame around the top to hold a wrap-around shower curtain. The upstairs had three dusty rooms with old magazines left scattered on the floors by the previous owners.

Loretta seemed pleased. "There's so much you can do with an old house like this," she said. "I love the fireplace in the living room, the high ceilings, and the woodwork. I see you've already started stripping off that ugly paint from some of it. It'll be a beautiful house once it's fixed up. I see you've already finished the kitchen. I like the yellow; it looks so cheery."

After saying good-bye, Jim slipped his slacks back off, donned his helmet and sunglasses, and rolled his bike out of the breezeway once more. It was already two o'clock. Would he ever get out? The phone rang again. *Who could that be? Linda? Yeah, right. I've got a better chance of being called by the Publishers Clearing House. Ed McMahon, or whatever his name is, will just have to find someone else to give those million dollars to. I must get going. If it's important, they'll leave a message. I'll get it when I get back.*

As he rolled his bike out the gate, Jim said good-bye to his pets. "You kids be good now. See ya in two weeks."

So much for an early start. Where did the time go? He got on his bike and pushed off.

He felt relief as he started pedaling. He should've been on the road hours ago. He wouldn't make a hundred miles that day, but the pavement beneath his wheels sang to him. He felt his breathing pick up and his heart kick in as he pumped the pedals. It was joyous, even though the bike was so heavy all loaded down. His bike weighed around twenty-one pounds unloaded, but all loaded, it must have been more than sixty. In addition, the panniers, which carried his gear, seemed to create more wind resistance.

Twelve to fifteen miles per hour is okay, he thought. *I'd rather be doing the eighteen to twenty I'm accustomed to, but I'm probably a little out of shape for this being my first ride of the year, and I'm certainly not used to the load.* He was glad to have a little granny gear in the front to get up the big hills that were coming. His bicycle just seemed to float down the road, like a boat—a big ore freighter, not a speedboat—as the scenery drifted by.

Soon, Jim was pedaling on Upton Road, heading north. Freedom at last. No phone to answer. No schedule to meet. He hadn't felt this happy for months. His heart was smiling, and he wondered why he hadn't been on the bike sooner this year. It was a perfect day, sunny, not too hot, and a tail wind. What more could a fellow want?

Jim passed happy white Queen Anne's lace and joyous purple joe-pye weed along the roadside. There were gleeful red-wing blackbirds, hot chocolate-colored not-so-mourning doves, and occasional stately blue herons and soaring red-tailed hawks along the way. Happy butterflies flitted around: orange-and-yellow monarchs, gold-and-black fritillaries, yellow sulfurs, and yellow-and-black tiger swallowtails.

I ought to have a name for my bike, he thought. *Roy Rogers had Trigger. The Lone Ranger had Silver. I wonder what King Arthur called his horse? His sword was called Excalibur. Some people have names for their cars. What could I call my bike? Hmm. The Red bomber? No. The Red Streak? No. Old Faithful? No. Freedom? I need something that doesn't sound so … so dumb. Old Miss? No, sounds like Mississippi. Old Mich? No. Mitch? No. Nothing sounds quite right. Well maybe something will come to me later.*

Jim jogged left onto Round Lake Road and then right onto Shepherdsville Road.

He thought about the little shoe he had found that morning. It made him think of that pretty woman with the friendly smile and the dark eyes that he'd imagined. He thought about his neighbor, Dave, who was always pestering him about getting a wife; he thought it would do him some good. *But women are like cats,* he thought. *Even if I don't want one, eventually one will find me. Cats seem to sense who is compatible with them. A person doesn't choose a cat; the cat does the choosing.* He thought about his two dogs. *That probably explained why a cat hadn't chosen him yet. Yet Linda chose him and then left. Why? I'm always thinking about Linda. Linda on my mind. Isn't there a song about that? Probably.*

In truth, Jim, like a lot of men, was a little intimidated by women. And he was hurt. He found it was easier, safer, to be nice to them but stay uncommitted, uninvolved, than to deal with them. He didn't hate women; he respected them, but after Linda, he found it hard to trust them. Or was it himself he didn't trust? Besides, if he were married, would his wife come along on an adventure like this? Maybe she wouldn't even let him go off on an adventure by himself. *A man needs some space, some freedom. Relationships are uncertain. I can be free and lonely. What's the line in that song?" Freedom is just another way of saying nothing left to lose"? Or something like that. What would be the opposite? Free—tied down. Lonely—uh, hmm, loved, I guess. Maybe if I was truly loved, I wouldn't feel tied down.* It was a nice, warm thought, tied down, but loved, to have someone to love, not to own, but to love. *It seems like the whole human race, from the smallest child to the oldest adult, is lonely. It's a basic need to find love. Acceptance.*

The bike tires seemed to hum happily on the pavement. It made him feel like humming along, at least in his mind. Karen Carpenter's song, "On Top of the World," ran through his head over and over again. The beat was in his feet as they pounded the pedals. "I'm on top of the world, lookin' down on creation," and "the reason is clear it's because I'm biking here. My bike's put me on the top of the world."

Such a feeling came over him, he just couldn't be blue while he was riding.

After about twenty-five miles, he reached the corner of M-21 and Shepherdsville Road, and he was starting to tire. He stopped at the store on the corner, Tom's Market, and went in. He spent a couple of dollars on granola bars and some grape drink and went outside to rest and eat. There were a couple of milk crates outside the store window and a plank lay across them to make a bench. He sat on the plank and chewed a granola bar. A car pulled in the parking lot, and an attractive-looking young woman got out. With sunglasses, he could enjoy looking at her without being obvious about it. She had on a crisp black top with matching shorts. Her dark hair was tied back in a ponytail with a black bow. *She dresses very neat,* he thought, every hair in place, her makeup done nicely. *A good-looking face. The face, the most important part of a woman's body, and a smile the most important part of the face. Or is it the eyes?* But she had on dirty white sneakers with holes in them, and it spoiled the effect a little. Well, quite a bit, actually. As she went by, he smiled, and she stopped and asked him how far he had ridden. "Only about twenty-five miles, so far."

"Where are you going?" she asked.

"Up to the bridge," he said, meaning the Mackinac Bridge. *I'm really going much farther,* he thought, but there was no point in telling everything. *Most people can't even comprehend going to the bridge.*

"Wow," she said. "I have a hard time riding only a mile."

"Don't be so hard on yourself. Most people can ride five miles, even on an old beat-up one-speed Huffy. Especially around here; it's so flat."

"How far is it to the bridge?"

"About 250 miles."

"When are you going to get there?"

"Monday or Tuesday."

"Are you staying with friends?" she asked.

"No, I'm camping."

"Do you do this often?"

"I've done a lot of biking and a lot of camping, but this is the first time I've done them both together. It's a new experience for me."

"Well, good luck," she said and walked into the store.

Funny, Jim thought, *how people dress so nice and then have one thing out of place.* Her shoes; it ruined everything. He guessed she probably just slipped the shoes on for a trip to the store. She probably had black flats at home. *Why would she wear tennis shoes instead of flats, which would have been just as easy to slip on?* On the other hand, she could have been a real knockout in black heels.

She came out of the store carrying a jug of milk, a two-liter of Diet Coke, and a box of … Pampers. *Oh well … I guess women have other things on their mind besides looking good, especially when they have a family.*

"Bye," she said as she walked back to her car.

He returned the "Bye." He watched as several more cars stopped and people went in and out of the store—none of them as pretty as the woman in black.

It was after six in the evening when he felt rested enough to hit the road again. He pulled his bike away from the wall and eased it out into the road. His legs were getting tired, and it made him think of the time he rode his bike in a tour across Iowa. It was called RAGBRAI, the acronym for Register's Annual Great Bicycle Ride Across Iowa. On RAGBRAI, there were baggage trucks that carried his tent and things, but on this trip, he'd have to average almost a hundred miles per day and carry his own luggage to win the bet, and he certainly wasn't going to make the mileage today. A baggage truck sure would've helped. He'd have to settle for lesser mileage the first few days until his legs adjusted to the extra weight and started getting back in shape.

He thought of the over seven thousand registered riders on the weeklong trip, maybe fifteen thousand people altogether if all the people who went along that weren't registered were counted. All day long, there would be riders on the road as far ahead as he could see and as far behind as he could see. He was never alone, riding with a couple of companions and all the others. There was plenty of company on that joyful trip. It was a fun-filled rolling party. Bikers owned the roads. Cars drove at bicycle speeds. In fact, most of the roads were pretty much blocked off from cars. It was just wonderful.

This trip was different; he was totally alone. Even though he wanted to be alone, he missed the company. *I'm going to be alone a lot,* he thought. *It sure would be nice to have someone to talk to, but it's just not going to happen. If another biker is only a mile ahead of me and I'm going a mile an hour faster, it would take me a whole hour to catch him, and before then, he would have likely turned off the road. There aren't many bikers on these roads to begin with.*

Hmmm, he thought. *I could always imagine a companion. Maybe that will help the loneliness. I don't have to tell anyone. It's a kid thing to have imaginary friends, but for me, it will just be fun to use my imagination. To create. Now let's see, what kind of a friend do I want? An alien? A mouse? A cat or dog? Something different. Something small. A grasshopper? I know, a cricket. He could sit on my handlebar and keep me company. A cricket, because it sings. I always enjoyed hearing a cricket chirp at night. But not Jiminy Cricket. What should I name it? Joe? Something that starts with a "C" so it alliterates. Chris? Something that rhymes? Picket? Kickit? Wickit? Stickit? No. Stick that! I can't even come up with a name for my bicycle; how can I name an imaginary companion? Back to Chris. Christopher. Christopher Cricket. I like it. All right, Chris for short. Chris Cricket.*

"Well, Chris, we're in Bannister now. Let's stop for a spell." He stopped on a grassy lot on the north side of town. Bannister used to have a grocery store, but now it just had a bar. He unrolled his blanket and laid down to rest a bit. "Looks like the tires are still holding air. We did a pretty good job fixing that flat this morning, aye, Chris?" Chris wasn't even around this morning, but if Jim could imagine Chris at all, he could also imagine he was there when he fixed the tire. It felt funny to talk to an imaginary cricket, but people talked to their cats and dogs, didn't they?

They rode three miles to M-57, turned west, continued for a mile, and then headed north again. "Hey, Chris, the sun's getting low. Any ideas about where to put up our tent tonight? Oh look, a State Game Area. Perfect." He had only gone forty miles for the day when he came to a state game area on the right. "Just perfect. What do you think, Chris? It's probably not legal to camp here, but someone will have to catch us first. Camping is allowed on game areas at certain times of the year in Michigan but not during the nesting season. Also, campsites are supposed to be posted, and we don't have any forms. But since we're not building a fire or hunting or leaving trash around or hiking around scaring up game, do you think anyone will mind or even notice? Hey, look at this place, all grown up with weeds, I bet we could hide in there. It's a parking place, and by the looks of it, there hasn't been a car here all summer. Do ya think I could put my tent up in here?"

"Pitch it," Chris Cricket said.

Hmmm. The little critter's starting to answer me, Jim thought. He chuckled and unrolled his tent, which was a small, six-sided dome tent. Then he put the poles together. The three poles were shock-corded; that is, they were hollow fiberglass with an elastic cord running through them. They just needed to be unfolded and joined end to end, and the elastic would hold them together. Jim ran the poles through the sleeves on the outside of the tent. When he went to put it up, he found that he put the poles in the wrong sleeves. He felt dumb and looked at Chris. "No crickitcism from you, Chris. Don't even think it. This is only my first night camping in a long time. I'll get it right the first time tomorrow." So he pulled the poles out and made sure the sleeves on one side of the tent were lined up with the sleeves on the other side of the tent and tried again. This time, he was successful. He left the rain fly off since it was quite warm out and he didn't think it would rain that night. It would be cooler that way.

Finally, he unloaded his bike and put everything inside the tent. "Okay, Chris. Hop in." He climbed in, zipped up the door, rolled out the ground pad, and lay down on it.

His fanny pack was digging into his back. He took it off and set it beside him. As he thought about the day's ride, he remembered the silver shoe and took it out. As he held it in his hand, an image came to his mind. It was the same woman he had thought of earlier. *Who? Just my imagination,* he thought. While he sat there holding it, trying to decide what to do with it, he felt good. Happy. There was a small metal loop on the back of the heel, probably where it had been attached to a bracelet or earring or maybe a necklace. If he could find a piece of string or something, he could make a necklace out of it and wear it under his T-shirt. But he didn't have any string. Besides, a shoe as nice as this deserved a real necklace made out of metal. He wasn't going to buy something like that until he got home, or he would lose his bet. A nice metal chain would probably cost a lot. When he got home, this trinket would make a nice souvenir of his trip. He put it back in the pack.

Jim lay back down and a cicada's shrill sound pierced his brain. It sounded like it was under or right next to the tent. "Hey, Chris, tell that cousin of yers to hush. He's hurt'n my ears."

I should've brought earplugs, he thought. He covered his ears as best he could and soon was fast asleep, dreaming about game wardens and what he would say if he got caught. "But, Officer, I'm not really camping. I'm just sleeping here. There's no fire. I'm not cooking anything. I'll be gone in the morning." Sometime in the night, he got out his wool blanket and pulled it over himself.

4
Go Where You Wanna Go

The first time Jim woke, he looked at his watch—5:30 a.m. It was already getting light out. He stretched, and his hand bumped against the wet tent fabric. *I'll just curl up and sleep some more,* he thought. *When the sun gets up high enough, it'll cook me out of here anyway, and by then, everything will be dry. I don't want to pack a wet tent, and besides, it's Sunday. I doubt the little store down the road is even open yet.*

Jim awoke the second time to Chris chirping away. He tried imitating him. After a while, he could make a whistling sound that wasn't a bad imitation … for a human.

"Hey, Chris. You gittin' hungry yet? I think there's a little store up the road where we can get some snacks before moving on. Since it's Sunday, it probably won't be open before ten, so we can take our time. I don't remember any other places to eat for a long way, but we'll find someplace good before the day's over. We'll find at least one good place to eat today and every day, but not at McDonald's or Burger King. I can eat at those places in Lansing. Give me a small ma-and-pa-type restaurant where I can sit down and rest while waiting for my food."

Crows were cawing. Other birds were chirping, singing, twittering, scolding, and drumming. Insects were buzzing and humming. He wondered how anyone could sleep with all the noise. He fell back to sleep anyway.

The sun rose higher, and it started to get hot in the tent. All the dew was dried off, and Chris was chirping madly. Jim woke a third time, looked at his watch, and then started counting chirps; as the temperature went up, the crickets chirped faster. In fifteen seconds, there were thirty chirps. *That means,* he thought, *it's what? Thirty plus forty is seventy. About seventy degrees. But Chris is down on the ground where it's cooler. It must be warmer than that in here. Oh forget it! I don't need to know the temperature to know that it feels warm. And humid, too. Whew! I better get my stuff packed up.*

He put the silver shoe in his fanny pack and then loaded up his panniers, unzipped the door, and threw them out. "Okay, Chris. Out! Hurry up. Out! Out! Out! Hop back on those bars, and I'll be with you in a minute." He took down his tent and found that one of the three fiberglass poles was cracked, so he wound it with electrical tape. *I sure hope this holds for the rest of the trip,* he thought. *I'll have a hard time winning the bet if I have to buy a new tent.* An occasional car roared down the road while he rolled up his tent and put it in its sack along with the tent poles and rain fly and then secured everything on his bike.

As he walked the bike out of the tall weeds, he noticed tiny white flowers on the heads. *Are those sweet alyssum? Nah,* he thought. *More like a wild guess. Hah. Wild guess. That's a neat name for a plant. But sweet alyssum? I don't even know if it grows in Michigan. I must have just heard the name somewhere. I'll see if someone along the way knows what it is. Seems like I know practically nothing about wildflowers and birds and insects. I wish I knew more. I'm going to be quite close to them for a couple of weeks.* He picked some, and a couple of minutes later, he was on the road.

Oh joy! On the road again! It sure feels good. Pumping the pedals sure gets the blood moving.

Chris spoke up. "Wild turkeys ahead."

Jim looked up. Sure enough. He counted fifteen of them in the field on the right.

A southeast wind today, he thought, *that's good. It feels like there'll be rain later, but it's nice to have a tailwind.* The wheels hummed on the pavement, and every now and then, he heard small pieces of loose stone, almost like a coarse sand, make a sort of soft crunching sound under the tires. *It's never completely quiet on a bike,* Jim thought, *no matter how hard I try. Sure, it's a whole lot quieter than a car. I can sneak up on deer or other animals. I can ride by houses, and people never notice. Still, if I coast, the free wheel clicks. The chain makes a soft clicking noise. Handlebars creak. Every time I roll over a little bump, something rattles. And once I get going, there is the constant wind noise in my ears.*

"Time for some music, Chris. I don't have a radio so you'll have to listen to what's in my head." *It plays over and over,* he thought, *not an eight-track, but a one track. I got a one-track mind, not a train track, a bike track. I make tracks. The song for the day is … "I gotta go, go where I wanna, wanna go, do, do what I wanna, wanna do …" The Mamas and Papas, "You Gotta Go Where You Wanna Go." What great harmony! What a great message. What a good feeling. I just can't help being happy today.* Chris joined in, helping out the tambourines. *"California Dreamin'" is another of their songs. Makes me think of a trip to California to see Loretta. Maybe I'll do that one later, but today, I'm goin' where I wanna go. Doin' what I love to do.* He never played the whole song, just parts of it, over and over, sometimes changing the words to fit his mood or situation.

A little after ten o'clock and about five miles later, Jim came to the little store in Sickles and stopped. The store had an old-fashioned wood porch and railing, made from planks torn from an old barn. He leaned his bike against it and went in. On the way in, he saw the headlines on the *Detroit Free Press* telling of a bombing at the Olympic Games in Atlanta, Georgia. Senseless! He looked around the store, got some Gatorade with peanut butter and crackers, and went up to pay. At the counter were some fresh-baked goods, so he bought a cinnamon roll. The owner was a big man, and he was using those gigantic hands to wrap tiny rolls in cellophane. Jim laughed inwardly, huge hands, little cinnamon rolls. Actually, the rolls were average-sized, but they just looked tiny in the grocer's hands. *He should be hammering iron at a forge, or at least doing carpentry work. Maybe he should be playing center for the Detroit Lions.* Exhibition games were starting soon, weren't they?

He paid for the food and started up a conversation. The grocer was friendly enough. He told Jim about Mr. Sickles, the founder of this nontown, a surveyor who had originally founded Elsie, a dairy town on the east side of Clinton County. Later, Mr. Sickles worked for the county in St. Johns and then decided to survey and plot out

Sickles, but Sickles just never took off the way Elsie did. That was years ago. *Maybe it was because Elsie had the Borden cow advertising for them,* Jim thought. Sickles didn't have a cow. If they did, who would buy products from a Sickles, sickly cow. It would be sick, not slick, advertising. Jim chuckled inwardly at his sick joke.

"By the way," Jim said, "do you know what these little flowers are?" He showed him the weeds he had picked.

"Nope. Seen 'em all my life, but never knew. I bet my grandpa woulda known. Back in the days when people walked everywhere or rode a horse, people paid more attention to nature. And if they didn't know something, when they met someone on the road, they could ask. Today, we zip by in a car, and if we should happen to notice something, we go by so fast we don't have time to examine it. And if we do stop to examine it, when we meet someone, we zip by so fast that we can't ask, all sealed up in our little transportation machines. So we spend our entire lives in ignorance of some of life's simple pleasures."

Jim had to agree. Chris couldn't help him, since Chris, being part of Jim's imagination, didn't know any more than Jim did. He decided he'd let this mystery go, but keep his ears and eyes open for information. On the way out, he ditched the little flowers. Literally. They were wilting anyway. Maybe he'd buy a book on wildflowers when he got back.

It was time to hit the road again. The gravel crunched softly under his tires as he started off. A couple of miles later, he was back on Barry Road, heading into Midland County.

"We just crossed the county line, Chris. Look at these roads, mostly white because the tar has worn off and left the white stone to poke through, but black spots where the county crew patched them recently. Kinda reminds me of a Holstein. Black spots on white, a popular pattern of the day. Was Elsie a Holstein?"

After a while, he said, "Look, Chris, another 'road closed at bridge' sign. I've been seeing enough of them lately. I wonder if we're going to have to detour. Maybe a car can't get through, but my bike can go a lot of places a car can't. I think I'll risk it." Eventually, he came to the bridge. The road was barricaded with not one, but three strips of guardrail, one on top of the other, of the kind used on freeway overpasses. It would be a job to climb over them.

He propped his bike up against the rail and walked down the bank to the water's edge. *Maybe I could wade across the river. It doesn't look too deep. Nah. The banks are too steep; it would be just as easy to climb the guardrails.* He walked back up, stopping to pick and eat some wild black raspberries on the way. *Raspberries? This late in the year? I'd've thought they'd be all done by now.*

Back at his bike, he said, "Okay, Chris. Hop off. I know you don't weigh much, but this bike is heavy, and I need all the help I can get. You'll have to cross the bridge on your own. Watch out for birds." It wasn't just that the bike was heavy; it was also bulky. He could barely lift it without unpacking it, but he managed to get it over the barricade.

In the middle of the bridge, he said, "Watch out for the hole, Chris. No wonder they closed the bridge. A car could lose a tire in there." There were no signs that the old bridge would be repaired. On the north side of the Pine River, he climbed over another set of guardrails.

"You can get back on now, Chris. I'll wait for you." It was quiet and peaceful there by the water's edge on a sunny day, with no traffic because of the bridge. It was around noon, and Jim had gone only fifty-eight miles since he left home.

"Chris, let's take a breather. This is a great place to stop." He unrolled his ground pad, spread it out, lay down, and stared up at the shady trees. *Aaah, this feels good. I must be more tired than I thought. I'm not used to biking with a heavy load, and it was quite an exertion to get it over the guardrails. Twice.* Jim sipped Gatorade from his Camelbak and thought, *No radio. No television. No telephone. No one to talk to, 'cept Chris,* and he was enough. He had a feeling Chris was going to start getting lippy. No cars. He closed his eyes. *Imagine … Listen to the river softly grinding away at rocks in its bed. Isn't it noisy! And that fish swimming by, the roar of its fins pushing against water. And those daisies over there, the ones that are budding. Hear the awful grating noise they're making as they open up. I can almost hear those things; it's so quiet. Almost, if it wasn't for the nattering of busy squirrels and chirping of happy birds and the hungry buzzing of a mosquito. A mosquito!* Jim slapped at it.

He remembered the silver shoe he'd wrapped up. He got it out and looked at it. Yesterday's image came back to him. "This is weird, Chris. Why do I keep getting this image? If this shoe could talk, I bet it would have an interesting story to tell." He felt good as he held it.

He thought of a glass slipper. *How impractical! Glass doesn't exactly bend, it would be stiffer than a bicycle shoe, and bicycle shoes are made stiff on purpose for more efficient pedaling. If the glass slipper didn't fit exactly, it would be very uncomfortable. Not to mention that it would be slippery to walk on, giving additional meaning to the term* slipper. *It wouldn't even be safe! And if all those obstacles could be surmounted, what would keep it from breaking the first time one stepped on something hard? It would be a cracked slipper. A broken slipper. Now there's a neat name, the "Cracked Slipper Corral" or the "Broken Slipper Ranch." And a glass slipper sliver could make a bloody foot. Ouch! I'm not even going to go there.*

Maybe I should think of this as a magic slipper. As if! He didn't believe in magic. He thought of Sméagol, also known as Golem, from J. R. R. Tolkien's *Lord of the Rings*, who liked to hold his "precious," the magic ring. The magic ring made its wearer invisible to mortals. It also worked its evil and eventually controlled its wearer. But this silver shoe wasn't like that. He certainly wasn't invisible. So he liked to hold the shoe. So what? Maybe it was a lucky shoe. That didn't make it magic or evil. He was just trying to get over his broken relationship with Linda.

He thought of Linda. *She just didn't work out,* he thought. *I wonder if anyone could ever work out for me. Sure, it would be nice to have someone pretty. But for a relationship to last, maybe it needs something more than mere physical attraction. A lot of people get married and then a little while later, poof. Divorce. There are lots of pretty women out there, too. Look at the lady in black outside the store on Shepherdsville Road. I wonder if she'll be divorced five years from now. Maybe she's a single parent already. They teach sex education in the school; why don't they have a class on relationships? Why does everything have to be learned the hard way, usually from a bad experience? Probably a man and woman should have something going for them besides attraction. A common interest, maybe. Something they can do together. Men connect by doing things together, like Dave and me. We play chess and work with wood. Why can't a woman do that? But women connect by talking, which is something maybe that I'm not very good at. At least according to Linda. Maybe if Linda biked, I would have spent more time listening to her. Now I'm just depressing myself. This is too beautiful a day to get depressed. I better get going.*

He tried to get up. "Oooh, my lower back hurts," he groaned. "I'm not used to the hard ground. I better stretch." Lying on the ground, he slowly pushed the arch in his back down against the ground, held it there for a count of ten, and then released it. He did this several times and felt much better. "You're lucky, Chris. With your exoskeleton, you never get a sore back."

He got back on his bike and pedaled on. It was only a few pedal strokes to Pine River Road where he turned right. Four miles down the road, he stopped at a Shell station in Gordonville and went in for some Gatorade and a sandwich from the cooler. Chris was on his shoulder. "I forgot about this store, Chris. We get to eat sooner than I thought. But It's c-c-c-cold in this air conditioning," he chattered. "I'm going back out where it's warm and sit in the shade of the station to enjoy this food."

A couple of young ladies drove up in a black Skylark. He enjoyed looking at them through his sunglasses. One of them, a brunette, stopped to chat, while the other one, with reddish-brown hair, went in the store. The brunette's hair came to her shoulders and was rather straight but looked nice. She had on a light-blue eye shadow. Somehow, the eye shadow just didn't look right to him. *And I don't even know why,* he thought. *Linda always had a perfect face, and she used eyeliner, eye shadow, mascara, and probably a whole lot of other things, but I don't have any idea how she used them or what it's like to put them on. Perhaps I should've asked her when I had the chance. I wonder what she would have said.*

The brunette had a pretty smile and was wearing a black halter top and blue jean shorts with a pair of white sandals. He estimated she was in her early twenties. Other than the eye shadow, he liked her looks.

"Nice bike," she said, looking at his red Schwinn.

"Thanks," he said. "Want to trade it for the Skylark?" He gave her a big smile.

"No, thanks." She laughed. "Where are you going?"

"To the bridge."

It was the same old questions he got asked all the time, especially by women. Men just tended to keep to themselves more. *Why is that?* he wondered. *If I was a woman, would more men speak to me? Yeah. Probably. Especially if I was attractive. Maybe some women find me attractive. Linda did. At least at first.*

Soon, the lady with the auburn hair came out with some bottles of Diet Coke, and when she saw her friend talking to him, she started asking questions, too. Her shoulder-length hair was thick and luxuriant, her one outstanding feature. She was wearing a white top, blue jeans, and white tennies. She wore the same blue eye shadow. They wished him luck on his trip as they left.

What's with the eye shadow? he wondered. *Did it do anything for them? Not for me, anyway, but maybe others like it. Red lipstick would have looked a lot better on either of them. I'm sure glad they didn't have on pink or orange lipstick, but some women wear that, too. Is there some sort of secret code that women have to pick their colors? Still, it was nice meeting them.*

He biked north on Gordonville Road to Sanford. US 10 ran east and west through Sanford. Just before he got to US 10, the road went down a hill and across a river, and there, to his surprise, was a bicycle trail, converted from an old railroad. "Let's ride the trail a ways, Chris. I wonder where it goes." He rode on it for about half a mile, just long enough to meet a couple of people on bicycles and man and a woman. Both were wearing tan uniforms and carrying first-aid kits on their bikes. They looked like they might be college students working a summer job.

"This trail wasn't here the last time I was up here," Jim said.

"It's new, just opened this year," the man said.

"How far is it?"

"Twenty-two miles. It runs from Midland to Coleman."

"Well, I guess I can't take it then; I'm heading north, not east or west."

It was quite warm out. Jim noticed the water bottles on their bikes and thought about his Camelbak. "I don't know if you guys have tried a Camelbak before, but I really like mine. They're great on a hot day like today because they keep your drinks cold and they hold a lot, almost two quarts. That's a little more than three big water bottles."

"No, I've never tried one," the man answered. "I've heard they're good, but aren't they hot? I don't think I'd like one on my back."

"They're neither all that hot nor uncomfortable. Just like you, I was skeptical of them at first. But after I finally tried one, I kicked myself that I didn't try one sooner. Not only does it keep my drink colder, but they're easier to use. I can drink with no hands; I just put the little tube in my mouth, bite down on the end to open it up, and sip. I don't even use water bottles anymore."

"You have a bottle on your bike."

"Oh yeah," Jim said. "But I don't drink from it. I carry some water in it and on a hot day like this, it warms up. Later tonight, I'll use it to wash up."

It was 1:40 p.m., and Jim had only gone seventy-two miles since he left home. The humidity had been high all day; in fact, there were some light sprinkles. Clouds in the south looked threatening. It was getting darker out, so he took off his sunglasses and put on his regular glasses. He went west on US 10 for a about a tenth of a mile to the next road, turned north, then rode up the west side of Sanford Lake, and eventually turned right on Curtis, riding up a steep bridge high above a river and into Edenville. He had only gone about ninety miles total so far and knew that he had to start making better time if he was going to make it to Ironwood.

"We gotta start pushing it, Chris, before the rain really comes." He rode hard on M-30 to Winegars and stopped at a little party store. He got some more Gatorade and peanut butter and crackers. He ate some and stashed the rest in his panniers.

The skies looked even more threatening, so Jim continued pushing north to Wagarsville Road and zigzagged over to F-97. "F-97, Chris. Do you think the 'F' stands for 'Federal,' since the road goes through the Huron National Forest for part of the way? Or maybe it stands for 'Forest.'" The skies kept getting darker and darker, and the sprinkles kept getting heavier. Jim had to stop and take off his glasses; they were fogging up from the humidity and rain, and he couldn't see out of them anyway. Since bugs, the main reason for wearing the glasses, didn't usually fly during a rain anyway, he'd risk it; he really didn't have a choice.

Darn! I don't have raincoat. I must have forgotten it. No, wait. I left it home on purpose because I wasn't planning on riding in the rain. I was going to stay in my tent if the weather was bad, or if I was on my bike and it started raining, I'd put it up and wait it out. I didn't think I might actually get caught in it. There is no good place to put a tent up here.

He laughed to himself. "I told Dave I was ready for anything, Chris. This time, I outsmarted myself." He turned north once again, keeping an eye out for possible shelters in case it started raining hard. It was really too early to camp for the night, and he was trying to make it to St. Helen before dark or rain, whichever came first.

Just as he turned onto F-97, rain started coming down steadily, and he was getting soaked. It was almost six o'clock, and Jim spotted a church on the left, Cornerstone Baptist Church, an attractive-looking church with a stone front. The building seemed fairly new, and it looked open. People were there. Ah. Sunday evening service.

"Any shelter in a time of storm. Let's go to church, Chris. You don't want to get any wetter, do you? I sure don't." He headed for the shelter of the porch and asked if he could come in. He'd only gone 110 miles since home and was roughly ninety miles behind schedule. The people were happy to let him join their service, bike shorts and all. Jim took a towel out of his pannier, dried off, and put on a warm sweatshirt. He hoped that the storm would blow over soon. "Hop on my shoulder, Chris. You can come in with me, but you have to promise not to chirp during the service. And be careful that no one sees you. Someone might knock you off and step on you, or some woman might scream. We don't want to cause trouble here."

He was thankful they didn't take an offering in the evening service since he didn't want to give from his limited resources. They sang four or five songs, and then some man spoke about something, but Jim wasn't paying attention. He was just glad to be out of the rain. He wondered how much money he had left. He knew he could only spend a little over fourteen dollars a day, and he had stayed within that amount so far. He also assumed that things would be more expensive as he went farther north, and he would need fare to cross the bridge or take the ferry.

Unfortunately, after the service, it was raining even harder, and there was also thunder and lightning. It was a real storm, not just a light rain. He asked one of the men of the church if he could spend the night at the church and camp in the yard. He told Jim, "Okay."

One of the senior ladies even invited him to spend the night at her house. Jim thanked her but turned her down. He told her he wanted to see how well his tent worked in the rain. He didn't tell her about the bet because he wasn't sure if the church people would think betting was wrong. Besides, when he made the bet, he fully intended to sleep outdoors, rain or shine. It was part of the bet and the adventure he wanted. It was part of the deal, no staying with friends or relatives.

Soon, all the church people were gone, but Jim stayed underneath the roof on the porch since he didn't want to pitch a tent in the pouring rain. Unfortunately, the roof was high up and some rain blew in every now and then. He got out his ground pad, laid it on the concrete porch, and put his wool blanket over himself and his space blanket, an aluminized plastic tarp, which was waterproof, over that. He huddled next to the building in the driest spot he could find.

"This concrete is way too hard, Chris. I gotta put that tent up as soon as there's a break in the rain. This concrete can't be doing my back any good, not to mention my hips and shoulders." Sometime in the middle of the night, the rain stopped and Jim got up to pitch his tent. This time, he got the tent poles in right on the first try. The tent pole that he taped up that morning held up. "So far, so good.

Scoot in there, Chris. I'm right behind ya." He crawled in and started to zip up the flap, but the zipper on one side of the tent flap broke. Fortunately, the zipper on the other side pulled all the way over so the flap still closed, but he knew he would have to be very careful with his tent for the rest of the trip.

It only took about five minutes to put the tent up, and shortly, there was more thunder and lightning. From time to time, the rain just poured down. The tent was on a high spot, so he wasn't worried about being flooded out, but he wondered about being struck by lightning or the tent being blown down. It got quite windy at times. Chris's continual chirping comforted Jim.

During the night, a nature call woke Jim up. It was pouring outside. Rain had already soaked through the tent, and there were little puddles on the tent floor in the corners. Jim took a washcloth, sopped up the wet spots, and wrung them outside the tent door. He found an empty plastic Coke bottle in his pack that he was saving to collect Michigan's ten-cent bottle deposit. His urgent need seemed more important than the ten cents, so he got a jackknife out of his pack and cut the top off. He used the bottle to relieve himself and then stuck the bottle outside and emptied it. "Pretty neat, Chris. I'll keep this bottle, and I'll never have to leave my tent in the middle of the night again. I bet it comes in handy where there are a lot of mosquitoes, too."

He stayed huddled in the center of the tent. At least he was staying warm and mostly dry. A little water would dry out later; after all, it was summer. Staying warm was the important thing.

5
I'm Feeling Lucky

Dawn came, and several times, he heard a strange noise, like an old Model T or some sort of small single-cylinder engine, a steady but fast tick, tick, tick, tick all the while accompanied by a rumbling sound. He finally opened up the tent and poked his head out to see what it was. Amish people were going by in a horse and buggy. The ticking was the horse's hooves on wet pavement, but Jim was far enough back from the road that he couldn't feel the hoofbeats through the ground. The rumbling sound was the carriage wheels.

It was still sprinkling or threatening rain, so he stayed in the tent and rested. He tried reading, but the dim gray skies and the dark maroon-fabric of the tent kept it too dark inside to comfortably read. Besides that, he couldn't sit up very long, as it was too uncomfortable.

He took his pulse, something athletes often did, but which he hadn't been doing regularly lately. It was ninety. His normal pulse before he left was only seventy. When he was biking regularly and in top condition, his resting pulse was as low as forty and usually below fifty. Ninety meant that he was quite stressed from the past two days of riding. His heart rate just confirmed what he already felt; he was tired.

He stared up at the roof of the tent and asked, "Chris, what am I doing here, laying on the hard ground, in this tent in the rain, by myself in this strange place, brooding?"

"Nothing."

"Nothing?"

"Yeah. Nothing. Didn't you come out here to get away from it all? To do nothing. Well, you're doing it. Nothing, that is. You're not repairing your house. You're not playing chess with Dave. You're certainly not at work. You're not doing any of the activities you normally do. You're doing nothing. But don't let that bother you. Sometimes it's really important to do nothing."

"But, Chris, didn't I tell Dave that sitting on the beach doing nothing is a vacation. That I was going on an adventure, not a vacation? And you tell me doing nothing is important?"

"Yeah. But in your case, at this moment, nothing is part of the adventure. If it was sunny out, you'd be on your bike eating up pavement. But the storm has stopped you. It was unplanned and even unwanted. Now you're going to be even further behind in your schedule. An even greater challenge awaits you. So doing nothing is still part of the adventure. Yet, doing nothing is important for another reason. A worker in a forest sees all the individual trees, but sometimes, he goes up on a mountaintop and looks down at the forest, so he can get the big picture. He can see if the forest is getting bigger or smaller, if it's diseased and dying out or growing healthy. It's hard to get the big picture when you're looking at individual trees, planting new ones, cutting down diseased ones, harvesting old ones, and what all. So up on the mountaintop, you leave your normal place in life, and by doing nothing, you can look at the big picture."

"What's so important about that?"

"When you get the big picture, then you can assess. Evaluate. Right now, you're physically stressed. Look at your heart rate. You're also depressed. The forced rest will help you recover physically. And taking a time-out to look at your life can help you get it into perspective and help you decide what to do about it."

"So … sometimes doing nothing is what's really important in life?" Jim asked.

Chris said nothing.

The rain continued off and on for most of the morning, so he stayed in his little tent until nearly noon. He didn't want to ride on wet roads because the front tire threw water back, mingled with grit, on the rider's feet, and after a few miles, the rider ended up with wet shoes and socks. Not only that, but grit got on the chain and worked its way back to the freewheel where it gradually ate up both chain and gears, and if the gears were worn enough, the chain skipped annoyingly whenever pressure was applied, making it hard to ride. Worn parts would not help him on this trip.

He was getting hungry. The peanut butter and crackers he had stashed the day before were gone. It looked like the rain might be over except for an occasional sprinkle, so he crawled out of his tent and loaded the bike. He checked his fanny pack to see that he still had the silver stiletto. Everything was ready. "On your perch, Chris. And stay off the bike computer. I can't read it when you're covering the numbers." It would take him over an hour to ride to the next town, St. Helen.

When they arrived in St. Helen, Jim said, "Chris, what do you think? Grandma's Café?"

Chris chirped, "Yes."

He put Chris on his shoulder, and they went in. Jim pulled out a heavy wooden chair and sat at a table.

Sitting on the hard chair, he realized his butt was starting to get tender. "I got spring butt syndrome, Chris. After being off the bike all winter, my butt has softened up. It hurts a little. But it should toughen up in a few days if I'm careful. Then I could sit on an iron brick, and it wouldn't matter. Well, maybe not an iron brick, but right now, it feels good to sit on something other than a bike seat, even this hard wood chair."

Grandma came and took his order—an omelet with cheddar cheese and ham, along with hash browns and wheat toast. In order to save money, he just had water for a drink, something he planned on doing for the duration of the trip in order to meet his budget.

"St. Helen is a nice-sized small town," Jim said, "yet it's so far off the beaten path, I doubt that many people have even heard of it. Not unless they're from around here, that is. I'd never heard of it until I made up this bike route through here."

Grandma said, "I grew up here, so I wouldn't know. But we do have at least one claim to fame. It's the hometown of Charlton Heston, who had a big old house not too far from here. It would have made a nice tourist attraction, too, but some arsonist burnt it down a few years ago."

While he waited, an older guy with a Detroit Tigers baseball cap came in. Jim nodded at him and gestured for him to sit at his table. The guy took him up on it. "Are you a Tigers fan, or did someone just give you a free hat?" Jim joked.

"It was a free cap. No one I know would admit to being a Tigers fan this year." The guy chuckled.

Jim thought it was great how two guys who didn't know one another could sit at a table and talk and joke like they were old friends without even knowing the other's name. He wasn't going to ask either. What was the point? He'd probably never see him again. "So what's going on?"

"Nothing much. I asked my wife what was for lunch, and she told me to go ask Grandma. So here I am."

Grandma came up and asked, "The usual, Fred?"

"Yeah," he grunted. She went back to the kitchen.

"This will probably sound kind of dumb," Jim said. "It's certainly off the wall. Yesterday, I saw a couple of nice-looking young women when I was stopped at a store in Gordonville."

"That doesn't sound dumb."

"It was good, actually. Both ladies looked nice, but they had on a light-blue eye shadow. To me, it just seemed so out of place. Neither of them had blue eyes. In fact, neither of them had anything on that even matched the color, the closest thing was their jeans. Do you have any idea why they'd be wearing it? Or am I the only one in this crazy world who doesn't understand this kind of thing?"

"Beats me." Fred laughed. "All I can say is that there are different kinds of women. Some of them don't care so much what they look like as long as they're comfortable and what others think isn't too important to them. A lot of those don't even bother with makeup."

"I've known women like that," Jim said. "Generally, they tend to be older. They've probably already raised their family and are not too concerned about attracting men, probably because they're fed up with men anyway." He was thinking of Grandma.

"Right," Fred continued. "Then there are those that actually dress to please men. They are the minority. Usually, they are young and have a slim body, and they enjoy the looks they get, the power they have over men, and the ability to use it, and some of them even get rich with it. Some of them may be hookers, but a lot of them are shrewd businesspeople or perhaps born teasers. Movie stars and models belong to this group. They know how to put on makeup that is attractive, and they don't necessarily care what others think about them either. They enjoy being glamorous and sexy. They are the lucky few who have a good self-image.

"Then there's a third group, the largest group. They dress to please other women. I don't mean sexually but socially. They are the group which calls the second group sluts, even though that might not be true. They are the group that would wear eye shadow because all their friends are doing it, even if it doesn't enhance their beauty. It makes them feel good about themselves. Accepted. They may not have any more clue about eye shadow than you do. In fact, I suspect that some of them, maybe not knowingly, but unconsciously, actually sabotage their beauty, just so they fit in. They are concerned what other people think, especially other women, and they want to be considered respectable. If all their friends are doing it, it's respectable. It's okay to be pretty but not too pretty."

"Women dressing to please other women? Now there's a thought."

Grandma brought out Jim's omelet and Fred's burger, fries, and coffee. Jim dug in while he pondered Fred's answer. The two ladies in Gordonville would be in the third group, and maybe the lady in black and Linda would be in the second group, but Linda was definitely not a slut. *It's interesting to think that women generally dress to please other women,* Jim thought. *I'd never thought of that before. Come to think of it, women probably don't think of it either; they just do it. It's a cultural thing.*

He enjoyed the meal, and it was the best he'd eaten on this trip. Actually, it was the first restaurant he'd stopped at on this trip and his only real meal.

Just as Jim went outside and started to get on his bike, there was a sudden rain shower. Fortunately, there was a partial roof over the front of the restaurant, so he just waited it out. The sudden shower convinced Jim to buy some sort of rain jacket in St. Helen. After stopping at a drugstore and a hardware store, he finally found one in a sporting goods shop for three dollars.

He also stopped at another little store and bought some Powerade and some more snacks to carry in the pannier. He diluted the Powerade with water in his Camelbak to save money. He liked Powerade better than Gatorade, which was too salty, but a lot of stores didn't carry it. He liked All-Sport, also, but because of the carbonation, he wasn't sure the Camelbak would hold it safely. The fizz might burst the bladder. Soda pop was out of the question.

As he pedaled out of St. Helen, "I'm Feeling Lucky" by Mary Chapin Carpenter, a talented country singer, kept going through his mind as he pedaled. "Chris, I'm so lucky to be out here, away from everything, to have survived that storm last night. Maybe not everything is going my way, and this isn't the nicest of days, but a bad day on the road is still better than a good day at work. So chirp away, and help me sing this song in my mind." He would have liked to sing it aloud, but he needed his breath to pedal.

The terrain was hilly and sandy, having been formed by glaciers. There was little farmland; it was mostly forest, spotty forest, and open areas with a few trees, mostly jack pine. He rode by areas protected for the endangered species, Kirtland's warbler, a small bird that nested in Michigan and almost became extinct but was on the rebound. Recently, a few nesting pairs had been found in neighboring states.

Jim kept riding on F-97 until it joined M-78 for a little ways. M-78 ended, and he followed F-97 still further. He was riding without glasses again since there were some occasional light sprinkles but not enough to make it worth opening up the package with the rain jacket. A few long, steep hills had him out of breath pedaling even in his lowest gear.

It was still early in the evening, and Jim went through Lovells. He was almost to Lewiston when he decided to stop for the night. He found a place in the woods far enough from the road so people wouldn't easily see him alongside a snowmobile trail. He put up his tent among the pine trees and thought about his situation. Three days and he still hadn't gone a hundred miles in a day. That day, he'd only gone sixty-five miles. Worse, his butt was getting sorer, even though his legs were fine. He realized that maybe he hadn't trained enough to reach his goal. In fact, he hadn't trained at all. He was counting on experience, but training counted too. *Well, give it some time,* he thought. He'd known even before he started that his first week would be tough. He also knew from experience that his second week would be better, just as long as he didn't have any saddle sores.

In the woods, there were some birds making a sort of piping sound. "Hey, Chris. Hear those birds piping? I don't know what they are, but it sure sounds pretty. How about a few chirps to help out the symphony?"

He sat in his tent and got out his water bottle and washcloth, something he did when he couldn't clean up in a lake or stream. Showers? Ha. King Arthur didn't have showers. His ancestors in wagon trains didn't have showers. Even on *Star Trek*, they didn't have showers—well, sonic showers maybe but not real ones. He was just washing up in the old time-tested manner. The washcloth was still damp from the day before. He put a few drops of dish detergent from a small plastic bottle on the cloth, added some water, and squished it in. Then he gave himself a sponge bath inside his tent. After washing, he rubbed some alcohol and hand lotion on his tender bottom to disinfect and act as a lubricant on the bike seat.

He put on his last pair of clean bike shorts and his last clean T-shirt, a dark-blue one advertising a bike ride in the Detroit area. Tomorrow, he would have to stop and wash clothes somewhere. When he was finished, he felt almost as good as if he'd taken a real shower. He felt fresh, clean, and relaxed; sleeping would not be a problem tonight.

The pine woods seemed to magnify sounds. Piping bird sounds echoed from all over. For someone who lived in the city, it was quiet and peaceful and yet at the same time, so noisy. In the city, one didn't notice all the little sounds because one was used to them and because sound didn't penetrate the hard walls of a house nearly as easily as it penetrated a tent. In the woods, every little sound just seemed a lot louder, echoing in the trees.

Jim lay in his tent listening to the birds for a while. Then he asked Chris, "Why am I depressed?"

"It's because you're not connected."

"Not connected? What do you mean by that?"

"We all have this idea in our mind of who we are, a self-image. Usually, it's a pretty good image; we think we're pretty cool. Some people call it ego. There's just one problem. This image doesn't mean a thing unless others confirm it for us."

"Confirm?"

"Yeah, we need someone to share this opinion of ourselves to validate it. Affirm it. As we go through life, people tell you that you're not cool, you're dumb, you're square, or you're a nobody or worse. When enough people contradict your self-image, you start to doubt yourself. You might even lower your self-image. Or if you have a real strong self-image, you just keep trying to prove to these people over and over again that you really are cool. If you can't get anyone to share your self-image, it gets depressing. When you finally get someone to agree with your self-image and you agree with their self-image, you connect. You accept and respect one another. It's a mutual admiration. You have a friend. You're connected."

"And I'm not connected?"

"Not very well. Connections can be of different strengths, like string, rope, or steel cable. You seem to have just a few strings."

"That doesn't sound very good."

"Think about it. How many friends do you have?"

"Well, there's you. And Dave."

"Anyone else?"

"No one close. Linda maybe. Some of my biking buddies."

"There you are. Dave is like a rope, a pretty strong connection for you. You play chess and banter and admire each other's building skills. And you have this crazy bet going. If it wasn't for Dave, you might be totally nutso."

"Well, what about you?"

"I only count as much as you believe in me."

"I guess that's true. What about Linda?"

"Think about it, Jim. How were you connected to her?"

"Well, uh, she wowed me with her looks."

"And she liked your looks, too. But how does that confirm your self-image?"

"Uh …"

"Men connect by doing things together. What did you and she do together? Did you bike?"

"No."

"Did you play chess?"

"No."

"Did you go to concerts?"

"Yeah, but she liked hard rock. I like soft rock, or even country or oldies."

"So music didn't connect you?"

"I guess not."

"Linda painted. Did you paint with her?"

"No. But I admired her paintings."

"Did that make you feel connected?"

"I guess not. I probably didn't understand them. I have a hard time even drawing stick people."

"What else did you do with her?"

"We went to movies."

"Did that make you feel connected?"

"I guess not. I like sci-fi, fantasy, and adventure. She likes chick flicks, romance, tear-jerkers. But I enjoyed being with her."

"Women connect by sharing. After the movie was over, did you tell her how it made you feel? If you were watching one of her chick flicks and you told her afterward that it was boring, do you think that made a connection with her?"

"Chris, you have a way of hurting a guy."

"If you watched a sci-fi movie together, did she share with you how much she enjoyed it?"

"I don't think so."

"What else did you do together?"

"Went out to eat."

"How did you feel about that?"

"I eat out all the time. So what? I probably would have been happier if she had cooked a meal for me. I have mixed feelings about eating. I'm trying to keep my weight down. I want to stay in shape so I can bike faster. I felt guilty, spending too much money and eating too many calories, so except for being with her, I probably wasn't too happy."

"How did she feel about it?"

"Linda? She was always watching her calories. It's no wonder she looked so good. She'd order a big dinner and just pick at it. I don't think she likes to cook. Maybe she'd've been happier if I brought her a frozen yogurt."

"So eating out wasn't really connecting you. What else did you do?"

"We watched TV."

"And did that connect you?"

"I guess not. But we picked out the house together. We were going to live in it after we were married. I spent all that time and money remodeling it."

"And how did that make you feel? Was this your project or hers?"

"I suppose it was hers. I didn't really want a big house to live in. I would've been happy with an apartment or something a lot smaller. I did it for her."

"So the house didn't really make you feel connected. Do you think all that work you put into it made her feel connected?"

"I guess not. I couldn't seem to please her."

"So, Jim, what is so special about Linda? You appear to not have been connected to her at all, yet you're saying you love her. Why do you think you love her?"

"I guess I love her for the way she looks. And she is a nice person."

"And why would she love you? How did she connect to you?"

"My looks? I don't know. Maybe she didn't."

"Do you think you two were just in love with the idea of being in love, of being married, having someone to care for, and having children someday? The American dream? A beautiful spouse and a big ol' house?"

"Yeah. I think we did share that."

"But you weren't really connected, were you? She was just someone to play a role for you. A trophy wife."

"Ouch."

"So why do you suppose it hurts so much to lose her?"

"Because … uh … my dreams are shattered? I have to find someone else to fulfill my dreams, and it's going to be hard to … well, I'll probably never find anyone else like her."

"You remind me of someone who just bought a brand-new Maserati sports car and had it stolen. No wonder you're depressed. You just lost your biggest toy."

"Chris, you're making me feel bad. You know, that's not healthy for somcone of your size. You know what I do to mosquitoes."

"I'm sorry, Jim. I was just trying to help you with connecting."

"All right. I know you mean well. So I'm only connected to you and Dave. Not Linda."

"How do you think Linda feels? Maybe her dreams are shattered, too."

"She must feel awful. I've been told that women are more into feelings than men, like the difference between color TV versus black and white."

"Perhaps she was sabotaging your remodeling because in her own way she … felt … that there was no connection between you. She might not have realized it consciously, but subconsciously, she was trying to either connect or get out of the relationship."

"I see. So how would I connect with her?"

"Share your thoughts and feelings with her. If she felt about things the same way you do, you would connect."

"There's not much chance of that."

"Why not?"

"I just don't think I had the same thoughts and feelings she did. Most of the time, I was just doing things to be with her, not because I had the same tastes she did. I put all that time and money into that old house for her. It wasn't really something I wanted, but I thought she wanted it."

"So in effect, you were a slave to her beauty?"

"It appears so. I think men would do anything for a good-looking woman."

"And she didn't want a slave. She wanted a partner, someone she could connect with, share with."

"But I still love her."

"You always will, on some level. In some ways, you may have been connected, but the connections were more like strings. They weren't strong enough for a good marriage. But it's okay, Jim. It's not reasonable to expect that you can connect with anyone or everyone, even if they are attractive. Most people only have a very few steel-cable-strength connections in a lifetime. Some people never get any. And back to confirming a self-image, when she left, it was a big hit to your self-image. It's no wonder you're depressed."

"That's it! I can see now I was being dumb in trying to connect to someone who was so different. It just wasn't meant to be. Maybe I can find a girl who is a little more like me the next time."

As the birds kept on piping, Jim dozed off, feeling like he had just solved one of life's great mysteries. He thought about how Linda must hurt, about how they never really connected and yet they got engaged. They were each trying to live out their own dream but not really relating to each other. During the night, it rained off and on at least three more times, just gentle sprinkles. The sound of little drops hitting the tent relaxed and soothed him; Mother Nature's little tears were sympathizing with him, comforting him. He slept well.

6
I Get Around

On the fourth day, Jim rose late again, partly to avoid rain. After making sure he had the silver shoe in his fanny pack, he rode into Lewiston, billed as Timbertown, to find a place to eat. He parked his bike at the Village Restaurant, leaning it carefully against the side of the building, both so it wouldn't fall and so it wouldn't scratch the paint on the building. "Chris, you coming in? Hop on my shoulder. But no chirping." Chris hopped up, and Jim went in and sat down. The waitress, Mary, according to the nametag on her black blouse, looked to be about his age. She was of average height and had dark hair in a perky cut and a nice smile. Was she wearing eye shadow? He couldn't tell. *I guess that makes it a no.* She was wearing natural-colored hose under her short black skirt, with white socks and tennies. The socks and tennies were clean and bright and her blouse and skirt wrinkle free. She looked nice, clean, fresh, and cheerful. Mary left a menu and a glass of water, which, as soon as she had gone, he surreptitiously emptied into his Camelbak, ice and all.

When Mary came back to take his order, he thought about making a smart remark about her being a "cute dish" but then had second thoughts. This wasn't the movies, and in his job environment, one always worried about sexual harassment suits, even if what was said was meant as a compliment. This worry carried over into private life, even if it was unfounded. He ordered scrambled eggs with corned-beef hash, and while he waited, she brought him a second glass of water, which he again surreptitiously emptied into his Camelbak.

A few minutes later, she came back with his food and said, "You must be real thirsty today. I'll get you another glass." Jim smiled. She was a good waitress; he could get her to come again and again. The thought did not displease him.

While Jim was eating, she came back again, this time with a pitcher. She filled his glass and left the pitcher on the table. Jim surreptitiously poured the water and ice from the pitcher into his Camelbak. There was just a little left, so he drank the water in his glass and emptied the rest of the water from the pitcher into it.

When she came back to see if he needed anything else, she spotted the empty pitcher and nearly empty glass. "Have you been pouring this on the floor?" she teased, and she bent over to look under the table. "I just can't believe you drank all that." Jim smiled. He enjoyed the view she gave him bending over. Talk about sexual harassment. And she never even knew! Or did she? Maybe she was flirting with him! After all, he hadn't asked her to bend over.

"I get thirsty on the bike," he said.

That prompted Mary to start asking him all the usual questions about his bike trip, and then she suggested that instead of going north out of Lewiston, he head east about nine miles and turn left by the county dump. It was paved now and less traveled, probably a better way to go than going north first and then east on M-32. It also avoided some big hills.

Jim decided Mary was pretty nice. She had given him a nice tip about the roads. The food was good, and he spent only about five dollars for it. He usually tipped a dollar, but he left two for her as he left.

When they got outside, Chris chirped, "Why did you leave a double tip?"

"She gave good service, didn't she?"

"Yeah, but why double?"

"The food was good."

"Jim, after all the pedaling, you were so hungry, worms would have tasted good."

"Because she gave me a route tip?"

"It wasn't worth that much."

"Because I liked the view?"

"Ah, that I believe. She had pretty nice legs for a human. Nothing as nice as a cricket's legs of course, but for a human, darn nice."

"So what's your point?"

"The point is—Grandma could have given you the same good service, the same good food, and the same tip about a route change, and she would have only got half the tip. It's not fair. It's discrimination."

Uh-oh, Jim thought. *I knew this critter was going to start getting lippy. I'll argue with him about it later. I want to get going.* "Hop back on the bars, Chris. We'll discuss this later. I can't believe that you, a male, are siding with the opposite sex."

The road was scenic and had some long, slow climbs but no knee-busters. There were a few good fast downhills. He was glad he had taken the new route; it gave him an opportunity to see the south side of Atlanta, which he hadn't seen before. Mary was right; the route was better. It avoided a lot of fast traffic and some killer hills. The reason he hadn't tried this route before was that he didn't know it was paved; his map showed the road as gravel.

"Chris, we're getting around today. How about some chirping to mix with the harmony?"

"I Get Around," a song by the Beach Boys, kept going through Jim's mind. He liked the harmony and beat of most of the Beach Boys' songs, and he felt like he was really getting around on his bicycle.

Jim's pedals kept gettin' "round, round, round, round" into Atlanta where he stopped to get some grape drink and added it to the water in his Camelbak.

Then Jim continued getting those pedals "round, round, round, round" to Onaway, taking M-33 North, which was a good road; it had a paved shoulder and was wide, fairly smooth, and lightly traveled, even though it was a state highway.

There was a stiff wind from the west, which was almost as bad as a headwind. It was a good sign, though. It meant better weather was coming. By the time Jim got to Onaway, he was very tired and his Camelbak was ready for some more water.

It was four thirty when he stopped at a little ma-and-pa restaurant named Denny's (not the chain). He went inside, ordered a hamburger, and just rested. It wasn't busy inside, but there was a young couple with two small kids who were running around and screaming, generally having a good time. They weren't bad kids; they were just acting their age. Still, Jim was annoyed (or was that annoised) since he was tired and just wanted some peace and quiet. He wished they would go away.

The waitress was a teenager who wore a name tag with "Donia" on it. He decided to forget the water trick and just asked her to fill the Camelbak for him, which she did. After eating, Jim went to the register, took out his wallet to pay his bill, and asked her if her father's name was Don.

"Yes, do you know him?"

"No."

"Then why did you ask?"

"Just a hunch. It seems natural for a girl named Donia."

Just then, her father, Don, came into the store, and she introduced him. On the way out, Jim left a dollar tip for her.

In spite of the little rugrats, Jim felt a lot better after the burger and the short rest. He stopped at a little store across the street and got some more goodies to carry with him. This time, he bought a bag of Cheetos, some corn nuts, and some more drink mix.

He "got around, round, round," west two miles and then north on Black River Road. He followed this road all the way past the UAW camp and Black Lake. He came to a little bridge that went over a stream. A man, who looked like he was in his twenties, with long, dark hair, was sitting on the railing of the bridge. As Jim rode by, the man caught sight of him and began singing, "The sands of time are running out on me."

Jim smiled, waved, and rode on, thinking about the words. *The sands of time are running out on me, too,* he thought. *I have to start getting some miles in if I'm going to make it to Ironwood.* He wondered if the words were from a popular song, or if the man had just made it up. If it was from a song, he didn't recognize it.

It was getting late as he rode by the little town of Alverno, which had just a church and a store. He was trying to think of where he could spend the night. There weren't many places between Alverno and Mackinaw City. So when he found a little Christmas tree farm, he decided to take advantage of it. "Merry Christmas, Chris. This should give you something to chirp about." He walked his bike far enough in that he couldn't be seen from the road, set up his tent, and crawled in.

He had gone seventy-five miles in spite of his late start and the headwind, and it had ended up a nice, sunny day. *That wasn't too bad,* he thought. On the other hand, he was having serious doubts as to whether he could make it all the way to Ironwood. He had lost too many miles. Worse yet, his butt was getting even more tender. He didn't have any saddle sores yet, but he figured he would have to take it easy another day or two. A short day tomorrow wouldn't be a bad idea. Not a bad idea at all.

"Chris, I've been thinking."

"Yes."

"About discrimination. It seems to have gotten a bad name, but some discrimination is good. Complaining that it isn't fair does about as much good as complaining that Florida has all the warm weather in the winter and they ought to share some of it with Michigan. That's not fair either, but it's true. And if somebody likes Pepsi, but not Coca-Cola, should he drink equal amounts of both so he doesn't discriminate against one of them? If someone likes an Apple computer instead of a PC, should he be forced to buy one of each? Discrimination is built into life itself. And what one person calls fair is often discriminatory against someone else. Even crickets must have some form of discrimination."

"How so?"

"Well, I've been told that the big male crickets eat the legs off the younger males so they can't grow up and mate with the females. All of nature manifests discrimination. Lions prey on the young and weak animals. It's called survival of the fittest or smartest or fastest. Even beauty has a part in it; red-wing blackbirds that have larger red areas on their wings are more likely to get a mate. And in humans, the prettier women are more likely to get a mate. The only nondiscriminatory way would be to have a lottery. Every male and every female of eligible age should be put into a big computer database, and the computer will randomly select who marries whom. That would be truly nondiscriminatory. The same lottery procedure could be used to determine who gets what job, who lives where, or any number of things. But let's face it, nobody would be happy. If I happened to draw a woman who was feeble-minded or crippled or who weighed four-hundred pounds, I might kill myself first. Maybe there are some women who would feel that way if they drew my name. And how would a Jew feel if he drew a Muslim or vice versa? I guarantee you, discrimination works. It's just not fair. But it's the way God made things."

"Are you saying God's not fair?"

"Probably. I don't know. God has his own ways; I don't understand Him. Who can say whether He's fair or not? But it's certain that He made us all different. To some people He gave brains, money, or beauty. Others are born crippled and poor. He probably has a way of working it all out in His grand scheme of things so that it's fair, but we as humans can't see this 'grand scheme.' It certainly appears to be unfair from a human viewpoint.

"But let me tell you this. If Grandma had waited on me at the restaurant this morning and gave me the good service, the good food, and even if she had bent over to look under the table and given me the view and also given me a route tip, I still wouldn't have enjoyed it as much. It sure wouldn't be fair to me to have to tip her the same amount as Mary. Besides, I didn't cheat Grandma. She got her tip. I was just extra nice to Mary. Why should that be wrong?

"If you stop to think about it, the antidiscrimination laws in this country don't actually stop discrimination, they just set down rules so you know how you can or can't discriminate. For a job, it is legal to discriminate based on a person's training, education, experience, testing, or ability to give a good interview. It's not legal to discriminate based on a person's age, religion, sex, or race. And yet these last items often affect the first ones. What an employer really wants is someone who not only can do the job but is also honest, responsible, and dependable. The last three items are impossible to gauge in an interview. I suppose that's why references are provided."

Chris just listened.

Jim lay in the tent and thought about the job his cousin Loretta spoke of. Was she just talking? Obviously, she was discriminating in asking him to work for her. Her company sounded like it was a lot different from other companies. Did it recruit its personnel by personal invitation only? Could she really get him a job with her company? It seemed too good to be true. He was very unhappy with his current job. Sure, it paid well. The epitome of irony was that the thing he liked best about his job was all the time off. He could take vacations like this. If he quit, where else could he get a job that paid this well or offered as much time off? He might end up working twice as hard for half as much somewhere else. He felt trapped, as if in a cage of gold, his soul sold to the company. He had good benefits. Working conditions were good.

So what didn't he like? He'd rather work for Loretta than Mr. Bigshot. Mr. DontHaveTimeforYou. Mr. DontTrustYou. Ah, that's it. He'd get assignments, and they'd end up stuck forever on his boss's desk simply because the boss never had time to look at them because he was busy with more important things. His boss wouldn't delegate work. It was too important, and he couldn't risk having someone make a mistake. His boss didn't have time to train him to do new things. It made Jim feel little, unneeded, and frustrated.

But what about Loretta's job, he thought. *Would I take it? She wouldn't make me feel unneeded. She'd give me important assignments. I'd get training with her company. It sounds like a dream job. Would I take it? Yes. I'm young. I'm single. I can go anywhere in the world that I want. I'm only tied down by my current job, which I don't like. Maybe it doesn't pay as much, and I hear the cost of living is a lot higher out there, but I think I'll take it. I'm tired of repairing the old house. I'll sell it when I get back, get what I can out of it. Start enjoying life again. California has a lot better biking weather than Michigan. I can even bike all year round out there.* Having made that decision, he slept better.

7
California Dreamin'

On Wednesday, July 31, it rained lightly almost all morning. Jim was glad for the rest it gave him in his little tent. It was almost noon before he was able to get on the road again. "Whew. Chris, I'm getting hungry. My stash is all gone. Have you had anything to eat?"

"I'm fine," he chirped.

Jim wondered what crickets ate. He didn't think it was the same things people ate, but he could imagine Chris had a good breakfast even if he hadn't.

They turned north on Butler and then west on US 23 to Cheboygan and stopped at the first nice restaurant they could find, the Flame, which had a beautifully etched glass front door. The door reminded him of Linda—classy, his former flame. It was light and airy inside, pleasant. He sat down at a booth, and when the waitress came, he ordered a codfish dinner with French fries, a roll, cottage cheese, and the usual water. No tricks on the waitresses this morning. Besides that, he couldn't get Linda off his mind. He didn't even notice the waitress. Once in a lifetime, he figured, a man would meet someone like Linda. *Once in a lifetime. She's the only woman who ever made me feel that way. That way. How could he describe it?*

* * *

The time I first saw her, I was coming out of the grocery store. She was all in black, her pumps, her hose, her perfectly fitted dress, her every hair in place, her eyes, her smile. I was smitten, as if someone took a sword and slashed open my chest and my heart fell out on the floor where everyone could see it. I was speechless, unable to move, stunned.

Then she batted her eyes at me; those long lashes melted me. It was like a magic spell, she could have asked me to kill myself, and I would have done it. Gladly.

Instead, she said, "Hi."

I was unable to answer, my mouth dry, my tongue stuck in my mouth. Other people were walking by like nothing was going on. Apparently, she only affected me that way. She asked me if I was all right. I nodded. Nodded yes, that is. Then I dropped my groceries. I felt like such a clumsy idiot.

She stopped and said, "Let me help you pick those up."

I picked my heart back up off the floor and put it back in my chest. I spoke, weakly, "Thanks." I bent over to help her pick them up, as if I were helping her, not the other way around. I don't think anything was broken. I can't even remember what was in the sack—probably some hot dogs and buns, maybe some plastic bottles of Coke.

Then she said, "My name's Linda." I nodded again. She had a nice voice. "Well?" she said.

I didn't say anything.

"Well?" she said again.

"Uh, well. Well what?"

"Well, what's your name?"

"I … I'm Jim. Would you like to go for coffee? I could sure use one right now." I don't know how I managed to ask her.

"Sure. That would be nice. Put your groceries in your car and meet me here by the door. I'll be out in a few minutes."

I put my groceries in my car, and when I came back to the door, I could see her in the checkout line. I didn't know whether to go in and check out with her or just to wait for her like she said. I waited. Like an obedient puppy. Stay, Jim, stay. She came out in a couple of minutes and said, "That's my red Oldsmobile over there," pointing to an Aurora. "Get your car and follow me." I would have followed her to the next star system, but she led me to Sarah's Place on Michigan Avenue. We went in and had some coffee together. I was able to settle down and relax as we talked. She was sweet and witty, a charming, caring person. That's how and where I met her, one of the happiest days of my life.

* * *

"Jim? Jim! Wake up, Jim!" Chris was jumping up and down on Jim's shoulder, trying to get his attention. "What's going on with you today?"

"Huh? Okay, okay, I'm awake now." He looked down at the bill on the table. His food was gone. He left the waitress a tip. He felt full, but he didn't remember eating. He looked at the empty dishes. "Chris, did you eat my dinner?"

"No, you did, Jim. I saw you."

"Good, I'm glad you were watching. If someone took me to court and asked me to swear to it, I couldn't right now. But I do feel full."

He took the bill up to the counter to pay. There were cute little dolls for sale and other handicraft items. Jim couldn't afford to get any, nor did he have enough room to carry extra things on his bike, though he was tempted. But for whom? He had no one to share them with.

The lady at the counter asked him, "Was everything all right?"

"Uh, yeah." What else could he say? He didn't remember a thing. He paid his bill and walked out.

As he put his helmet and sunglasses back on, he said, "Thanks for waking me, Chris. But it was a very pleasant daydream—about when I first met Linda. It was about taste. As they say, 'there is no accounting for taste.' *Taste* is just another word for *discrimination*. When I first met Linda, I was stunned, bowled over, whatever you call it. But I was the only one. Everyone else just walked by like she wasn't even there. She didn't have that effect on everyone, just me. It's a good thing, too. If every man felt about her like I did, there would be World War III fighting over her."

One thing that had been bothering Jim ever since he went by Black Lake and heard that man singing on the bridge was the rear wheel on his bike. It had a slight hop in it, which meant that whenever he was riding, even on a really smooth road, it still felt slightly bumpy, as if the wheel had a flat spot on it. Thinking it was the rim, Jim stopped at a bike shop in Cheboygan to see if he could do something about the wheel. Unfortunately, they didn't have any new rims that would fit his bike. At most shops, they had a lot of mountain bikes, which were becoming very popular, but not much for "roadies," as people who had road bikes were called, whether racers or tourists. At least he didn't spend any money, if he'd bought a wheel; he would have lost his bet for sure. His butt was tender enough that he would have been willing to spend a lot for a smoother ride.

After thinking about Loretta last night, "California Dreamin'" was running through his mind. It was a good biking song with lots of harmony on such a summer day.

Would he go to California? It was a risk. Things might not work out. Shoot, things weren't working out now. Even if he didn't take the job, he would at least go out there for the interview and to see his cousin. He would probably take it. "How'd you like to go to Los Angeles, Chris? I bet you'd like the warm weather."

So he dreamed about California while pedaling down the newly paved US 23 toward Mackinaw City. About halfway between Cheboygan and Mackinaw City was a roadside park, on Lake Huron, where he stopped and rested. In spite of earlier rain and clouds, the sun came out, and it felt nice and warm. The grass had dried. He spread his blanket on the green grass, got out his dirty clothes, and took them down to the lake to wash them in the cold water. He waded in and rinsed the salt and grime off himself. The water was refreshing but too cold to enjoy swimming, and the beach was rocky and slippery, not sandy like on Lake Michigan, so he had to step carefully. He wrung out the clothes and spread them in the sun to dry and then stretched out on his blanket. He watched people come in and out of the park, some to feed the seagulls, some to picnic, some to wade, and some bikers even came in to fill their water bottles at the pump. He began to get drowsy in the warm sun, so he put his towel over his eyes to blot out the sun and fell lightly asleep. Chris chirped contentedly.

* * *

Sandy Hill rode south on US 23 toward Cheboygan. She had spent the night with her sister, Judy, at their aunt's house near Moran, a small town north of St. Ignace. Judy didn't ride a bike, so she carried Sandy's clothes and whatever other things she needed for her two-week vacation in the car. They were spending the nights at relatives' houses. This way, Sandy got to ride her bike in the UP, visit her relatives, and take care of one additional mission. Sandy was just an average woman of average height with light-brown hair and dark-brown eyes. There was nothing special about her that would make her stand out in a crowd. She wore her hair in a shoulder-length ponytail most of the time. She came from a big family and just sort of fit in with everyone else. She stayed fit by running and biking and even competed in triathlons sometimes. She had just ridden down to Mackinaw City and was now heading to Cheboygan. About halfway there, she stopped at the roadside park on Lake Huron. She walked her bike in and spotted a red Schwinn loaded for touring, just what she was looking for.

*   *   *

Jim woke when he heard someone walking nearby. It was a young woman with a purple helmet, a purple top, black shorts, matching purple socks, and bike shoes, and she was walking a purple Trek. He put his sunglasses back on. There was a rainbow decal on her helmet and another one on her bike, and she had a rainbow tattoo on the side of her leg just above her socks. She had light-brown hair bleached by the sun, in a ponytail. The ponytail looked cute sticking out under her bike helmet. It was hard to tell since he was on the ground, but he estimated that she was of average height, about five six.

She stopped to talk to Jim. "Hi. Where you headed?"

She had a rich alto voice, and Jim was startled by its musical quality. It was deep, like Anne Murray's or Karen Carpenter's.

She wasn't asking the usual questions. Instead of "Where are you going?" she said, "Nice bike. How many speeds do you have?"

"Uh … twenty-one, three on the front and seven on the back." She seemed so pretty that he stopped breathing for a moment, as if taking a breath would make her disappear. What a nice way to wake up. *Or am I awake?* Jim pinched himself.

"Careful, Jim," Chris said. Jim looked at his handlebar where Chris was giving him the eye.

"What size is your granny gear?"

"Twenty-six."

"That's pretty small; most the ones I've seen are a thirty."

"Yeah, I ordered it special. I'm hoping to ride it out west in the Rockies someday."

"Oooh, that sounds like fun. Have you ever been there?"

"I have, and believe me; you can't get too low a gear. If the steep roads don't get you, the thin air will. But what a thrill when you cruise down at fifty miles per hour or even faster!"

"It is fun. I've been as fast as forty-five on a few hills in Michigan. Are you headed for Mackinaw City? It would be fun to have someone to ride with." She gave him a pretty smile and added, "If you can keep up, that is."

Oh, a challenge! Who wouldn't want to ride with her? But he kept his cool. After all, he did have his own priorities. He'd come there to recover from a relationship, not start a new one. He would be nice to her, enjoy her company for a while, but he wouldn't let her get close. "I'm drying my clothes in the sun right now. Also, I'm pretty tired and need some rest. It's only a little way to Mackinaw City, and I can easily make it before dark, but if you want to wait around a while …" He thought that waiting would discourage her.

"That would be good. I could use a little rest myself. May I sit down with you?"

So she wasn't going to be discouraged, he thought. There was a certain camaraderie that bikers shared on the open road by virtue of their common sport and perhaps their common vulnerabilities, such as flat tires and autos. Jim might have turned her down because of his hurt and bitterness toward women, but he couldn't turn her down because of her bike. "Uh … sure." If Grandma had come in on a bicycle, she would have been more than welcome. But this person was pretty. It made him uncomfortable. He moved over to one side of his blanket, and she sat down on the other side but said nothing; she just stared out at the lake. Jim rolled over on his stomach and tried to continue his nap. If the woman had been chattering, it probably would have irked him. Still, he might have been able to ignore her and go back to sleep. Her silence was even more irksome. After a while, he couldn't stand it.

Finally, he began talking to her. "I'm Jim, from Lansing. Are you from around here?"

"I'm Sandy Hill, from Flint."

"Where are you going?" Now he was the one asking the usual questions.

"To the UP. I've got relatives up there."

"Are you by yourself?"

"Yes and no. My sister, Judy, is going on this trip with me, but she doesn't bike. She's driving her car and carries my things for me, and we spend the night at relatives' homes. I'm mostly by myself during the day."

Suddenly, Jim thought she looked familiar. Where had he seen her? "Don't I know you from somewhere?" he asked.

"No." She smiled. "But you don't need to use a pickup line on me after the conversation has already started."

"I … I wasn't," Jim said, sounding surprised. "I just think you look familiar. Or maybe my mind is playing tricks on me."

"Really? What's your last name?"

"Sanders."

"Where are you headed?"

"To the UP. They tell me it's God's country up there. Maybe I'll run into Him." He chuckled.

"Any particular place?"

"Ironwood. I'm headed out US 2. Camping the whole way."

"Then you're staying at the Straits State Park, just across the bridge?"

"No, I'm staying somewhere along the side of the road. I don't intend to pay camping fees when I'm not cooking or using electricity or even building a campfire."

"Would you like to stay with my sister and me at my aunt's house tonight? I know she wouldn't mind."

"I'm not sure yet where I'm staying tonight, and perhaps under other circumstances I would be delighted to stay with you but not this trip. I can't." *I sure am glad I made that bet,* he thought. *I've got an out.*

"Oh." She sounded disappointed.

Not wanting to make her feel rejected, he continued, "How long are you going to be up here?"

"Two weeks. I started my vacation Saturday, the twenty-seventh."

"That's the same day I started my vacation," Jim said, "and I've got two weeks also."

"Too bad we're going to different places; maybe we could've worked something out to ride together. At least part of the time," she added.

"A possibility. Which way are you going?" he said, trying to be nice.

"North. To Paradise."

Sandy seemed to be lost in thought for a while and just stared out toward the lake. Finally, she said, "Jim?"

"Yes." He sat up next to her and stared out toward the lake, too. He saw two ore freighters, one headed west toward the bridge and one headed east. They passed one another in the distance. *Two ships passing in the … er … day. Yep,* he thought. *That's all we're gonna be, two ships passing.*

"Why can't you stay at my aunt's house?" she asked hesitantly.

Jim was torn between wanting to avoid her and wanting to be with her. In a way, he felt sort of silly, but a bet was a bet and he hated to lose. "I made a bet with my neighbor. I have to spend less than two hundred dollars on this vacation to win. Part of the bet was I wouldn't be staying with friends and I'd buy all my own food. If I stayed at your aunt's house, I'd be cheating on the bet. I have to be on my own."

"Oh." She thought about it. A minute or so later, she said, "Would you watch my bike for me? I'm going down to the lake."

"Of course." In a way, he felt relieved that she was leaving, if only for a few minutes.

She took off her helmet, shoes, and socks and walked to the short, rocky beach. He watched her walk down, enjoying the view. Her shoulder-length ponytail waved gently in the breeze off the lake. Seagulls screeched overhead. While she was wading, Jim had a sudden urge to see the little silver shoe. He pulled it out of his fanny pack, unwrapped it, and held it in his fingers. It was she, he thought, the person in the image he had when he'd first held the shoe. Why did it make him think of her? Who was she really? How or why was she connected to the shoe? It looked like she was coming back. He quickly rewrapped the shoe and put it back in his fanny pack.

When she got back, she took a paperback out of her fanny pack and asked him, "Do you like to read?"

"I do. What have you got?"

"A book on King Arthur. I enjoy reading about him." She showed him the book.

"That's volume two of the Pendragon series; I just got through reading this same book before starting this trip. It was really good. In fact, King Arthur is what inspired me to take this trip. I wanted some adventure of my own. I brought volume three with me to read. See?" Jim dug into his pannier and pulled out the book.

"You're not very far along in it."

"No, I thought I would have time to read, but I've been tired from all this biking, and reading seems to put me right to sleep. The few times I wasn't tired, I was in my tent staying out of the rain, and there just wasn't enough light in the tent to read comfortably. A maroon tent on a cloudy day just doesn't cut it for me."

They talked about King Arthur for a while until Jim noticed the sun was going west behind the trees at the edge of the park. It was after five o'clock.

"I think we should be going now. My T-shirts are dry, but bike shorts take forever to dry because of the chamois padding inside. This late in the day, the sun just isn't very warm in Michigan. "You can't even get a tan after five. We're just too far north." He gathered his clothes and repacked his bike. He rolled the blanket up last and put it in a stuff sack on top.

Sandy filled her water bottle at the pump. Then they pedaled toward Mackinaw City.

Jim was all loaded down, but Sandy wasn't, since Judy carried most of her things in her car. She pedaled hard, and he struggled to keep up. It was a good thing it was only seven miles to the city and it was pretty flat, or he was going to have to beg for mercy and ask her to slow down. He hated to think a woman could pedal faster than he could, even if he was loaded down. She was good.

They rode into the city together and then stopped at a fudge shop. Jim bought some caramel corn, and Sandy bought some cherry walnut fudge. They went outside and sat on a bench while they ate. "I'm going to cross the straits in the morning, Sandy. I've gone far enough for one day. Maybe we can ride together again sometime. It was fun riding with you. Thanks." He planned to go back and camp in a place he'd seen just outside of Mackinac City. He knew Sandy had her own plans.

Sandy pulled a business card out of her fanny pack. "Give me a call at work when you get back. Matt Assenmacher has rides from his bike shop in Swartz Creek. Maybe you'd like to ride with the Flint club sometime."

"Sure." He put the card in his wallet without even looking at it. "Thanks. I'll call you when I get back." Maybe he would, he thought, if he felt like it, but he wasn't really planning on calling. He didn't mean to lead her on, but he wondered, *How does a man say bye to a woman without hurting her?* Women seemed to take this "I'll call you" thing seriously. Was saying, "I'll call you" a promise, a lie, or just being polite and keeping one's options open? He hoped she would take it as being polite.

He got on his bike and headed back out of town about a mile with his eye out for the place he could camp.

He had enjoyed the ride with Sandy. Linda never rode with him. Of course, he would have enjoyed riding with anyone. It got lonely on the road.

He soon found the place to put up his tent, possibly still within the city limits, not far from I-75 since he could hear the freeway traffic, and it was still within sight of US 23. It was a wooded area in a right-of-way cleared for power lines. He had only gone twenty-five miles for the day. He thought about the time he spent in the sun at the beach and the good rest he'd had. He also thought about the ride/race with Sandy. It'd been fun! She had been fun. He was thinking of her in terms of a fellow biker, rather than as a woman. And yet, he couldn't quite forget that she was a woman, as well as a good rider. Could someone like her replace Linda? Why was he even thinking that?

He put up his little maroon tent and climbed in. Chris followed. Jim had packed two pairs of black tights to keep him warm, either while sleeping at night or while riding if the weather turned cold. He had a light pair and a winter pair for colder weather. He was planning to sleep in the winter pair, but he couldn't find them. *Darn,* he thought. *Did I leave them back in Alverno? Did I leave them at the park? Did they fall out of my pannier along the way?* He was sure he'd had them in Alverno so he must have lost them somewhere in between. It was too late in the day to go back looking for them now.

"Chris?"

"Yes?"

"That was a good discussion we had about connecting. Do you think I need to make new connections?"

"Examine your life, pal. How many friends do you have? There's me, and there's Dave, and that's not saying much. You're disconnected at work. You've disconnected or maybe never were connected with Linda. You've pretty much disconnected from your biking buddies by not seeing them. In order for connections to stay strong, they need attention. You're pretty much alone. When was the last time you called your parents? How about your brother, Leo? Family connections can mean a lot. It's no wonder when Linda left, you were devastated. She was pretty much your whole life."

"I think you have a point there. So how do I connect?"

"You could start with your family. Call your parents. Try to be friends with them. They would probably love to hear from you, and they could be the easiest to connect with, since you've known each other all your life. Call your brother, Leo. Connecting with them would be a mutual benefit. One thing about connecting is that it often takes forgiveness. Since your family knows you best, they might have more to forgive of you than a stranger. You might have a lot to forgive of them. But it's hard to connect when you hold a grudge."

"I don't hold any grudges. That shouldn't be a problem."

"Really? Maybe not with a single person, but what about a group of people?"

"A group?"

"Women."

"Okay, I confess. I don't really hold a grudge against Linda, per se, but guess I do have one against women in general."

"So because of one person's action, you condemn all women?"

"Yeah. It doesn't seem right, does it?" Jim thought for a moment. "I suppose I better change my thinking. Not all women are bad. There are a lot of good women. Maybe I don't always understand them, but even Linda isn't bad. It did hurt that she left. Now that I see that we were not really connected and understand why she might have done what she did, I can forgive her. I'll just have to be more discriminating about who I fall in love with next time. Beauty isn't enough. I want someone I can really connect with.

"Tell me something else, Chris. How do I connect with people?"

"With guys, you do things together, like you do with Dave. Play chess, play baseball, build a road, root for a team, or even go biking. Guys connect by doing things together. When you find someone who you enjoy doing things with and who you admire and respect because they do it well and when they admire and respect you because you do it well, you connect. You support each other's self-image. That's why team sports are so important to guys. It's a connecting mechanism. I know you're not on a team, you're a loner, but you can find ways to connect. You did with Dave."

"Okay, so how do I connect with women?"

"Simple. Share with them. Tell them your thoughts and feelings. Listen to their thoughts and feelings. You don't have to prove to them how good you are, just be yourself. Be a human. I know it's really hard for a guy to do this because it's not in your nature, but if you try it, you'll find you have a lot more in common with women than you ever thought."

"Okay, Dr. Christopher. Thanks for the lesson. I don't see any way I can connect while I'm on this trip by myself. Maybe if I had a cell phone, but I don't. I'll work on it when I get back. At least I'll call my family. Maybe I'll even drive to Detroit and visit them. What have I got to lose? I never really meant to leave them or disconnect from them."

"So what are you going to do about Sandy? Will you connect with her?"

"Probably not. It's not likely I'll see her again, and even if I do, I'm probably going to move to California. I don't believe in long-distance relationships."

The sun went down, and the stars came out. Jim fell asleep, but in the middle of the night, a loud noise awakened him. It sounded like the screech of a large bird. Was it a screech owl? He'd never heard anything like it before. Weird! At the same time, he felt hoofbeats on the ground. It was a dragon! Jim's imagination ran wild, and he sat up in the tent and shivered. Any second, flames would come down out of the sky and turn his little tent into a puff of smoke. He would be barbecued.

Calm down, he told himself. *There are no dragons here, just a tired biker with a wild imagination.* He wished there was some sort of window in the tent so he could see out, but all he could do was unzip the door and stick his head out to see behind the tent, which he didn't really want to do. It would probably just let mosquitoes in and he wouldn't be able to see anything in the dark anyway. *Think. Hoofbeats. Maybe it's a deer.* He didn't think there were any bear there, and a bear probably wouldn't make hoofbeats. What was the frightening noise? Maybe there was both a deer and a screech owl. Finally, the hoofbeats went away and Jim went back to sleep. *Whatever it was,* Jim thought, *at least it didn't try to attack me. A tent doesn't offer much protection against wild animals, but it does hide me from their view.*

A small part of him wished it really was a dragon and hoped that the dragon would find him and end his misery. During the day on the road in the bright sun, it was easy to forget about the cares of life and be happy. But tired, in the middle of the night, cold, on the hard ground, his depression came back. He just didn't care. Chris must be sound asleep. He hadn't made a chirp.

*   *   *

Sandy watched as Jim pedaled away and called her sister, Judy, on her cell phone. Then she rode further into town to the kite store and waited for her. Judy drove up in her big red Oldsmobile, and Sandy put her bike on the rack behind the trunk and got in. Then they drove up to their aunt's house in Moran.

"I found him today," she told Judy.

"What's he like?"

"I'd say he is of average height, sort of lanky, around six feet, short brown hair, about thirty years old, in pretty good shape, no potbelly anyway. He looked yummy! He kept staring at me with those gray-blue eyes, as if he had never seen a girl before. He's riding a red Schwinn, all loaded down for touring, just like I was told. You can't miss him. I sat with him in the park, and we talked about King Arthur. Who'd'a thought? He's even reading the same series of books I am. I enjoyed being with him. He wasn't rude to me, but I think something is bothering him. He was aloof. We rode together back to Mackinaw City. I tried my best to lose him, but he just wouldn't give up. By the time we got to Mackinaw City, his tongue was really hanging out." She giggled. "If there had been some hills, I would've dropped him, but it's pretty flat in that stretch. If I'd dropped him, I'd've waited for him, though. He must be a pretty good rider to keep up with me, especially with that load. He seems very determined to carry out his plan. He told me he was going to camp out every night and once he got to the UP, he was going west on US 2. Even though I offered to let him stay at Aunt Dora's house tonight, he turned me down. I was surprised when he told me about a bet he made with

his neighbor, Dave, and it doesn't look like he's going to cheat on it."
She told Judy about the bet.

"Are you going to see him tomorrow?"

"I have to try." She wanted to say that she'd love to see him, that
she could hardly wait, but didn't want to sound too enthusiastic to
her sister, who was holding a grudge against men in general because
of a bad experience she'd had. Sandy liked him and suspected they
had a lot more in common than just King Arthur and biking. She
wanted to find out more about him.

"How do you think he'll cross to the UP?"

"Good question. My guess is that he'll take the ferry. But which
one … who knows? They come every fifteen minutes, and there are
three different ferry companies. He might decide to call the Bridge
Authority and take a ride in a pickup truck for two dollars. It would
be a way to save money over the ferry but not near as much fun."

"I'll tell you what. Ferry your bike to the island tomorrow, and
keep a lookout for him. I'll take the car and watch for him on US 2.
Whoever spots him first will call the other. When you do see him,
see if you can get him to go north to Paradise. It will be a lot easier
for us to watch him than if he goes west. I'd like to meet him."

8
Ready for the Times to Get Better

The next day, Thursday, August 1, Jim lay in his tent and leisurely ate the leftover caramel corn for breakfast. He got the silver shoe out of his fanny pack and enjoyed holding it for a few minutes, thinking about Sandy, wondering what the connection was. Around ten o'clock, he took his tent down, packed up his bike, and rode back to the roadside park to see if he could find his missing tights. He was afraid he'd get cold at night without them. No luck. It would be a fifteen-mile round-trip for nothing. He sighed. Sweatpants would have kept him warm, if he had brought some, but they were bulky and weighed more than the tights he had altered especially for himself. He was going to miss those tights.

"Chris, did you see my tights fall off the bike?"

"How could I see back there? You're in the way, blocking my view."

"I guess you can't. Well if you *hear* something fall off, let me know, okay?"

He had one last chance to find the tights, if perhaps he had lost them where he camped in Alverno, he could find them on the return trip. He didn't think he did, but if so, it wasn't likely that anyone would find them. He decided to stop there on the trip back home to look for them.

The day was warming up and full of sunshine, which brightened Jim's dark mood. Riding back to Mackinaw City, he was pondering what song he'd mind-sing. *What's my theme song today? "Bridge over Trouble Water" might be a good one, since I'm crossing the straits. Only thing is—I'm not taking the bridge, and the beat is too slow for pedaling. Ah, Crystal Gayle has a song that has a nice beat and says it all, "Ready for the Times to Get Better." "It's been a too long a time, with no peace of mind, and I'm ready for the times to get better."*

He was two days, maybe three, behind schedule. But Jim knew that if the tenderness on his butt went away, he could go a lot farther than a hundred miles in a day. With good weather, he had gone as many as two hundred miles before dark in the past, although not with a loaded bike. He could still win his bet with some hard riding later. The real question was, how long would it take for the tenderness to go? It was stupid of him to go on a tour like this without doing a few training rides beforehand.

Riding a bicycle or walking across the bridge was not normally allowed. To get to the UP, Jim would have to call the Bridge Authority and pay a dollar for them to take him across in a pickup truck. However, he opted for the other way to get to the UP—by ferry. It cost a lot more, but Jim had planned on this from the beginning, providing the weather was nice. He would take the ferry to Mackinac Island, laze around the island for a while, and then take the ferry to St. Ignace. The ferry took longer, but it was scenic and restful. He really needed the extra rest more than he needed to get back on schedule.

Odd, he thought, *two places with similar-sounding names and yet spelled differently. Mackinaw City. Mackinac Island.* Both places were pronounced "Mack-in-awe," but only the city was spelled that way. He wasn't sure if it was a French name or an Indian name. He could picture rich people driving a car that was pronounced "Cad-i-law" but spelled Cadillac.

There were three ferries to the island—Star, Arnold's, and Shepler's. Jim had no idea which was the best way to go, so he just took one. It turned out to be Shepler's and was twelve dollars for an adult ticket and another four dollars for the bicycle. He was definitely overspending his budget that day, but he had planned for this.

The ferry was a large boat that would probably hold a couple hundred people. The lower deck was enclosed, which was nice in cold or stormy weather. He rested on the lower deck during the twenty minutes it took to get there.

The big attraction at Mackinac Island was the horses. The island also smelled like horses, he noted. Cars were banned on the island, and that made it ideal for people who wanted a horse-and-buggy ride or for walkers and bikers. People staying at the Grand Hotel had their luggage pushed up the big hill on carts by young men in bright uniforms. There was a blacktop road about seven or eight miles long that went all the way around the island, State Highway M-185. Other roads went up to the top of the island. Jim took one of those roads at random, not knowing or caring where he was going. He eventually ended up at the airport on the island. *Odd,* he thought, *cars are outlawed, but planes are not.* The airport had a nice mowed lawn and a picnic table, so Jim spread out his blanket and lay down after setting out some of his still-damp clothes on the table in the sun to finish drying. He took his helmet off and set it on the ground with his glasses inside while the little tune, "Ready for the Times to Get Better," kept running through his mind. Chris joined the percussion section.

It was going to be a good day. He felt the times were already getting better.

* * *

Sandy sat on one of the high places on the island and scanned the docks, looking for a red Schwinn. Finally, she saw it. She watched to see which way Jim was going. It looked like he was going up to the center of the island rather than taking the path around it. She took out her cell phone and called Judy.

"I've found him," she said. "I'll call you again this evening."

She hung up and followed Jim from a distance. It looked like he was just exploring, not going to any particular place. He stopped at the airport. Perfect.

* * *

"Ready for the Times to Get Better" was still running through his mind when he heard someone call his name.

"What do you want, Chris?" he said without looking.

"I'm not Chris," she said.

Jim turned and looked. He put his sunglasses back on. "Sandy! Where'd you come from?" She had on sunglasses and was wearing a biking jersey with rainbows on it and purple socks, but what had happened to the tattoo on her leg? It was gone. It must have been one of those temporary tattoos sold at the mall. "I certainly didn't expect to see you here. What a pleasant surprise!" he said and smiled.

He really wanted to be alone, but since it was his nature to be nice to people, he wasn't going to tell her to get lost. After all, there was no way she could know how he felt, and he wasn't about to tell her. He could still enjoy Sandy's company as a fellow biker, although he didn't want her leading him in another race like yesterday—not then, but on another day, when he was feeling perkier, it would be fun to give her a run for the money.

She smiled. "I just came up the hill. Who is Chris? I don't see anyone else here. And I didn't see you with anyone yesterday."

"Chris is … I … uh …" What could he say? "None of your business." That wouldn't have been very friendly. He didn't want to admit he had an imaginary friend. Chris was made up on a whim, but Jim didn't want to look crazy to Sandy and he didn't want to have to explain. It was not the type of thing an adult would admit to. He looked at his handlebar. "Chris is a biking friend of mine. I must have got your names mixed up. I do that all the time, call a person by the wrong name, that is. I'm sorry. I'll try to get it right the next time."

"Well, I'm glad we bumped into one another," she said. "Did you sleep well last night?"

"I was jolted awake in the middle of the night by some sort of animal. I thought I heard hoof beats on the ground, but it made a low-pitched screeching sound. Almost like a cough. I really can't describe it. It was very strange. Being tired and half-asleep in the middle of the night, I imagined it being a dragon."

"What was it?"

"Beats me. Maybe a deer. I tried to get a look, but there are no windows in my tent, and I couldn't see anything out the door. It was too dark anyway."

Hmm, Sandy thought. *It sounds like he really did spend the night in the tent last night. With Chris?* She had an idea.

"What's your tent like, Jim? Would you set it up so I could see it?"

Jim thought this was a strange request. "I guess I could. Are you thinking about camping?"

"Yeah. I'd like to know how you do it."

Jim pulled the tent off his bike and set it up; it only took a few minutes. "As you can see, there's really only room for one in there. It was probably advertised as a two-person tent, but two people would be really crowded in there, especially with the gear. It's really just a kids' tent; I think I bought it at Kmart for about twenty dollars. One of the poles is broken; I have it taped together. And one of the zippers on the door doesn't work. It's pretty rickety; I hope I can make it last for the rest of this trip."

Sandy crawled in. No signs of a woman in there, no perfume or other signs, and it was pretty small. She couldn't imagine a woman spending a night in there. She couldn't even image Jim spending a night in there. Well, maybe he could. She sat down inside to think. She decided that a woman probably hadn't been in the tent. Then what? Did he have a pet mouse or something? Why did he look at the handlebar when she mentioned Chris? Hmmm. She crawled back out. "It's amazing that someone would sleep in something like this for two weeks. Couldn't you find one bigger?"

"Oh sure, but it's all about weight and space. I am carrying it myself, and I don't have a lot of room on my bike."

"That makes sense. I hadn't thought of that."

Jim repacked the tent, and they sat together and watched six airplanes take off and land in less than an hour. "Sure is a busy airport today," he said.

"Yeah. Perfect day." She sat at a picnic table and stared at the runways. Jim started to doze off again.

Finally, Sandy broke the silence. "Jim, have you ever ridden across the US on your bike?"

"No, but I'd like to someday."

"Me too. But not by myself."

"It would certainly be different from this trip. Obviously, it's much farther. At a hundred miles a day, it would still take a good month or two and it's hard to get that much time off work all at once. Also, I would want to carry an extra Camelbak. It's a long way between watering holes out west. I might even need panniers on the front of my bike, but I don't think I'd like them. I know they would help balance the load on the bike, but I think they'd make steering in a crosswind much harder. I'd also want to take a second blanket and some sort of pillow. It's funny, but that's what I've missed the most on this trip. I've been using my bike helmet for a pillow, filling it with extra clothes, if they're dry, and even the mosquito netting, whatever I can find that's soft. Who'd a thought? I'd also take a camera; I can't imagine crossing the country without a camera. If I had a camera, I'd take a picture of you right now."

"Jim, how sweet." Sandy began posing.

Jim gulped. "And I'd take a few extra clothes," he managed to continue. "Not much more than I'm carrying now, though."

"Would you try to do it for only a hundred dollars a week?"

"Actually, I think it could be done. But I'm not sure I would. It might be nice to allow myself more just in case."

"In case of what?"

"In case I wanted to spend a night in a motel. In case I wanted to visit Disney Land. Who knows? Just in case, that's all. I'd probably have some bike repairs and unexpected expenses on a trip that long."

"Would you take BikeCentennial's route?"

"I don't know. It's a possibility. But I've always wanted to ride US 2 all the way west to Seattle. I don't know what I'd do east of Michigan. And I'd rather do a round-trip, but then I'm talking about taking a whole summer. What about you? Do you like to tour?"

"I like adventure. I've never done anything like you, but I'd sure like to try it sometime. If I had someone to go with, that is."

"It would be more fun to ride with someone than riding alone. I'll grant you that. Probably safer, too."

They enjoyed the solitude and peace together for a while.

Jim finally spoke up. "Sandy, this is sort of off the wall and might sound kind of dumb, and I don't want to get personal with you or anything, but do you ever use eye shadow?"

"Sometimes. What brought this on?"

"On the way up here, I stopped at a little store in Gordonville and I met these two ladies there. They were both wearing a light-blue eye shadow, and it just seemed way … wrong, out of place somehow. At least to me, like they were wearing the wrong color or something. I mentioned it to a guy I met along the way, and he gave me an interesting explanation, more than I bargained for anyway. I just thought I'd like to hear it from a woman's view."

"I don't know what to say, Jim. I'm not wearing any today, but if I were, what color do you think I should use?"

"I'd probably be wondering why you were bothering to wear it behind sunglasses. I'm no expert on this … so this might be a really dumb answer, but you've got on a purple top. I might expect you to match the purple. You've got dark-brown eyes. I might expect you to match your eye color. If you had on rouge or lipstick, I might expect you to match that. But you look nice the way you are, so why bother at all?"

"Thanks for the compliment. It's just a lot of work to put on all that makeup every day, and you're right, people with glasses have a hard time with it. It works better with contacts because glasses tend to hide the eyes anyway. I'm not trying to look special for anyone today, but if I were and did use eye shadow, it would be to make my eyes look bigger and enhance their shape, to make them more attractive, not to match a color."

"Oh."

"Today's woman would rather not be thought of as something to look at, some guy's sexual fantasy, or a possession. We are a person, someone to respect, someone with feelings, ideas, and dreams of our own. Not an object of lust. We feel that we should be accepted the way we are and not have to wear makeup, hose, and heels, etc., to be accepted."

"I understand that. But as a woman, don't you like to do those things anyway? Don't you like to feel like a princess? If you have on a pretty dress, doesn't it make you feel good? If you make heads turn, don't you enjoy the attention?"

"Actually, I do. I guess there is a balance. I want to be thought of as a person, not a sex object, but I also enjoy being a woman. I like being pretty."

"As a man, I respect women. I know they're people with feelings and desires, dreams and goals. In some ways, they're not that much different than men. But they are not the same. Men enjoy when women dress up and strut their stuff. We have certain feelings, certain reactions, certain likes and dislikes that are actually hardwired into our brain from birth, not something we have a choice over. We have the choice to cover up our thoughts, or modify our actions, but we don't have the choice to change the basic reaction. Let me give you an example. I was at a 4-H fair one time, and there was a woman dressed up as a clown there, big red nose, white face paint, short and dumpy, nothing sexy about her at all, right? She had these huge fake eyelashes. They were an inch long, maybe two inches. They weren't meant to be sexy; they were meant to be funny. Well, she put them on and then batted her eyes at me. I kid you not; it put butterflies in my stomach. I melted. I'm still in love with that clown today. Well, not really in love, but you see what I mean. I was so surprised by my own reaction that I never forgot either her or the reaction. Women have figured this out about men over the years and now use mascara to lengthen their eyelashes. There must be a basic instinct, at least in some men, that likes long eyelashes. On an intellectual level, it's dumb. But it's not dumb, it's biology."

"Oh. Long eyelashes. Hmmm. I'll have to remember that."

"I guess what I'm trying to say is—any good-looking woman will attract the attention of a man. He can't help looking, and he can't help enjoying because it's hardwired into his brain. It's the way God made us. To expect a man to not notice would be like expecting a dog not to chase a cat or bark at a person passing by his house. It's unrealistic. It's basic biology. If men weren't that way, the human race would probably die out. Relationships are hard to figure out and make work. If we had to do everything strictly on an intellectual level, we probably wouldn't do it at all. It just wouldn't be worth it."

"I don't like men undressing me with their eyes."

"Perhaps not, but you can't stop it from happening. To expect men to not do it is unfair to them, because they really don't have a choice about it. Some men are more obvious about it, indiscreet, but we all do it. That doesn't mean we will act on it, but if given opportunity, there're very few men who could resist looking at an attractive woman."

Jim continued, "Now how did we get on this subject, anyway. I was just curious about eye shadow. I guess I'll never understand it; it's another one of those mysteries of the opposite gender. You women wrap us around your little finger with your good looks and then complain because men rule the world. I think women rule too, even if they do it behind the scenes. Men so often do what women want." Jim was thinking of Linda, how she wrapped him around her little finger. The things he would do for her if she only asked! He was sure Linda knew the hows and whys of eye shadow, but he wouldn't be getting a chance to ask her.

Sandy said nothing but glared darts at him behind her sunglasses. She wondered if Jim was undressing her with his eyes. Yeah, he probably was. *I guess I should feel complimented,* she thought. *And he's probably right, there's nothing I can do about it except, well, get ugly. I don't really want to do that. But does he really respect me as a person? Maybe.*

"The shadows are lengthening," Jim said. "Maybe we should get going. I'd sure like to have some whitefish for dinner tonight. I'm starved!"

They rode their bikes carefully down to the ferry, avoiding *road apples,* that is, horse droppings, and wet spots on the pavement that were probably a little stronger than just water. By six in the evening, they had ferried to St. Ignace and ridden their bikes to a sports bar. When the waitress came, Jim ordered the whitefish dinner. It cost almost fourteen dollars. Now he had really gone over budget for the day.

She just ordered a salad. The food was good, and he enjoyed her company. They talked some more about King Arthur.

"If you were alive in King Arthur's time," Jim asked, "who would you want to be? Guinevere? Enid? Elaine? Someone else?"

"That's a hard question. I never really thought about it before. Let me think … We have it so good today; it's hard to even imagine what it was like back then. I think, though, I'd still have to be me. Even if I was a peasant girl. Queen or peasant, princess, lady, or pauper, I'd accept life's challenges and face them head-on. I think I could do any of them. It's not so important the station in life as how one lives it. Inside, I'd live nobly. Inside, I'm a queen, even if no one else sees me that way. But living nobly doesn't mean lording it over people or always having your own way. I think it means loving others, serving them, being humble. And being humble doesn't mean self-deprecating. One can have a good self-image and still be humble. I think I have a good self-image, but I must be rambling. How would you answer the question? Would you be a knight?"

"Not necessarily a knight. I could be king!" Jim laughed. "Seriously, though, I think I'm like you. But I'd want adventure, so a knight might be a good choice. They went out seeking challenges, trying to do good, protect the weak and innocent, and establish the law in the land. Many of them also got themselves killed. The ones you read about were either the really good ones or the really lucky ones. Not everyone was a Lancelot, though I'm sure many died trying. I can see why the prestige and camaraderie of the Round Table were so attractive. I'm drawn to it myself.

"Perhaps," Jim continued, "I'd rather be a Merlin. A diplomat, an advisor, a thinker. There must be some adventure in that as well. Fighting, or knighting, is for big people, strong people. I don't think of myself as big and strong, as I like to think of myself as light and fast. Smart like a fox. There's the chessboard with the fighters on it. And then there's the mind behind the board that moves the pieces. That's me."

"So you're a manipulator?"

"I guess that's the way it I made it sound, but I'm not sure that's what I meant. It seems like in real life, I'm the one being manipulated, not the other way around."

"Aren't we all!" She laughed.

"I really like your thoughts about being humble and having a good self-image. I think both men and women need a good self-image. But it doesn't mean you have to be proud, either."

"Yeah," Sandy said, "I have a good self-image because I believe God loves me. And if God loves me, it doesn't matter what anyone else thinks. All I need to do is please God. And that means loving others and living honestly and fairly. I don't mean to say that I'm perfect; I'm not. But God loves me anyway, so I just do the best I can. And I know when I screw up, God will forgive me."

"What a pleasant thought. I've been so unhappy with my job lately, simply because my boss won't give me the chance to screw up. Not that I want to screw up. I think I do good work. But he won't approve it or allow me to follow through on it. It makes me wonder why I even work for him. I'm so frustrated. I need the freedom to screw up and the wisdom not to."

"God does give you freedom. We're not His puppets on a string. And He'll give you wisdom, too, if you ask."

After a moment, Sandy asked, "Jim, would you consider changing your destination? I mean, would you go to Paradise tomorrow so we can ride together? I've really enjoyed your company, and I'd feel a lot safer with you along. You could be my knight."

"What? And lose my bet? No way." Jim couldn't believe she would even ask this of him.

"No, I don't really want you to lose your bet, Jim. But was your bet about a place and a distance or about the cost? Maybe your neighbor doesn't care if you go all the way to Ironwood. He just didn't think you could go on a vacation for only a hundred dollars a week. Would you call your neighbor and ask him? Please?"

Jim didn't like that she was asking him to change his plans. It might make it easier for him to win his bet if he didn't have to go so far, but he'd rather lose than change his goal. Still, what could it hurt?

Dave would probably make him stick to his plan anyway. "All right, I'll call, Dave," he grumbled, "but don't expect anything to change."

Sandy gave him her cell phone, and Jim dialed the number. On the third ring, Dave answered.

"Hello, Dave? This is Jim."

"Jim! Is everything all right?"

"Yes, everything is fine."

"It's good to hear from you. Where are you?"

"In St. Ignace."

"I thought you'd be further along by now."

"I would have, but I had some bad weather. Don't worry; I'll get back on schedule. I just had a question about our bet."

"Shoot."

"Was our bet about the cost only or did it include the destination also. Two hundred dollars for fourteen days and fourteen nights. Also I have to go all the way to Ironwood, right?"

"I guess your plan was for you to go to Ironwood. But in my mind, it doesn't matter. Why should it be any cheaper somewhere else? Do you want to change your destination?"

"What about going to Paradise? I know it's a lot closer, but I'll go to some other places as well."

"Paradise! That sounds like a good place to meet a girl. Is someone else with you? A girl?" Dave teased.

"Come on, Dave; give me a break. You don't know me very well if you think I'd change my plans for a girl. How could you think such a thing? If you insist that I go to Ironwood, just say so. It's no big deal. Otherwise, I was thinking of going north to Paradise instead."

"You can go to Paradise if you want. No problem. But the two hundred for fourteen days and fourteen nights still stands. Whatever you do, just have a good time. And be careful, okay? Ride safe."

"Okay. Thanks. I'll see you when I get back."

"See ya." They hung up.

"So your neighbor is Dave? What did he say, Jim?"

Jim was stunned. "I can't believe it. He said the destination didn't matter. I can go to Paradise if I want." Jim stood there shaking his head. Why was Dave letting him off the hook? "Paradise is as good as Ironwood as long as I camp out and buy my own food," he said weakly. Paradise was only about fifty miles north of the bridge but too far for him to make a detour and still go to Ironwood, especially since he was already behind schedule. It would mean a whole new route and destination in the UP part of this trip. Where would he go after Paradise? He didn't like this idea.

"Oh good. Where can we meet tomorrow?"

"I don't know, Sandy. Are you sure you really need me? This is a big change for me. I sort of had my heart set on Ironwood."

"I would really like you to come with me," Sandy said. "You told me yesterday that King Arthur inspired you for this trip. What do you think King Arthur would do? Just leave me here to fend for myself?"

Jim thought about it. She had a point. She was comparing him to King Arthur, and it made him feel good. He felt … noble. She had appealed to a basic instinct of a man to be … protective. And it would be nice to ride with her for another day. He'd still have the whole rest of the trip to himself. He thought about his tender butt. The change would cut some miles off this trip. His butt won out in the end. At least that was what he told himself. "Okay, I'll go with you. But just tomorrow," he grumbled. "You're on your own after that. Agreed?"

"Agreed. So where can we meet tomorrow?"

"I don't know. You got any ideas? I don't know the area and have no idea where you're staying tonight. I don't even know where I'm staying."

"There is a little town on M-123 called Moran. I'll wait for you there. At the store on the corner. How about eight?"

"Store on the corner?"

"It's a very small town. It's the only store on the only corner."

"Okay."

Jim said good-bye to Sandy and started north on Mackinac Trail Road. When he got to M-123, he headed west and rode past the store in Moran. A little way out of town, he found a clearing in a wooded area, well hidden from the road, and he pitched his tent. *It was a good day,* he thought. *Restful. Scenic. Good food. Someone intelligent and attractive to talk to. And now, someone to ride with tomorrow.*

Jim looked up at the sky. It was cloudless, and without clouds to hold the heat in, he figured it was going to be a cold night. He could already feel a chill in the air. "Chris, it looks like it's gonna be a cold night. You can crawl under the blanket with me, but be careful. I don't want to find a crushed cricket on my ground pad in the morning."

"Don't go with her, Jim."

"What? Why not? I already said I would. Is there a problem?"

"Yeah. You can't keep me a secret from her. She already has her suspicions about me. Why do you think she was inspecting your tent? If she finds out about me, I'm going to have to leave. It's either me or her, Jim. You can't have both of us."

"Jealous?"

"Not jealousy. Reality. I don't want to leave. I enjoy riding with you, and I'm possibly the best-traveled cricket in the world now. I enjoy singing for you. Most people don't appreciate my … abilities."

"So you can stay until she finds out, right? I'll just have to make sure she doesn't find out. I already told her I'd go tomorrow. Hey! It's only for one day. I won't see her again after that. You heard her. She agreed I'd be on my own after tomorrow."

He went to sleep wondering about the next day. *Well, she is a fellow biker, and I don't have anyone else to ride with. And she is pretty. If she wasn't such a good biker, I would have told her no, though. Maybe it won't be so bad. I hope she doesn't make me kill myself trying to keep up with her. How did I let myself get talked into this? Somehow she made me feel good about myself.* He fell asleep smiling.

It got colder during the night, and Jim woke to put his sweatshirt on over his T-shirt. He already had on his biking tights along with his socks. There wasn't anything else he could put on to stay warm. He got out his aluminized "space blanket" and put that over the top of his wool blanket. It felt much warmer than just the wool blanket alone. He huddled up on his ground pad, which was only four feet long and a foot and a half wide, and covered himself completely, even his head, with the blanket, leaving a little opening so he could breathe fresh air. He wasn't quite shivering, but he wasn't as warm as he'd like either. It was going to be a long, cold night. He wished for the morning sun to warm things up.

*   *   *

Sandy waited until Jim was gone and then called Judy. "I'm at the sports bar in St. Ignace. Come get me."

Judy drove up a few minutes later in her red Olds '98. They loaded the bike up and drove back to Aunt Dora's house.

"Did you get him to go to Paradise?" Judy asked.

"Yes. He didn't want to, but I convinced him I needed someone to look after me and appealed to his male chivalry by comparing him to King Arthur. He is a romantic of sorts. Adventurous. Noble." *Yes, noble,* she thought. *That's it. What an interesting person. I've got to know him better.*

"So what's the plan tomorrow?"

"He agreed to meet me at the store in Moran. We'll just be there when he shows up tomorrow, around eight. You can meet him yourself."

"Great! I can hardly wait."

"I also noticed that his socks don't match. What do you make of that?"

"Color-blind?"

"Probably not. The letters on one are blue; the other is red. I haven't heard of a red/blue combination of color blindness, or it's awful rare. Usually, it's red and green that get mixed up."

"Could be any number of reasons, then."

"I think I have an idea. Also, when I surprised him on the island, he called me Chris. I asked him who Chris was, but he wouldn't tell me. I think there's someone else. I thought maybe he spent the night at Chris's house somewhere, but his story suggests he spent it in the tent. I think he heard a deer in the middle of the night. He set up his tent for me, and there were no signs that a woman had been in it. It seemed too small to have two people in it anyway."

"So Chris is just the girl back home."

"Well, if she was home, why would he be calling me that here?"

"He was dreaming?"

"He said he gets names mixed up easy, but for some reason, I don't buy it. He's hiding something from me. It's funny, when I mentioned Chris, he looked at his handlebar. There must be a clue there. I intend to find out what's going on."

"You better. You just can't trust a man. If you're starting to like him, you're heading for trouble. And the better looking they are, the less you can trust them."

9
Breaking Up Is Hard to Do

Friday morning, as cold as it was, Jim was amazed to find his tent door covered with mosquitoes. *There must be water nearby,* he thought. *Mosquitoes seek carbon dioxide from breathing; maybe they also can detect heat. If so, my tent must stand out like a beacon in this cold.*

He tried to pick campsites away from wetlands, by listening for frogs and looking for cattails, willows, red-winged blackbirds, and other signs. He hadn't seen any of these signs when he'd chosen his camp; he must have missed them. Maybe he'd been thinking about Sandy. Nah! They must just have been out of sight. At certain times of the day, frogs didn't croak; in the middle of the night, there would be dead silence, and then a little while later, the whole pond-swamp-marsh would come alive with the noisy creatures. Jim packed quickly, not only because of the mosquitoes, but also the cold. If he hadn't told Sandy he'd meet her at eight o'clock, he'd've slept in longer, waited until it warmed up, maybe until ten o'clock. At least the skies were blue, the sunniest weather he had seen on this trip so far, and it would warm up. Chris was too cold to chirp, but it did sound like his teeth were chattering. *Do crickets have teeth?* After checking his fanny pack to see that he still had the silver shoe, he quickly dragged his bike back to the road through the weeds and mosquitoes and hopped on, leaving the cloud of mosquitoes behind as he headed back to Moran.

Sure enough, Sandy was waiting for him inside the store. The store was rather tiny and the prices high. There were tables, and one could order breakfast there. He quickly gave Sandy the once-over. Her fingernails were not long but looked nice. They were painted purple with little stars on them. Not rainbows? But there was a rainbow on her arm just below the sleeve of her butterfly-print bike jersey. She was holding a pink biking jacket and wearing black tights, and … and … Jim swallowed … socks that didn't match, a pink one on her right foot and a purple one on the left. The pink one picked up colors from the butterflies in her top; the purple one matched her bike. She looked nice, but why did she mismatch her socks? And yet, were they really mismatched? They looked nice with the clothes she was wearing. He looked at his own socks, red on the right, blue on the left. *Silly me,* he thought, *to think no one would notice. I noticed hers right off, didn't I?*

Sitting at a table with her was another woman with short, shiny black, healthy-looking hair dressed in black slacks and a red plaid blouse. She wore a Western hat and boots.

"This is my sister, Judy," Sandy said. "Judy, this is Jim Sanders; he's the brave knight who is going to ride with me today." Judy had the same pretty smile as Sandy, the same brown eyes, and the same jutting chin. Sandy's nose was more angular, straight like his own, while Judy had a button nose, cute.

Then Judy surprised him when she asked, "Sandy and I were discussing *Star Trek* when you arrived. Are you into sci-fi?"

"Not before breakfast." He bought a cinnamon roll and sat down. Then he raised his right hand, palm forward, fingers up, the middle and ring fingers spread apart, making a double-fingered V. The thumb was also spread apart so his whole hand was making a kind of lopsided W. "Live long, and prosper," he said.

Judy raised her hand in like sign and replied, "Peace, and long life." Like *aloha* on Hawaii, the Vulcan sign was both a farewell and a greeting, first given by Spock on *Star Trek*.

"It's hard to believe," Jim said, "but that sign has been around for almost thirty years now, as long as I have. My mom gave me a birthday card once that had a list of events that happened in the year I was born, 1966. I was surprised to find the first *Star Trek* episode aired on my birthday, September 8. Just out of curiosity, I looked it up. It was called 'The Man Trap' and is about a creature that could take on human form and kill people by draining their bodies of salt. I grew up watching reruns of *Star Trek*."

"What a coincidence," Sandy said. "My birth date is June 3, 1969. My cousin, King, is a real Trekkie, and he told me it was the date of the very last *Star Trek* episode of the original series. It was titled 'Turnabout Intruder,' and Dr. Janice Lester took over Kirk's body with help from an alien device. Kirk was trapped in Lester's body, and that body was dying from radiation poisoning. I loved watching all the old reruns."

Jim said, "I remember coming home from school and plopping down in front of the TV every day and watching those reruns. It was a ritual. Some of the earlier episodes were not even in color. Or maybe we just didn't have a color TV back then."

"There are still a lot of people who don't know anything about *Star Trek*," Judy said, "but whether they know it or not, it's part of the American culture now. There's never been a time in our lives when we were without it."

"Before you came," Sandy said, "we were sort of discussing time travel. It seems to be a popular subject among Trekkies."

"I don't particularly care for time travel," Jim said. "I know it's a popular subject, but I've never read a book or seen a show with it that made sense to me. I suppose it's fun to think about it, but there's always a paradox involved. For example, if you traveled back in time a year and met your former self and shot him dead, would that be suicide? And if you were dead back then, how could you be alive now to shoot yourself? They may make interesting stories, but they never make sense to me. What do you think?"

"You make a good point," Judy said. "What I really like about sci-fi is that it lets you suspend reality for a while. Then you can take an objective look at yourself from another viewpoint and discover who you really are. It expands your imagination. Take Spock, for example, a half Vulcan and half human. In reality, I don't think there is any way such a creature could exist; they are too different biochemically. A Vulcan has copper-based green blood. A Vulcan has a heart located in a different part of his chest. Any interspecies breeding would not be able to produce a live offspring with such differences. But with reality suspended, Spock has been one of sci-fi's favorite characters and has let us explore the differences between basing our actions on logic or emotion. And in so doing, we find there are benefits in both. And there have been a lot of other benefits from his character as well."

"Sort of like Data," Sandy added, "of the *Next Generation*."

"Yeah, that's right," Jim said. "I like the thing about Vulcan Pon Farr. It's another side of humanity. You know, when the Vulcan gets the mating urge every seven years? Vulcans base their whole lives on logic, and when Pon Farr hits them, well, they are mystified. It's not logical. But the urge is so strong that if they don't act on it, their bodies deteriorate and they die. So they end up doing extremely illogical things to satisfy that need. I guess in the show they compared the urge to that of salmon swimming upstream to spawn. Well, humans have those biological urges, too. Sometimes they surprise us. I was sharing with Sandy yesterday how long eyelashes affect me. Fortunately, we can control our urges; we don't have to die from them, and we don't have to hurt others because of them, either."

Judy baited him. "But men are so dumb. It's like they have their brains in their crotch."

Jim took the bait. "You women think you're so smart. I would think that women especially would realize how biology affects what we do or think. That monthly cycle of yours makes you get crotchety often enough. And we men have to put up with it."

"You men should have a little more sympathy. How'd you like to have to go through that monthly process?"

Jim didn't like Judy's men bashing. "At least we're aware of it. And we do our best to cope with it. And if you were on the pill, it wouldn't be a problem. But you women are not even aware that men have a similar malady."

"Go on. Give me a break."

"It's true. Our bodies produce semen continually, and it builds up. If that buildup isn't released, we get testy. The thing about it is—we don't have a choice; it's going to be released. Somehow. But in the meantime, it's like a pressure is building up in our bodies. It's not painful, and I can't say that we feel it physically, but we sure feel it mentally. So how does it get released? A little bit is lost when we empty our bladder, but not enough. If we don't have sex, then eventually it will be ejected in our sleep and it makes a little mess in our bed, usually while having an erotic dream. Or we could have sex with someone and release it that way, but since that's not socially acceptable, especially for single men, almost all men masturbate. At least that way, the mess is caught in a tissue, which is a lot less messy. After it's released, we're a lot less testy, more relaxed, and easier to get along with. It doesn't sound good, but it's biology; it's the male cycle, similar in some ways to the female cycle."

"So is that why you're getting testy? You haven't been getting any?" Judy was really riding him.

Sandy spoke up. "We better get going, Jim. Judy will have us here all day talking about *Star Trek*. She and King will drive you crazy if you let them. Besides," she whispered, "Judy had a bad experience with a guy once, and she's sort of a man hater. She'll eat you alive if you let her get to you."

Jim took the clue, got some Gatorade and a few snacks for his panniers, and went to pay. He really didn't want to talk about male sexual problems; Judy had baited him into it. At the counter, Sandy introduced her aunt Dora, the cashier. Dora looked to be in her fifties, with dyed red hair, and a little on the dumpy side, but she had the same smile as Sandy and seemed cheerful enough. She was wearing jeans and a plaid shirt. "Good luck," she said to them as they went out the door.

As they rode, Jim continued the conversation. "Well, I just don't think it's right for Judy to be down on men because we are differently sexually oriented than they are. We're biologically pushed into it. Like Pon Farr."

"Okay, Jim. You made your point. Let's talk about something else."

Jim was quiet for a minute and then said, "I guess I got carried away, didn't I? Well, I never intended for it to go so far. I'm sorry I got carried away in there."

"It's okay, Jim. I know how she is. But about time travel, I'm with you; it doesn't make sense to me, either. But a lot of people like it. It seems to be a very popular subject with Trekkies."

"Well, what about parallel universes? Do you think there can be another you somewhere else in another universe?"

"Not really. I think I'm one of a kind, in any universe, and I happen to be in this one, not any other. I know that mathematically speaking, it is possible to have parallel universes, but that doesn't make it truth. There's a big difference between reality and possibility. On the other hand," Sandy continued, "Judy's point about suspending reality so we can examine ourselves is a good one. To me, good sci-fi not only examines science; it also examines humanity. Sci-fi, by suspending reality, can help us take a look at ourselves from a different viewpoint."

"Sandy, wait." Jim had stopped on the side of the road. Sandy turned around and went back to him.

"Got a kink in my back," Jim said. He was off his bike and stretching. "And I missed about half of what you said there. It's so hard to talk while riding. Either I'm out of breath from pedaling uphill, or I'm going downhill so fast I can't hear anything because of wind noise. If we're going to talk, we really have to ride side by side and go slower. Better yet, maybe we should just stop from time to time. If we don't, we'll be there before lunch, and I'm not in that much of a hurry."

"I'm all for stopping, especially after it warms up. It's too cold to stop now. What you said about wind noise," she continued, "I wish there was something that could be done about wind noise. I've tried earplugs, but they don't seem to help. It makes everything quieter, but the wind noise is still there. I even tried those wind deflectors you attach to your helmet straps. They didn't help much; it just made me feel like Mickey Mouse!" She laughed. "Or at least a Mouseketeer."

"I solved that one a while back," Jim said. "It is possible to stop wind noise. I made a soft foam appliance, which I wore like headphones that sheltered the ear from wind, sort of like if you put your left hand in front of your left ear, palm back. That works, too, but can you imagine trying to steer with your elbows? My wind silencers worked; they just weren't practical. The foam was nice in cold weather because it helped keep my ears warm. But on a hot day like today will be, they got sweaty and grimy. Also, they didn't hold their shape well. I finally gave it up. It would be safer to have a wind silencer, though, because I could hear cars coming up behind me a lot easier. Some cars really sneak up on me. Maybe someday helmet manufacturers will build wind silencers into their helmets. It could be done."

Jim finished stretching, and they started out again.

They rode together to Trout Lake, and there, they stopped at a sports bar. They leaned their bikes against the front of the building, went in, and sat down at a table near the front window. They could see their bikes parked outside. The owner came over and took their orders for hamburgers.

The bar was full of sports memorabilia; Jim thought the owner must have spent a lifetime collecting it. Pennants, footballs, pictures, trophies—the bar was covered from one end to the other, even the ceiling.

After taking in the surroundings for a few minutes, Jim looked at Sandy again. "I couldn't help but notice that your socks don't match," he said, "not that I'm one who should be talking. But they look nice with the outfit you're wearing." He chuckled.

Sandy looked down at Jim's socks and feigned surprise. "I see what you mean. But yours don't either. Do you always mismatch them?"

"Nah. I've never done it before, at least not intentionally. I just decided to do it for this bike trip. I thought it might bring good luck. It's silly, I suppose. I don't know anyone else who does it, so I thought I'd try it. You don't normally do it, do you? I mean, if I remember right, your socks did match the last two days."

"I just thought I'd be different today. Maybe it will bring me luck, too."

Jim changed the subject. "I had an idea for the Federation," he said, referring to *Star Trek*. "The Romulan cloaking device is supposed to bend light around a starship so you can't see it. It takes an awful lot of energy to do that. What if they put a dual-polarized filter field around a ship? If they turned the two polarization fields perpendicular to one another, it would look almost like a black hole. Radar or any other sensor waves would be absorbed or blocked. At a distance, it would be almost impossible to detect. It would be almost as good as a cloaking device and probably a lot more energy efficient. Theoretically, I think it could even serve as a shield for the ship. Maybe that's how shields are created on *Star Trek*. Any electromagnetic charge, like a phaser or disruptor, fired at the ship would simply be absorbed or blocked."

"Interesting," Sandy said. "I always wondered how they did that. Now you've told me how to stop wind noise on a bike and how to make a defense shield for a starship. Do you have any other inventions?"

"A few. How about aerogel balls to fill up your tent in cold weather. They are extremely lightweight and would keep you warm in the coldest of weather. I haven't made any, but I think it might be possible. I practically froze last night; that's when I came up with this idea. The only question is, can they be compressed so I would have room to carry them on my bike?

"I did make a heat-exchanging mask for cold-weather biking that absorbs heat from your breath when you exhale and warms up the cold air that you inhale. Some people, like me, can't exercise in cold weather because their lungs hurt. With a heat-exchanging mask, I can go running outside even when it's freezing with no problem. I could have used the mask last night, but I didn't bring it with me. I'd've been a lot warmer. A lot of body heat is lost just by breathing cold air."

"I can see how that would help. But I think it's amazing that you come up with all these ideas and inventions. Have you made any money from them?"

"Unfortunately, not yet. But that may change. I'm going to talk with my cousin Loretta about them when I get back. She would know what to do."

The owner brought them their burgers, and just as they started eating, two men came in.

"Hi, Sandy," one of them said. "What are you doing here? I heard you were in the area."

"Well, Beetle Bailey and Elmer Fudge! I don't believe it," Sandy replied. "I'm on a biking vacation. Come and sit with us. I'd like you to meet Jim Sanders; he's from Lansing and is biking with me today. Jim, these are a couple of my cousins, Benjamin Bailey, who we call Beetle, and Elmer Bailey, a.k.a. Fudge."

Beetle looked to be about thirty. Light-brown hair stuck out from under his baseball cap. He was wearing vertically striped overalls, like an engineer, and work boots. The thick, heavy glasses on his face kept slipping down. The overalls looked fairly clean. Fudge appeared to be the same age as Beetle. He had black hair sticking out of his baseball cap and was wearing jeans and a plaid flannel shirt with his work boots. He wore glasses, too, but they seemed to be staying in place.

"Nice to meet you, Jim," Beetle said. "I'd like to join you, but we were going to sit over at that table and play chess. We got a match going." They shook hands with Jim, went over to the other table, and then ordered burgers. Jim watched as Fudge got out a small chess set and began setting up the pieces. Beetle got out a clock, which was actually two clocks side by side in one frame, and put it next to the board. Fudge pushed a pawn forward and then pushed a button on top of the clock. Beetle did the same. Pretty soon, they were pushing pieces and hammering the buttons on the clock. Less than ten minutes later, the game was over. They were laughing and poking fun at one another, bragging about who was the best and who was going to beat who the next time. Then they reset the board and repeated the performance.

Sandy told him how Benjamin, in the third grade, had caught a great big black stag beetle from under a rock and took it into the classroom. When no one was looking, he put it into the desk of one of the girls. Later, when she opened the desk and saw the giant beetle, she let out a scream. Well, Ben, being the nice guy he was, started feeling guilty about it, so he went over to her desk and took it out for her. He became the class hero and thus earned the nickname Beetle from all the kids. It wasn't until years later that he confessed to being the one to put the beetle in the desk in the first place.

Elmer was in 4-H and entered some fudge in the county fair. He took first place. He was so proud he went around showing his blue ribbon to all the kids. That earned him a nickname, Elmer Fudge. Later, they found out he was the only entry.

Jim told Sandy how he used to do some bike racing. His other bike was like a speedboat, so light and fast. The bike he was riding that day felt like an ore freighter, a ship; it was a good bike, slow but steady, built for comfortable touring, not racing. Sandy shared that she had done a few triathlons.

"Biking is a great way to keep fit," she said.

Jim agreed.

Sandy asked, "Why are you wearing T-shirts, Jim? Don't bikers usually wear jerseys?"

"I thought I'd be more comfortable in a tee. They're cotton, and I sleep in them. The jerseys I have are synthetic material and look nice, but I'd rather not sleep in them. I do miss the back pockets, though. I don't have enough room to carry both. That's why I'm using a fanny pack."

After finishing their burgers, Jim and Sandy went over to watch Fudge and Beetle play chess. Sandy said, "They're playing speed chess."

"Oh, yeah. Dave told me about it, but I've never played it."

Beetle said, "Would you like to try a game?"

Jim looked at Sandy.

"Go ahead," she urged.

"Okay. I think I can get the hang of this."

It was just like Dave had described. They set the pieces up. Since Jim was white, he moved first. He pushed the king's pawn two spaces.

"Push your button," Beetle said.

Jim complied.

Beetle answered with his king's pawn and pushed his button. Jim thought for a moment and moved his king's knight.

"Push your button," Beetle reminded him.

"Oh, that's right. I'm not used to this."

A little while and a few moves later, Beetle had him checkmated. Jim looked at the clock. Beetle had used less than a minute. On the other hand, Jim's flag had almost fallen.

"Wow! I've never been beaten so fast in my life."

Beetle extended his hand. "Thanks for the game. You'll do better next time."

"Thanks." Jim had sort of a dazed look on his face.

Sandy looked at Beetle and said, "We have to go now. It's been nice seeing you two again."

Once they were outside, Jim said about the loss, "The worst thing is—I don't even know how he did it. I mean, it happened so fast I don't even know what I did wrong. It's one thing to play a game and see yourself slowly get beat piece by piece. At least you understand. But this was like being conked on the back of the head. I never saw it coming. And I thought I was a pretty good player, too."

"Well, if it makes you feel any better, he does that to me also."

"You play chess, Sandy?"

"Sometimes."

"Well don't get any ideas. If that runs in your family …"

"Don't worry about it!" She laughed. "Only Beetle and Fudge play that way. Beetle tells me he's not that good, that he knows some guys who can clean his clock in chess, but I've never seen it happen. Besides," she added, "I like playing other games too."

Jim thought about asking her "What games?" but decided to let it go. He'd been beaten enough for one day.

They got on their bikes, and Sandy said, "I want to stop at a cousin's house here in town for a minute. He's a biker too, and I want you to meet him."

About two blocks down, they stopped at a house and saw a young man wearing a black T-shirt and jeans in the garage working under the hood of an older-model Chevy. They went up to him, and Sandy said, "Root Beer, this is Jim Sanders. We're riding to Paradise today. Would you like to come along?"

"Can't. Gotta get cleaned up for work pretty soon. They need me down at the little store. Sorry. Maybe next time." Root Beer started to stick out his hand out and then took it back. "I'd shake hands, but mine is kind of grimy right now. But it's nice meeting you. Have fun."

Jim noticed a tandem bicycle in the back of the garage. "Is that tandem rideable?" he asked.

Root Beer looked where Jim was looking and said, "Very rideable. I use it every chance I get. Would you like to try it? Help yourself. I gotta go get cleaned up. Sandy can help you. Just put it back when you're done."

"Well, yes. By all means. Thanks so much." Jim had never ridden a tandem before and wanted to find out what it was like. Some of his friends had them, and they looked like a lot of fun. If Sandy was willing to ride, he thought she would make a good partner. He walked the bike out of the garage and saw that it indeed was in good shape. It looked like a late model, a bright-red Santana. Seven speeds in back, a granny in the front, the drop handle bars—it was a regular road bike. Root Beer went into the house.

"What do you think, Sandy? Will you ride with me?"

"Sure. But why don't you take it out by yourself first just to get the feel for it."

Root Beer looked to be about Jim's size, so he didn't bother adjusting the seat. He got on the bike, and it felt good. He rode down the driveway, turned left on the street, and continued on for a bit. Then he stopped to turn the bike around. When he got back, he said, "This sure does feel different. I couldn't even do a U-turn on it."

"You'll get used to it. The wheelbase is a lot longer so it doesn't turn as sharp, but it is possible to do a U-turn on most roads. The key is to shift into a real low gear and go slow. Do you want me to stoke now?"

"Stoke?"

"The person in the back is the stoker, like the guy who shovels coal in the steam engine to get it going faster. The person in the front is the captain. That's you. You have to brake, steer, shift, and make all the decisions. All I have to do is give you a boost, like a supercharger."

It looked like the rear seat was already the right height for Sandy, so she got on. "I may have been the last one to ride with him," she said.

They rode down the driveway, turned left, and at the main road, turned right, heading back to Moran.

"Wow," Jim said. "This really feels different with you on the back. But it feels good."

Sandy told Jim his real name was Adam Nash Warren. "He really is a good biker. It was his initials, A. N. W., that got him the name Root Beer."

Jim chuckled. He was in heaven—blue skies, a warm day, a pretty woman on the back of a tandem. It made him feel like pedaling hard. Soon, they were going twenty to twenty-five miles per hour down the road. It was exhilarating. After about fifteen minutes, Jim decided it was time to turn around. He slowed down, put it in a very low gear, and asked, "Are you ready to turn around?"

"Yeah. I'll help you turn."

They made the turn with room to spare, and he asked, "How did you do that?"

"Simple, I leaned over. The person in the back can turn the bike by leaning. It makes it a lot easier for the person in front if he doesn't have to do it all himself."

They pedaled back, and Jim was laughing out loud.

"What's so funny," Sandy asked.

"Nothing is funny. I'm just having such a good time I can't help myself. This is wonderful. It's just laughing-out-loud fun."

When they got back to Root Beer's house, Sandy asked, "Aren't you glad you came with me now? Riding a tandem with me must be worth a change of destination, don't you think?"

"I have to admit, it was worth it. I'll remember this ride for the rest of my life. Did you enjoy it as much as I?"

"Oh yes. I certainly did. I'd love to ride with you again anytime."

They put the bike back in the garage and got on their own bikes. As they were leaving Trout Lake, a German shepherd came from behind a house and started chasing them, barking. Jim was behind, so the dog chose him as the easiest target. "Go on ahead, Sandy!" Jim yelled. "I'll take care of him." The dog ran in front of Jim, and he had to stop to keep from running into it. Then the dog ran behind him. Jim got off his bike, careful to keep the bike between him and the dog. He shouted threateningly at the dog and raised his arm like he was going to hit it. The dog backed off, and he was able to walk his bike away gradually. After a while, the dog left him alone and he was able to catch up with Sandy, who was riding slowly, waiting for him.

"You make good dog bait, Jim," she teased. "I'm glad you came with me today. See, I did need you."

Jim felt good that he'd been able to protect Sandy.

When they came to the Camp River Bridge, they stopped, not only to rest, because it was killing Jim to keep up with Sandy, but also to use the river to wash some of his clothes. Afterward, he wrung them out and strapped them on the back of his bike to dry in the sun while he was riding. Sandy watched while he waded in the stream.

There were a lot of flowers along the road as they continued on, and Jim asked, "Do you know what any of these wildflowers are called?"

"No, they don't have any in Flint, and I guess I just never asked any of my relatives who live up here."

"They're beautiful, so many colors, yellow, red, white, blue, and purple."

"And so many different kinds. I recognize thistle and daisies, but I have no idea what most of them are."

Jim said, "They sure are pretty on such a sunny day. Look at the bee flying among them. Imagine being a bee, flying among the flowers, each flower like a sun or planet waiting to be explored, exotic food to be tasted, heady aromas to be smelled. It would be like flying through space, maybe better. Our human existence is so limited."

Sandy said, "Look at that huge fly."

It followed them for a while. Jim batted at it and even tried to catch it in his hand. The fly circled around them and came back, buzzing alongside either Sandy or Jim or behind them and sometimes even in front of them. Jim was glad when it finally disappeared. It looked like it was an inch long; he'd never seen anything like it in Lansing.

They came to the mouth of the Tahquamenon River and stopped at the boat launch. Sandy watched as Jim went down to the dark waters, put his hand in, and brought it out again to taste the water.

The water was slightly brown from tannic acid leached into it from tree leaves in the forests upriver.

"Tastes like tea," he said. "Imagine, a river of tea."

Sandy laughed. "Yuck! You try just about anything, don't you?"

"I was thinking about bottling it and selling it. There's Arizona Tea. We could market it as Michigan Tea."

"Eeuw, gross!" Sandy made a gagging motion.

"I was just kidding."

Jim walked over to a grassy area and spread his blanket out on the soft ground, being careful to avoid goose turds. They sat down and rested in the sunshine, watching the river flow into Whitefish Bay.

Sandy said, "It's so peaceful here."

"Tahquamenon is a pretty name," Jim said. "It must be an Indian name. Michigan has a lot of places with pretty names. I always thought that if I had some daughters someday, that I'd like to name them after some of Michigan's places. I just love 'Menominee.' It's so musical. And doesn't Caberfae grab you? Livonia makes a nice name, too. If you like a Greek flavor, Atlanta and Sparta come to mind. There's also Crystal, Ravenna, and Ashley. Menominee is my favorite, though."

"Menominee is a pretty name, but for a son," Sandy said, "I like Flint. There's something very masculine about it. And there is a man named Lansing in my family tree. Lansing Bailey. I also like Leroy, Prescott, and Clifford."

"I like Flint," Jim said, "just as long as you don't use 'Stone' for a middle name."

"I wonder what it means," Sandy said.

"What, using 'Stone' for a middle name?"

"No, Menominee."

"I don't know. Maybe I should write the city and ask them. I'd hate to name a kid that and find out later in means something like 'horse droppings.'"

Sandy laughed. "Maybe it means something pretty like 'water falling over rocks.' When I say the name, I can almost hear water gushing down a stream, splashing around rocks. The name even sounds that way to me."

Jim thought Sandy's laughter was like that. It had a musical quality to it. It sort of gushed out, like water falling over rocks. They sat and stared out toward the bay in silence for a while.

After a while, Sandy asked, "Do you have a girlfriend?"

Jim wondered what he should tell her. Did he want to tell her? After a minute, he finally decided to tell her the truth. "No. I was engaged for a while, but Linda left me a few weeks ago. I came on this trip to help me get over her. I think I see why she left, but it wasn't pretty. I'm almost over her, but I'm not sure I'm ready for a new relationship yet. What about you? You probably have a boyfriend. I can't imagine someone as pretty as you without one."

"Oh, I've had my share of dates, but nothing ever came from them, and I'm not desperate. I can wait for the right man."

"Really? And what is the right man for you?"

"That's a difficult question. I've read several books on it and taken notes. I've read that you should make a list of the ten things you most want in a man and another list of the ten things you definitely don't want in a man. After you meet an eligible person, give him a grade. They advise that there is no perfect man but unless they get a grade of 80 percent or higher on both lists, they are probably not right for you."

"So have you been grading me?"

"Of course. Don't you guys grade women?"

"Ah, I think you got me there, although I usually don't do it consciously."

"I'm just an average girl, average height, average hair, average everything. I probably get only a five or six from you on a scale of ten."

"Are you fishing for compliments? Good heavens, Sandy. You get a lot higher than that. I thought you said you have a good self-image."

"I do. I wouldn't mind if I only got a five or six from you. My own image is a lot higher. It's just that I think that's where most men would put me."

"I suppose that if you asked a group of men to rate you, some would rate you around a five or six and some would rate you lower, but I think most would rate you higher. Everyone has different tastes. I would rate you a lot higher, maybe even a nine or ten. However, the rating is ongoing, isn't it? As I find out more about you, it could go up or down."

"One thing about us, Jim, is that the situation we've been in isn't artificial. When a man and woman go on a date, the man dresses extra nice, buys flowers, holds chairs and opens doors, lights candles, plays soft music, and generally tries to make things romantic. The woman puts on her sexiest clothes and her best behavior, and they try to impress one another. You and I have been as honest as dirt. There's been no pretense. I think I've seen you as you really are and you me. So far, I like what I see. But there are some things on the list I don't know about yet, so I can't make a final opinion yet. And I don't think you know me well enough yet, either."

"True." Jim wondered what she had on her two lists. Probably a sense of humor. Probably money. Good looks? It was too much to think about right then.

Jim lay back and looked up at the sky. After a while, he said, "It's such a pretty, sunny, warm day. It's sort of fun to daydream, to watch the puffy white clouds in the sky and make things out of them. Look at that cloud. What do you see?" He pointed.

"I see a shoe, a sexy white stiletto. No, make it silver."

"A silver stiletto?" Jim was astounded. He patted his back fanny pack.

"Yes, why? What do you see?"

"I see a white starship. No, make it a silver starship, either Klingon or Romulan, depending on how I look at it. But since Klingon and Romulan starships are both green, it must be something else."

It was Sandy's turn to be astounded. "A silver starship? I guess there is no accounting for imagination, is there?"

They both laughed.

"But now that you mention it, I think I can see a starship."

"And I think maybe I can see a stiletto."

"On days like this," Sandy said, "sometimes I just want to sing."

"Go ahead. I'll listen. Maybe I'll harmonize."

Sandy started softly, "This is my Father's world, and to my listening ears, all nature sings and round me rings the music of the spheres. This is my Father's world, I rest me in the thought of rocks and trees of skies and seas, His hands the wonders wrought."

Jim was mesmerized by her voice. "That's beautiful. Where did you learn it?"

"It's in the hymn book at church."

"Sing it again, but slower."

This time, Jim hummed along with her, trying to harmonize. He made her sing it three more times. By the time she sang it the last time, there was some pretty good two-part harmony.

"If only I could remember the other verses," Sandy groaned.

Jim laughed. "I really enjoyed that. You were wonderful."

"You were pretty good yourself. Where did you learn to harmonize?"

"Sort of by accident. Once when I was by myself, I turned on the radio and Elvis was singing, 'I Can't Help Falling in Love with You.' I started to sing with him, but I started out on the wrong note. I immediately knew it was wrong, or at least that it wasn't the melody. I was too high. But it sounded so cool. I must have accidentally hit one of the other notes in the chord. From then on, I was hooked, always trying to sing a little higher or a little lower than the melody. I don't always get it right, but it's fun to try, especially when I do get it right."

"In a chord, there are usually two or three notes that are not the melody. So practically speaking, two or three times as many harmony singers are needed as melody singers. Despite the need, most people sing the melody. I think that makes you sort of special."

"Thanks. In some ways, it's actually easier to sing harmony. You can always find a note in your voice range, and you don't have to memorize anything. It's kind of a lazy way of singing."

"There's a verse in the Bible that says, 'Behold, how good and how pleasant it is for the brethren to dwell in unity.' It's easy to dwell in unity; everyone just has to do the same thing, and it does make for easy living. But I always like to think of the verse as saying 'dwell in harmony,' implying that everyone has different skills and needs, and they accept one another and all contribute in their own unique way. Dwelling in unity is like a Gregorian chant. Dwelling in harmony is like the Mamas and Papas."

"I love the Mamas and Papas. I was 'California Dreamin'' on the way up here."

"Do you read music?" Sandy asked.

"Nah. I just listen. Harmonizing was a challenge at first. Still is in a way. Now I find that I get the melody and the harmony mixed up sometimes. Sometimes I lose myself and can't tell the difference. Maybe it's sort of a musical dyslexia. You know. People reading 'was' as 'saw' or 'god' as 'dog.' I get harmony and melody switched. Strange, huh?"

"Not really. Horizontal dyslexia is when one mixes up 'was' and 'saw.' Then there's vertical dyslexia when one mixes up 'M' and 'W' or '6' and '9.' There are probably other forms of switchings as well. Why shouldn't there be a musical dyslexia? I can tell you really enjoy singing."

"I've always enjoyed vocal harmony. I grew up listening to my parents' music. I didn't play the radio much back then, just old records. The Beach Boys, Mamas and Papas, and the Chiffons are some of my favorites. Back in the fifties and sixties, there were a lot of groups that sang together. Not so much anymore. Today, there are more individuals singing, not groups, and then they drown themselves out with their own instruments, and sometimes their singing sounds more like shouting. And they don't try to have a pretty voice anymore. A gravelly voice seems to be in vogue. They might be singing a beautiful love song, but their voice sounds strained, as if they're dying, not in love. Not very many really harmonize today. When I play the radio today, I tend to listen to oldies stations a lot."

"But you can harmonize with individuals. You just did with me."

"I can hear the harmony in my mind. I don't really know how I do it; it took me a long time to learn. It's all in my mind."

"Well, you have a good ear. I loved it. I wish …" She started to say, "You could sing with me all the time but said instead, "… more people could sing that way."

"Sandy, let me share something with you." Jim was remembering a conversation with Chris about sharing.

"Go ahead."

"I remember a few years ago when I connected with a guy I knew. I don't know how it started; we were just fooling around, I suppose, but one of us wadded up a piece of paper, and the next thing I knew, we were batting it across an imaginary net, like badminton, except with our hands, not rackets. We only did it for a couple of minutes, but I had such a good time, I've never forgotten it, or him, though I haven't seen him in a while. I think in that one silly moment we became friends for life. Maybe he didn't feel that way, but I did, anyway. It's how men connect, by doing things together."

Sandy stared out toward the bay but said nothing, as if she might be able to see out there what he was going to say. King had told her once that men have a hard time sharing what they are feeling or thinking sometimes. She sensed this was one of those times with Jim. King told her the best thing she could do during one of these moments was to be silent. "If you want a man who will share with you, don't interrupt," he said. "Give him lots of time so he can get it out. It doesn't come easy for him. Giving him the time he needs is also the hardest thing for a woman to do, because men are so slow, and it's natural for a woman to jump right in on a conversation. But if a man is glib, silver-tongued, he may be easy for you to believe, but he could just be saying whatever line he thinks you want to hear. The slower a man speaks, probably, the more he means it."

Jim continued, "Today when we sang that song, I … think … I just got that same feeling. It's so cool … when someone can hold a melody, and I can sing along and harmonize. And you did it without a piano or anything. You are good! We did something together, and suddenly, I feel like you'll always be a friend. We connected."

"Thanks. I appreciate that." Sandy was starting to feel connected because Jim was sharing. It made her feel important and respected. She thought she'd try to encourage him to share some more. "Do you also connect through biking?"

"Yeah, sometimes through biking. If I'm riding with a rider who is my equal and we have a good time together. If when I'm tired, he'll wait for me. If we take turns drafting and increase our overall speed by working together. I've felt real close to some of my biking pals. But this year, I haven't biked at all until this trip. I guess I sort of forgot about them since … well … this last year."

"Singing is somehow different. You take your voice and I take my voice, and we create a brand-new tone that is unique to us. No one else can make quite the same sound, just like a fingerprint is unique. We're making something together, not trying to outdo one another."

Sandy waited.

"Oh, I see what you're asking. Yes, I connected with you through biking today. That tandem ride was awesome. I really respect your abilities, and I appreciate that you wait for me since I'm all loaded down. I feel I'll always enjoy riding with you."

Sandy waited. Finally, she said, "Thanks, Jim. Since you're sharing with me, I'm starting to feel connected also."

Jim sat in silence for a few minutes and stared out toward the bay. He was still astounded that she saw a silver stiletto in the cloud earlier. "Sandy, do you think what we see in clouds is a reflection of our inward self?"

"It could be. Maybe it's like interpreting ink blots or dreams even. You saw a starship. That's a reflection of your love for *Star Trek* and adventure. I saw a stiletto. That reflects my love for shoes and dressing up."

"You like shoes?"

"Yeah. I love shoes. I must have over a hundred pair at home."

"But what you said yesterday, about not wanting to be a sexual fantasy for a man, yet you have all those shoes and enjoy dressing up. I don't get it. Are you trying to look pretty for other women?"

"I suppose that's one area in my life that I don't understand either. I do like feeling like a princess. But I only want one man, and I want that one man to only want me. I'm sort of old-fashioned that way."

"So what kind of shoes do you have?"

"I only have one pair of biking shoes. I suppose that's because they don't make them with high heels. If they did, I'd certainly have several pairs of those."

Jim laughed. "You're kidding, right?"

"No, really. I think they'd look cool. Even while riding."

Jim looked at his shoes and said, "Think how we look clomping around in these shoes with the cleats lifting the front of our feet up. It's like having shoes with negative heels. They're great for biking, but awful for walking. I wish my shoes had a better heel. I suppose you have some running shoes."

"Yup, three pair, two to train in, and one lightweight pair to race in."

"That seems practical."

"It seems to work, but then when it comes to fashion, well, I envy Imelda Marcos. I like all kinds, flip-flops, wedges, mules, stilettos, ballet flats, pumps, platforms, boots, and in all different colors, patterns, and materials. You get the picture."

"Yeah. You're looking for a rich man who can buy all the shoes you want."

"No, silly. I'm looking for a man who can love a shoe-crazed woman like me. A poor cobbler would probably work." She grinned.

Jim laughed. "So when you play Monopoly, are you the shoe?"

"Are you kidding? That's a man's shoe and not even fashionable. I like excitement. I like to think of myself as light and fast—like you. I want to be the race car. If it was a Corvette, I'd like it even better."

"I guess we can't play then."

"Why? Do you want to be the race car also?"

"Of course! But a bicycle would be better."

"Or a stiletto!"

They laughed.

Jim asked, "Do you play chess much?"

"Some. I just like to play for fun. I'm not serious like Elmer or Beetle. Actually, I think chess is more of a man's game. If someone could make a more feminine chess set, I'd probably like it better."

Jim laughed again. "You mean the pawns should wear skirts and the rooks dresses?"

Sandy laughed. "Something like that. And there's only one woman on the board, the queen. Why not a princess? Why not a maid? Woman are important in the world. For one thing, every man is born of one. They should have more importance on the chessboard."

"You make a good point, but don't forget, the queen is the most powerful piece on the board. It sort of mimics life, the king is ruler, but the queen is most powerful."

"There is that," she said.

They sat in silence for a while and stared off into the lake, enjoying the warmth of the sun and the peacefulness of the day. It was calming. It was like a bath for the soul, cleansing, refreshing.

Finally, Sandy said, "Tell me about your family."

"I have a younger brother, Leo, who lives in Detroit, near where my parents live. Dad is a custodian at Wayne State University. Mom works at the cosmetics counter in one of the malls. I have an aunt who lives in California, and her daughter, Loretta, who visited me Saturday. She wants me to come work for her company, and I'm thinking of taking her up on that. I also have an uncle in New York. I have a pretty small family, really."

He added, "I went to college at Michigan State and got a degree in business. I got a part-time job with the state and eventually a full-time job with them, and that's why I live in Lansing. There's not much to say really. I live by myself with two dogs in a big old house that needs a lot of work."

"So what are you doing on this vacation? It's not just the bet, is it? I mean, you could be vacationing with someone, like I am. Or you could be taking your car. Or you could be staying in motels or real campgrounds. Why did you make the bet? It seems like you're going out of your way to be alone."

Jim looked at her sideways; it was as if she were reading his mind. "You're right. I was in need of adventure. I was reading the King Arthur series and decided that as Arthur rode his horse across England, I would ride my bike across Michigan. Let's just say it's part of my recovery from the breakup with Linda."

He continued, "Also, there are certain feelings I get … I feel in charge of myself. Independent. Adventurous. Daring. I could go into a woods at night, and someone could find me there. I figure the worst that would happen is that I'd get kicked out, but I could get arrested or in an extreme case, an irate landowner could shoot me. But when I get all done, I'll feel like I've accomplished something. Proven myself. Conquered adversity. Won. It's a feeling that a man needs, but I'm not getting it on my job or at home."

"You don't seem to be too depressed. I think you told me you were getting over Linda."

"Yeah. That's right."

"Who's Chris?"

"Chris?"

"When you called me Chris yesterday, you said you got my name mixed up. I was just wondering who you mixed me up with. Apparently not a family member."

"Chris was, or is, helping me get over Linda."

"So Chris is a therapist?"

Jim wondered what he could say. He didn't want to talk about Chris. She wasn't even supposed to know about him. Now he felt cornered. He decided to just tell the truth. "Sandy, don't push me on this. I really don't want to talk about Chris right now. Some things are better off not known."

"I'm sorry. I didn't mean to pry."

"It's all right. I don't mean to be rude. It's just not a good time."

They sat in silence for a while. The song they sang earlier was starting to run through his mind. He started humming without even realizing it. He was startled when Sandy joined in, humming along with him.

He laughed. It was hard not to love her. Well, at least like her. He wasn't sure about love yet.

After a bit, Sandy asked, "What do you want out of life? Are you happy?"

Jim sensed that Sandy was accepting him for what he was. There was no hostility or mockery in her voice, just a gentle sweetness. After a few moments, he spoke. "The truth? I'm not very happy right now. In fact, I've been downright depressed, especially since Linda left me. Not suicidal or anything. But Linda and I picked out a house together, and I started fixing it up for her, and now … now that she's gone, I just feel like I'm stuck with it. What's the point? I guess what I would really like is a job I can enjoy doing, something that makes me feel useful, even if it doesn't pay that much. Right now, I'm getting paid pretty well, but it's killing me inside because I don't feel needed. I feel that if I quit, I probably wouldn't even get replaced. And I think I would like to have someone to come home to at night. A companion to share my biking and adventures. Someone I could take care of and who would take care of me and make me happy. Someone to have my children."

"And you don't have anyone."

"No. I guess I still need to heal. I'm not ready for someone else yet." Jim paused for a minute and stretched his legs out. "Actually, I was thinking about starting over. When I get back, I think I'll put my house up for sale and move to LA. My cousin, Loretta, thinks she can get me a decent job out there. It's a thought, anyway. I'm at least going out for the interview."

"That sounds wonderful. I always wanted to live in California. Michigan is beautiful in the summer; you just can't beat it. But we are one of the northern states, and it's so cold in the winter, it's hard to bike. Sometimes it's even too cold to run outdoors. In California, I could bike, run, and swim all year round."

"Really? You want to move to California?"

"Yes." She wanted to add that she wouldn't move there by herself, but only if she had someone to go with, but she thought that might sound like she was coming on to him.

Jim rolled over on the blanket and suddenly was asleep. It was so relaxing there.

Sandy watched him for a few minutes and lay down herself. She felt safe with him. She too was soon napping.

Jim felt much refreshed when he awoke. He saw Sandy napping, her breasts gently rising and falling. He watched her for a few minutes and then reached over and touched her shoulder. "Sandy," he said softly. "Sandy, wake up." Her eyes blinked open. "We need to get going, it's almost five o'clock."

They rode into Paradise, and they stopped at Tag's and ordered pasties, pronounced "past-eez." It was like a stew, only drier, and it came wrapped in pie crust, sort of like a northern burrito. It had beef or chicken in it and carrots, potatoes, onions, and spices and was very good but not peppery hot like a burrito. The miners' wives used to bake these for their husbands' lunches and wrap them in newspaper to keep them warm in the mines. Some people ate them with gravy on them. Jim didn't.

As they ate, Jim said, "Tell me about your family, Sandy."

"Mom and Dad live in Flint. Dad works for Buick. Mom teaches third grade. I have two younger sisters—Judy, who you met, and Lisa. I've got two older brothers, Bob and Bill. Bob is the oldest and Lisa the youngest. Lisa is still in college. Bob and Bill have gone into the heating and cooling business. I live by myself in apartment in Flint and work at Hurley Hospital. Judy is a beautician. We all live in the Flint area, but Mom and Dad have brothers and sisters around the state. We have a big family reunion every summer, which seems to be in the Flint area most of the time, but we've also had them in other areas, including St. Ignace, Sault Ste. Marie, Traverse City, Grand Rapids, and Detroit. There are usually a hundred or so people at these picnics, and it's usually held around the Fourth of July."

"It must be nice to come from a large family."

"It teaches you to get along. And in a big family, there always seems to be at least one special person you can relate to, someone who understands you and who you can go to for help. A mentor. King is mine."

"King?"

"One of my cousins. I have an uncle who is pretty special, too."

"What do you do at Hurley Hospital?"

"I'm in accounts receivable. I operate the billing system."

"What do you want out of life?"

"Just to do God's will."

"And what exactly does that mean? How do you know God's will?"

"We can find out a lot about what God wants for us by reading the Bible," she said.

"But surely the Bible doesn't cover everything."

"No. I think there are some gray areas. I can't imagine that God expects us to all be alike. You know, all dress the same and march to the same beat, like soldiers. If that's what God wanted, he could have made us robots, or clones. But He didn't."

She added, "I'm beginning to think that what we want is also what God wants. God gives each of us our own dreams or goals in life. One person wants to be a race car driver, another a football player, still another a mathematician or even a preacher. Sometimes He may want to alter the direction of our dreams. I think He gave us the Bible to give wisdom and guidance to follow our dreams and help us find success."

"So then," he said, "what you're saying is you want to be free to follow your dreams, because that's God's will. So it boils down to the dreams God gave you."

"Yes, I want to be able to follow my dreams."

"Yeah. Me too."

The pasties were gone. It was time for Sandy to go to her uncle's house for the night. "Thanks, Jim, for coming with me today. I enjoyed your company. It's so much more fun to ride with someone. It was a blast on the tandem. And thanks for keeping that dog away. And thanks for singing with me. I'd like to do it again with you. You really made my day."

"I sure enjoyed it, too," Jim said, and he wasn't just being polite. "But if I ever ride with you again, you have to carry a couple of bricks so I can keep up with you. You're a really good biker."

She laughed. "You're pretty good yourself, keeping up with me all loaded down."

He continued, "Tomorrow, I go off by myself again. Maybe I'll see you when I get back." This time, he wasn't just being polite; he thought he might really see her. He still had her card in his wallet, didn't he? He could probably contact her through Assenmacher's bike shop. He held up his hand in the Vulcan sign. "Live long and prosper."

Sandy held up her hand and replied, "Peace and long life."

He headed north out of town and found a place in the woods to set up his tent. He had ridden only about fifty-five miles for the day. As he lay in his tent, he thought about the things Sandy and he had in common, an interest in *Star Trek*, biking, King Arthur, names for children, the singing, and even mismatched socks. She looked so nice, her smile, her hair, her athletic body. *I think I'm falling for her. But I can't do that. If I move to LA, I might not ever see her again. Well, she might come with me. Still, I'm not ready yet. What if I fell in love with her and got engaged, and then later, she broke up with me, like Linda did. How could I ever get over it?*

He thought of the song by Neil Sedaka, "Breaking Up Is Hard to Do." The tune started running through his mind, and he wasn't even on his bike. Sandy had stolen his music from him. He hadn't thought of a song even once that day until then. Well, that was not quite true. She had taught him a new song. "This is my Father's world, and to my listening ears, all nature sings and round me rings the music of the spheres." Now this song was running in his mind.

He forced Sandy out of his mind. Tomorrow, he would be on his own again. But her song was still playing, even if he wasn't aware of it.

He got out his map and studied it.

"Well, Chris, it's you and me again. Want to go to Whitefish Point tomorrow? We could visit the falls afterward. Since I can't make it all the way to Ironwood, we may as well go to Drummond Island afterward. I've never been there before."

"Sounds good to me, Jim."

"How'd I do today? I kept you hidden, and she still doesn't have a clue. I told you I could pull this off. Ha!"

"Ha yourself!"

"What do you mean?"

"Do you really think you're out of the woods? She asked about me again. And she's still in the area somewhere. Don't you think she could find you again if she wants? Or she could just 'bump' into you by accident."

"So what. We bump into one another, say 'Hi,' and go our own way. No big deal. You heard her. She agreed I'd be on my own."

"Remember when you compared women to cats?"

"I remember. A cat can sense who will love it and who is compatible with it. You think Sandy is like that?"

"Meow."

* * *

Sandy rode south a little ways and stopped at a pay phone; her cell wasn't working. No signal. She called her uncle George. "I'm here at the IGA. You want to come and get me?"

After a little while, a slightly older man showed up in an ugly brown pickup truck. "King! Long time no see." He got out, and she hugged him.

"Good to see you, too. Dad sent me to pick you up. Let me put your bike in the back." He gently laid the Trek down on the bed. Then they drove off to his house.

"Judy is already at the house. She told me about this Jim you're following. How is he?"

"We had a really good time today. I found out he is imaginative and inventive. He came up with some really cute names for his children he hopes to have someday, and he also liked the name I had, Flint. Most people wouldn't even consider it. You know the name he had? Menominee! For a girl. And he sings. Not just sings, he harmonizes. We sat on the shore of the Tahquamenon and sang 'This Is My Father's World' together. It was so romantic. He played some chess with Beetle, who kicked his butt good. No surprise there. He also told me about an invention that Starfleet could use to make their ships appear to be a black hole. Not quite as good as a cloaking device, but useful. He likes *Star Trek*. You and he should get along just fine. And we had a blast riding Root Beer's tandem together. Don't tell Judy, but I really like him. He's still in the 80 percent or above on my two lists. But I have a problem. Tomorrow, he expects to be off by himself. And I have no idea where he is going."

"Let's think about it," King said. "Where could a person go from up here? There aren't many choices, the falls, Whitefish Point, or around the bay. What kind of bike does he ride? Since I work at the gas station in town, I can keep an eye out for him. He'll probably stop in town for breakfast somewhere, and when he leaves, I'll tell you which way."

"Okay. He's riding a red Schwinn, all loaded down. You can't miss it. The only problem is, if I show up, he might get mad."

"At you, Sandy? Didn't he have a good time today? He knows you ride your bike and that you're in the area. He couldn't possibly get mad if you were to 'bump into' him by accident. I think you can risk it. But if he is moody, then just don't talk to him until he's ready. When a man wants to be by himself, it usually means he trying to work out some problems on his own and he doesn't want to talk about them. So don't ask. And if he does ask you for advice, don't offer it, or if he insists, ask him what his choices are. Listen to him instead. If he talks the problem out for himself, he'll feel a lot better. Later, he'll really respect you for it."

"Thanks, King. I'll keep that in mind. He told me about his latest breakup and that Chris is helping him get over it. But he didn't want to talk about Chris. I wish I could find out."

"I can imagine, but don't push him. When you see him tomorrow, let him be alone. He'll appreciate you being there as long as you don't bug him to talk. Acceptance is what he needs. Hey! We all need acceptance. Remember the three 'A's of a good relationship: appreciation, acceptance, affection."

Sandy thought about it. She probably showed appreciation with his singing and biking, also his imagination and inventiveness. Acceptance, well, she hadn't pushed the issue with Chris. She accepted his interpretation of the clouds. Maybe she could work on this area. Affection? Uh-uh. Not that far along yet.

10
The Wanderer

Jim woke to the sound of a dog barking. Somewhere, there was a cabin nearby with a dog chained up that had barked all night, and he hadn't slept well. He thought how ironic it was that he should go on a vacation to get away from it all and find that he couldn't get away at all. Even way up there, one could not escape the sounds of cars, trucks, dirt bikes, four wheelers, and there, so close to Whitefish Bay, boats and Jet Skis. And if these were all quiet, then an occasional airplane. And the dog barking all night, he could have heard that in Lansing! But the barking penetrated the nylon tent walls much easier than the walls of his house. Jim thought that maybe he should've brought a radio after all. He could have put on headphones and drowned out the barking. Or earplugs. He was going to add earplugs to his travel checklist.

Jim looked at his watch. It was already nine o'clock. He was still tired, but his stomach was starting to growl. "Chris, are you hungry? Let's go eat. I sure would like a doughnut right now."

"Is that all you want? I'm a lot hungrier than that," Chris answered. Jim tried to imagine Chris eating more than a crumb. He definitely had eyes bigger than his stomach.

After packing up and checking his fanny pack to see that he still had the silver shoe, he held it in is palm for a few minutes and enjoyed the warm feeling it gave him. *Dang,* he thought, *even when she's not with me, she's with me.*

He put the shoe back in his pack and headed south, back into town. There was a little doughnut shop there, and he got a big cinnamon roll. While he was there, he decided to go back north again, all the way to Whitefish Point. It was only eleven miles, and he was easily there by ten thirty.

At the point, there was a lighthouse museum on a long, sandy beach with small pebbles at the edge of the cold water. Lake Superior was too far north and too deep to ever get warmed up. No one was swimming. No one was even wading. It was a bright sunny day, but there was a cold wind off the lake. He walked his bike up the beach until he got tired of lugging it through the sand. He laid it down in some dune grass and unpacked his dirty clothes. He took them to the water, waded in, and washed them. The water was clear, very clear, and it seemed to magnify and brighten up the little stones underneath it. There were some very pretty ones. If Sandy was riding with him, he'd pick up some for her just to slow her down, but he wasn't going to get any for himself. He gathered up his clothes and carried them back to his bike. Then he walked back to the parking lot, which was already filling with visitors. A huge boulder sat in the center of the lot in a grassy area. He climbed up on the rock and sat there while he wrung the water out of his wet clothes. Then he put the clothes on the back of his bike to dry and brushed the beach sand off his feet. He put his shoes and socks back on and walked around observing the lighthouse.

Up against the side of the museum was a purple Trek with a rainbow decal and purple helmet hanging from the handlebars. *Uh-oh,* he thought. *I've been here long enough.* He got on his bike, and just as he started riding south, he heard a woman's voice say, "Jim." He pretended not to hear it and kept riding. He wasn't ready to start a relationship yet, especially on a vacation. *I don't care how pretty she is,* he thought. *Even though I had such a good time with her yesterday.* He'd had a very good time with her yesterday. That was the problem. Part of him wanted to be with her again. But hadn't she agreed they would be on their own today? Chris said she might bump into him today. Was he reading her mind, too?

The Lake Superior beach made him think of the Beach Boys. *I should hum a Beach Boys tune today,* he thought. *How about "Barbara Ann"? No. I'll be changing it to Sandy somehow. How about "Good Vibrations." No. That one makes me think of Sandy too. I know, "The*

Wanderer." Dion. "And when I find myself a-fallin' for some girl, I just hop right on that bike of mine and pedal around the world, I'm the wanderer." Soon his bicycle was leaving behind brokenhearted girls all along the road. In reality, there was only one girl he was leaving behind. Sandy. *But how do I get her out of my head? Pedal harder! I'm the wanderer.*

A mile or so down the road was a boat launch, a big one. He turned in and walked out on the pier. As he went out, the water got deeper and deeper, but it was so clear he could still see all the way to the sandy bottom, even at the very end. Someone had told him that it was still safe to drink water right out of the lake, though it was not recommended. Seagulls flocked around, and fishing boats were berthed up on the pier. The day was warming up, and Jim enjoyed the walk in the sunshine. The parking lot was filling up with cars and vacationers launching boats. He stopped to talk to a man who had on a scuba-diving suit.

"That looks like fun. What do you see underwater around here? Or is this business?"

"No, just fooling around. Going to visit an old shipwreck."

"Salvage?"

"Oh no. These wrecks are protected. Michigan has declared them underwater parks."

"Parks?" Jim asked.

"Yes, Michigan has declared certain shipwrecks as state preserves, and there are some nearby."

When he got back on his bike and started to ride again, he noticed a ticking sound his front wheel was making. Jim stopped to examine the bike and found the magnet on the front fork was just nicking against the speedometer pickup sensor. He adjusted the magnet and pickup so it wouldn't tick. *I must have bumped it,* he thought.

Then he went out on the road again. This time, he noticed that every time he put it in high gear, the chain would rub against the front derailleur, so he stopped again and got out a little screwdriver to adjust the derailleur. After a while, he got it about as quiet as he thought he could get it—not perfect, but pretty good. He began to notice other noises on the bike, the handlebars and the seat creaked. Since it was such a nice day, he thought when he got to his next stop, he would work on the creaking handlebars. Working with his hands was therapeutic. It gave him a sense of accomplishment. Besides, now that he wasn't going to Ironwood, it seemed like he had to find ways to kill time, suddenly, he was way ahead of schedule. He wasn't going into Canada, and the eastern UP just wasn't that far. Funny how things worked out.

When he got back to Paradise, he stopped outside a little restaurant, and there was another biker getting ready to leave.

"Are you from around here?" Jim asked.

"No, I'm from Canada," he said. "Rode over here from Sault Ste. Marie this morning. I'm on my way back now. Actually, my wife is coming to get me. A hundred clicks is enough for one day."

"Have a good day, eh." Jim hadn't thought about being so close to Canada. A hundred clicks was a hundred kilometers, about sixty-two miles. *Sault Ste. Marie, pronounced "Soo Saint Marie," another of Michigan's funny pronunciations,* he thought.

Jim went into the restaurant and ordered a hamburger and a pitcher of water. When the waitress wasn't looking, he opened up his Camelbak and filled it up from the pitcher. The burger was great, Jim thought, nothing like a bike ride to work up an appetite and make even mundane food seem gourmet. The waitress came back and saw the empty pitcher.

"My, you were thirsty," she said. "Let me get you some more."

Before Jim could protest, she went out and came back with another pitcher. Jim drank some of it and left her a nice tip.

It was afternoon by then, and Jim headed west toward Tahquamenon Falls. The state highway M-123 was horseshoe-shaped with Paradise at the hump on top. Both legs of the horseshoe had an M-123 South and an M-123 North. Although the two M-123 Norths both went north, they actually went in opposite directions and met at the top at Paradise. The east leg of M-123 South went to St. Ignace. The west leg of M-123 South went to Newberry.

As he was riding to the falls, he met two hikers. "How far is it to the falls?" they asked as they were walking on the west leg of M-123 North to Paradise.

"In the direction you're heading, it's only about five miles to Paradise, but it's seven miles to the falls. I'd say you already passed the falls."

"You're kidding." It wasn't a question. These young men had been hiking in the woods and came to the state highway on the west leg. When they saw the sign M-123 North, they assumed it would take them to the falls, since they were camped in the state park south of Paradise but on the east leg.

"You were tricked by the road sign," Jim explained to them. "If the highway department had named them east and west roads, maybe that wouldn't have happened." He showed them his map.

The men were walking with two big dogs and carrying backpacks fully loaded. It was a hot day, and Jim thought they looked tired. They decided to hike to Paradise and then to the campground to get their Jeep so they could drive to the falls. He felt sorry for them.

Jim took off again, and a couple of miles down the road, a white full-size van was stopped on the shoulder on the other side of the road. Jim wondered why a van would be stopped there. He kept looking at it to see if someone was in it and what the person was doing. Finally, he got close enough to see a lady at the wheel, and she had one finger over her lips, telling him to be quiet. With her other hand, she was pointing to the other side of the road. By this time, Jim was almost past her. He had just enough time to glance quickly and see a cow moose and her calf standing in the grass. *Darn, if I hadn't been looking at the van, I would have seen them sooner. It's too late now; if I stop or turn around, I might spook them.* He'd heard stories about moose charging people, and that wasn't something he wanted to find out about firsthand. *Next time I see a vehicle stopped,* he thought, *I'll know to look for wildlife first.* He kept going.

It wasn't long, and he was at the Lower Falls. He had been there before, but he took a quick ride in and around and even stopped at the gift shop. The water level was too high, so the park wasn't allowing people to row to the island. It was too dangerous. He splurged on a Coke and went out to sit on a bench in the shade. It was really getting warm out.

Then he headed out for the Upper Falls. *Just like Michigan,* he thought. *We got an Upper and Lower Peninsula; why not have an Upper and Lower Falls?* The Upper Tahquamenon Falls was a few miles away and just across the county line. He pulled in and walked his bike to get a quick look at the falls. Somewhere, he had read that this was the second largest falls east of the Mississippi. Of course, there was no comparison with Niagara Falls. The tea-colored water flowed over it noisily. He had seen this on other vacations, and even though it was a great tourist site, he had other things on his mind. He didn't stay long.

He headed back to the parking lot, laid his bike down in the grass, rolled his blanket out, and spread his still-wet clothes in the sun to dry. It was a nice open area, and there didn't seem to be any bugs. The sun felt warm and inviting. It reminded him of yesterday when he sat in the sun with Sandy. He decided he would make use of the time to work on the creaking in his handlebars. "Hop off, Chris. I'm going to fix your perch." He got his tool kit out and took the handlebars apart, starting with the aerobars. After they were all apart, he used a rag he had found—someone's worn-out T-shirt—to clean the parts with some 3-In-One oil. The trick to keeping them from creaking was a light coat of oil. Sometimes bike mechanics used a little grease. Grease probably worked better and probably lasted longer too, he figured, but he didn't have any. He started to put it back together.

While he was working, a purple Trek pulled in the lot, ridden by a lovely young woman with a ponytail and a purple helmet. Her socks were mismatched but somehow didn't look mismatched. *Purple and pink must be her favorite colors,* he thought. Her biking shoes were black and seemed awful masculine, like his shoes. Fashion hadn't reached women's bike shoes yet.

Jim had his handlebars all apart; there was no escaping this time. She came over and sat down on the grass. She held up her hand with the Vulcan sign and said, "Live long and prosper." He just kept working. They had already agreed that they would both be on their own today. Why was she there? Sandy sat down on the grass out of his way and quietly watched him work. Jim didn't know what to say. He wasn't mad at her. Not really. In fact, he liked her, but he had planned on being alone that day, and he didn't want to talk; still, he didn't want to be rude to her. He was more irritated with himself than anything. He should've pedaled harder. He could've listened to Chris. He wouldn't have taken his bike apart where she could catch him. He should've, he could've, he would've. *Aw, what's the use?*

Finally, he held up his hand and said gently, "Peace and long life." She made him nervous but a good kind of nervous. He liked her, but he couldn't concentrate on his work, either. She was just too pretty, too distracting. She was wearing the typical black biker shorts, but she had on a red, white, and blue jersey with stars on it. Her ponytail looked cute sticking out from under her helmet. Her starry purple nailed hands matched her bicycle. Had she painted her toenails, too? Probably. There was a rainbow tattoo on the back of her hand. Her bike shoes even looked cute. It wasn't the shoes; it was the small size. He guessed she wore a size 7, but a woman's foot was usually just smaller than a man's. That would be only a size 5 1/2 in men's shoes. He wore a size 11. They were a lot smaller; of course, they looked cute, even if they weren't fashionable. She just had a woman's body, and he was biologically reacting to it. He wondered how she'd look in heels. Oh, man. A biker in heels, would that be cute or what? Not very practical, but he was getting turned on just thinking about it. He dropped his little Allen wrench. His hands were shaking. He dropped it twice more. He finally got it back together and then realized he had put the aerobars on backward. His heart was pounding.

She sat quietly and watched.

He took the aerobars off and put them back on again. This time, he got it right.

He turned and looked at Sandy. He studied the rainbow tattoo on the back of her hand now. Next, she'd be putting one on her cheeks. He tried to be calm inside, but his heart still pounded. He wanted to run away, but he didn't. He wanted to hold her, but he couldn't. He finally accepted the situation and got control of himself.

She was a fellow biker. She was being quiet, waiting for him. He took a deep breath and exhaled slowly.

"I'm glad you came," he said softly with a smile, and he really meant it.

"I'm glad I found you," she said, smiling. Her deep voice was calming.

It was getting near five o'clock, and Jim thought he should be heading back. He was getting hungry. "I saw a little fish house back in Paradise, and I've had whitefish on my mind all day. Would you like to eat with me there? At Brown's Fish House? I'm starved."

"Sure." She pulled some cookies out of her fanny pack. "In the meantime, would you like some chocolate-chip cookies? I made them myself."

"My favorite," he said. "But I'll take a rain check on them. I'm not in the mood for cookies right now; I want fish. Whitefish. Besides, I can't cheat on my bet."

"Really? You'd turn down my chocolate-chip cookies? For fish? You really don't cheat on a bet, do you? Have you ever cheated on a test at school?"

"Nope. Not me. I don't cheat on things I care about, but I have been known to cheat on the speed limit. If I were in charge, I'd change all the speed limit signs to 'Suggested Speed.' In fact, to be honest, I just like to go fast, not that I'm in a hurry. I just enjoy driving fast. You know, light and fast, the race-car driver on the Monopoly board." He laughed. "So what do you cheat on?" he asked casually.

"Me. Well, I never cheated on a test at school, and I wouldn't cheat on a bet either. I don't intentionally speed. But I've cheated on my diet sometimes. Like right now." She got a cookie out of her fanny pack and started munching in front of him. It had no effect on Jim. He had been thinking about whitefish all day.

Jim laughed. "You? On a diet? No way! You look fabulous. There's not an ounce of fat on you."

Sandy picked her bike up and started to get on it. "Way." She smiled. "But thanks." Sandy felt good that he had said that. He had no idea how hard it was for her to keep her figure trim—all that running and biking, swimming too, to burn off calories, and watching her food intake. When she made those chocolate-chip cookies, she was her own worst enemy. She liked to look good, but she also wanted to keep the extra weight off so she could bike faster and run faster. An extra pound really made a difference. It worked both ways. She kept the weight off to run and bike faster. And she ran and biked to keep the weight off. At least running and biking were fun, and she enjoyed the compliments.

As they rode back to Paradise, Jim told her about the moose and the hikers. At Brown's Fish House, Jim ordered the three-piece dinner with baked potato. Sandy got the same. When the waitress brought the food out, Jim didn't use his tartar sauce on the fish or butter the potato. "I like the taste of fresh fish and baked potato. Why make them taste like something they're not?" he explained. The deep-fried whitefish was like candy to him.

As they savored their food, Jim asked, "What's with all the rainbows, Sandy?"

"I love rainbows; they're so pretty. And they're a sign of hope. I like to think that things will get better, or at least that they could get better. You know, focus on the positive. It's hard to be depressed with a rainbow shining at you. You look like you could use one. I have some in my pack. Let me put one on you."

"On me? A rainbow? Nah, it's not my style. Maybe a dragon might be nice."

"Trust me, a rainbow is just what you need. It'll cheer you up. Besides, I don't have any dragons." She dug a little rainbow out of her pack. "I think this would look real good right above your knee. Hold still." Before he could protest, she peeled the clear plastic off the front of it and stuck it just above his knee. "Wait a minute; I have to soak the backing off now." The rainbow wasn't visible yet, just the circle of white paper that it was printed on. She got a napkin and soaked up some of the condensation from the side of her cold drink. Then she put the wet napkin over the circle of white and held it for thirty seconds. Jim held his breath. The wet napkin was cold, but he only felt her warm fingers on his bare skin. It was electrifying. Searing. Like a hot iron. Were her fingers really that warm, or was it him? She took the napkin off and then gently slid the paper off the tattoo. "Don't touch it. It will dry in a minute, but if you touch it now, it might smear. I've found that they work best where the skin is wrinkle free and doesn't have any hair on it. They last three to five days, sometimes a week or longer if you're careful with them. If you want to take it off, just rub it gently with some rubbing alcohol or baby oil. Water doesn't affect them; you can even go swimming with them. These tattoos don't cost much, and I don't use them all the time, but since this is my vacation, I think I'm entitled to a little fun."

Jim felt like he'd been branded. Just like a steer. Owned by the Rainbow Girl. Property of the Rainbow Ranch. He wondered if she'd stick one on his helmet or bicycle next. It did look kind of cute. Well, she'd be gone tomorrow and he'd take it off then. He didn't want to hurt her feelings.

They sat and enjoyed their food, the smell of cooking fish, watching people come in and out. They enjoyed one another, not talking much, just being together.

After a while, Sandy asked, "Jim, will you go to church with me tomorrow?"

"No way," he said instantly. "I don't even have any regular clothes, just these bike clothes, and I haven't shaved for a week. I'd really feel out of place."

"Please, Jim," she said softly. "It would really mean a lot to me." She looked at him with her dark-brown eyes. The light from the window sparkled off them. He didn't want to go, but he didn't want to be rude. He reached over with his left hand and gently touched her right hand.

"Please don't ask me that," he said softly. "I don't even go to church at home; I don't know what to do. How to act. I haven't said a prayer since I was a little kid. Would God want me there?"

"It's good that you're honest," she said quietly. "But yes, He would want you there. And I really want you to come with me. God doesn't look on your clothes but on your heart."

"That's just it. My heart is not all that pure, Sandy. I can't stand before God."

"God knows that. None of us can. My heart isn't all that pure either. But God loves me. And He loves you, too. I know. He would be glad to have you there. After all, there aren't any perfect people in my church, though maybe some of them think they are."

Jim stalled, but he could feel his resolve breaking down. "Where do you go? To the Catholic Church in town?" Jim knew the UP, like most of Michigan, was mostly Catholic.

"No, I go to the Baptist church. It's just a little church and very friendly. Not formal at all. You can ride your bike there. You can even wear your bike clothes there; they won't mind at all. They'll be happy to have you. Sunday school starts at ten o'clock."

Jim remembered seeing the little church as he rode into town the day before. He pulled his hand back but said nothing.

Sandy thought that maybe she could find him some jeans and get him a razor. The thought occurred to her that if she did that, it would be like telling him he wasn't accepted, that he wasn't good enough. But he was accepted, he was good enough; it was just his own opinion of his appearance that kept him away. "I'll tell you what," she said. "I'll wear my bike clothes tomorrow. You don't have to feel like you're alone. There will be two of us in bike clothes." There, that would show acceptance.

"You … you'd do that for me?" Jim recognized the sacrifice she was offering him. Many women just wouldn't wear bike clothes to church, not unless they really cared.

"Yes," she said softly. "Besides, it's only for a couple of hours. What harm could it do? It would mean an awful lot to me."

"Oh all right," Jim grumbled. *She did it to me again,* he thought. *First Paradise, and now this. Why can't I just say no to her? Am I a wimp or what?* Secretly though, he was glad she had asked him.

Jim finished eating his fish and was still hungry. It was so good; he wished there was more. Then he saw there was a smoked-fish smorgasbord platter on the menu and decided to order that, too. He had really blown his budget for the day, but it was a real treat for him, and he didn't get up there very often.

Just then, a big, husky man came in. "Hi, Dune," he spoke in a deep voice. "Mind if I join you?"

Dune? He's calling her Dune? What's that about? Jim thought.

Sandy said, "Have a seat, King. I'd like you to meet Jim Sanders. He's biking up here on a bet. Can you imagine that? Jim, this is Michael Hill, also known as King. King of the Hills. He's the cousin I told you about earlier, the Trekkie. My mentor."

King was a big man with thick black hair. Jim could see why he was "King of the Hills." *I wouldn't want to mess with him,* he thought. Jim estimated him at six feet four and at least 250 pounds. Muscular. Maybe a weight lifter. King looked to be in his forties. She treated him like a big brother.

King offered his hand and said, "Glad to meet you, Jim. I hear that Sandy enjoys riding with you."

"Hi, King. Glad to meet you." But he wasn't. Not really. He was enjoying Sandy's company, and now he was losing it.

King sat down next to Sandy, and they started talking away like old friends. Jim heard quite a few words that sounded like some foreign language.

Finally, Sandy and King got up. She turned to him and said, "Jim, I'm sorry; I have to be going now. King is taking me to my uncle George's house tonight. It was real nice having dinner with you," she said, taking Jim's hand and giving it a quick squeeze. "I'll see you tomorrow. Ten o'clock. At the church. Okay?"

"All right, ten."

She bent over and gave him a quick kiss on his cheek. "Q'plah," she said.

"What did you say? Kuh … what?"

"*Q'plah*. It's a Klingon word. It means 'success,' much like *shalom* is a Jewish word meaning 'peace.' A greeting. A farewell. I'll tell you about it tomorrow," she said and smiled.

Sandy and King walked out, leaving Jim to eat his smorgasbord by himself. He really liked the smoked fish, which he ate slowly. He should've stopped at one meal and left Brown's while still wanting more. This second meal was too much, and he was really stuffing himself. He picked at his food a little and finally decided not to eat the rest. With Sandy gone, he just wasn't hungry anymore. When

Sandy left, he felt like a cloud had just covered the sun and a chill wind had come.

He pulled the tiny silver stiletto out of his fanny pack and unwrapped it. As it warmed in his fingers, he felt better. He thought about Sandy having over a hundred pairs of shoes and chuckled to himself. He figured she'd wear shoes like this one. She probably had a pair already. He wrapped the shoe back up and put it back in his fanny pack.

He wondered what this "Dune," "King," and Klingon stuff was—not that he didn't like it. He liked sci-fi and watched *Star Trek* shows regularly. The original series wasn't being shown in Lansing currently, but *The Next Generation*, *Deep Space Nine*, and *Voyager* were still on. He read a book once called *Dune* by Frank Herbert. What did Sandy have to do with that?

He threw out the rest of his dinner and rode away from the restaurant. Alone. Sad. He looked at the rainbow on his knee, and it made him feel better. He pedaled down the road a ways until he found another place he could camp that was far away from the barking dog that had kept him awake the previous night and set up his little tent. The tent pole that he'd repaired earlier broke where he had taped it. He got a jackknife out of his tool kit and cut the broken end off. It was only an inch or so. Then he pushed the broken pole part out of the metal sleeve, maneuvered the metal sleeve over the fresh end, and taped it up again. The pole was an inch shorter now, but it still worked almost like new.

He crawled into his tent and decided to wash up. At least he could be clean for church. He couldn't find his washcloth. It must have fallen off the bike during the day. So he got a clean sock and used it instead. Adventurers had to improvise all the time, he thought. He was careful not to rub over the tattoo. Sandy would see it the next day. He'd wait another day to take it off. What could it hurt?

He checked his odometer and saw he had gone fifty-seven miles for the day. Then he counted his money and found ninety-eight dollars left. *I've been on the road eight days and spent just under half. I'll make it.* "It's been a good day," he wrote in his diary, detailing the events.

Chris said, "Jim, you really blew it today. You let her brand you. Now she owns you. You're never gonna be the same again."

"Come on, Chris. What's with you anyway?" he argued with his imaginary friend. "There's no way she owns me. Tomorrow, I go to church with her, and then poof, I'm outta here. This tattoo isn't permanent. It's coming off tomorrow night."

"She has you hooked, and you don't even realize it yet."

"You know what, Chris? I think a rainbow would look good on you." Jim blinked. When he opened his eyes again, there was a little rainbow on Chris's back. "There. Don't you look nice? You can keep that until I take mine off. We're in this together, pal, like it or not."

"Aaaaaargh! What are you doing? My beautiful shiny black back! Take it off. No respectable cricket would have such a thing."

"Tomorrow, Chris. It won't kill you for one day. Besides, who's going to see you but me?"

Chris was fuming, but Jim ignored him and drifted off to sleep. He dreamed of being on a spaceship with Sandy. He was lost. Navigation was down. Klingons were chasing him. Klingons. Funny, he'd never paid attention to Klingon words before. And King and Sandy were speaking it. And now Klingons were chasing him, and he couldn't get the ship to respond to the helm. No matter which way he tried to turn the ship, it would end up going the wrong way. Would he die out there in the coldness of space, shot down by Klingons? Sandy clicked over to him on her silver stilettos and took his hand. With her guiding his hand, he steered the ship in the right direction, and somehow, they escaped the Klingons. After the escape, he felt like James Bond, Agent 007, and he was looking for a place to be alone with her when he awoke.

He woke up with a sense of awe and wonder about Sandy. Had she bewitched him? He wondered how she knew where to go, how to steer the ship. Was it her woman's intuition? What did she see? What was his subconscious trying to tell him. Sometimes it took a woman to help a man get his bearings. But it was a woman who got him this way in the first place, wasn't it? Life could be so confusing, and sometimes, it seemed like there were no hard-and-fast answers. Still, it seemed a good dream.

* * *

"So how did your day go?" King asked when they were in his truck.

"I almost caught him at Whitefish Point, but he got away. I yelled at him, and I think he heard me, but he just kept going. I thought it would be best not to pursue. Later, when I checked in with you at the gas station, I found he was headed toward the falls. I caught him at the Upper Falls, in the parking lot. He was taking his bike apart and cleaning it or something. I did just like you said, and it worked. After a while, he started talking and even asked me to have dinner with him where you found us. You must have seen our bikes parked against the building."

"How is he treating you?"

"So far, he's been a perfect gentleman. He even let me put one of those rainbow tattoos above his knee. I also asked him to come to church tomorrow. I got him to say yes."

"Great! Do you think he'll show?"

"Yes, I do. Jim doesn't seem like one to go back on his word. Do you know, I offered him some of my homemade chocolate-chip cookies, and he turned me down? Didn't want to cheat on his bet. I have one left, would you like it?" She got it out of her fanny pack.

"You bet I would. Everyone knows you make the best chocolate-chip cookies in the world!" He gladly took it. "Mmmmm. You better be careful with those. The way to a man's heart is through his stomach, and more than one young man has ended up ruined … er … married because of cookies like these." He laughed.

"Don't worry about Jim. I was stunned that he turned me down. No one has ever turned down my cookies before. And for fish! I guess he really wants to win his bet fair and square."

"Well, at least he's honest."

"I know, and it makes me feel kind of guilty, following him around, even if it is fun."

That night, when she went to bed, she thought of Jim, sleeping in a tent in the woods somewhere. She said a little prayer for him that he would be okay.

King was right, she thought. By not pushing him today, I won his respect and friendship. I wish King hadn't come so soon; I would have liked to spend some more time with him. It was a delightful meal we had together. I wish I didn't have to wear my bike clothes to church tomorrow. It wouldn't be so bad, but I promised the pastor I would sing. Well, Christ went to the cross for me. I can do this for Him.

11

Amazing Grace

Jim woke up way too early to go to church, so he just lay there for a while until he dozed off again. There was nothing to do really, except wait until about nine thirty and then pack up and head for the church.

When he finally got up, his lower back was sore. He thought that maybe the hard ground was starting to get to him. He was careful to sleep on his side every night and even learned to like the lumpy ground underneath him; it let him find a comfortable place for his hipbone. He did some exercises for his back and started packing up.

He wanted to get to church early enough to see Sandy before the service but not too early. So he timed it to arrive at a quarter to ten.

Sandy was already there with her purple Trek. She had a tattoo on her knee, in the same place where his own was. Jim wished he had a Trek bike, too. But he wouldn't put a rainbow on it; he'd put some stars on it and make it a "Star" Trek. Somehow, a Star Schwinn just didn't have the same appeal. But he really liked his red Schwinn; it fit him perfectly, and he was comfortable on it.

He walked slowly over to Sandy and gave her the Vulcan hand sign. Thinking about the previous night, however, he changed the greeting to "Q'plah."

Sandy laughed. "A Klingon greeting with a Vulcan hand sign today? A mixed signal?"

"Why not? Didn't I tell you I had a little rebel in me?" He smiled.

"Q'plah," she replied.

"You know what I thought when I first heard that?" he asked and grinned. "I thought it had something to do with a cow using the bathroom."

Sandy broke out laughing. "I guess it does sound somewhat like that. But don't tell King. He may not be too happy about it." She continued, "You walked over here like an old man today. Are your legs sore?"

"No, it's my back. I think sleeping on the ground is getting to me. I'll be all right. But what did I hear Mike, er, King call you last night? 'Dune'? Does that have something to do with Frank Herbert's book, *Dune*?"

Sandy laughed. "No, silly. It's my name. Sandy Hill. Dune. Get it? King has been teasing me about that for years. You know, there are some weird nicknames in my family."

Now it was his turn to laugh. "I never even thought of that. I better be careful, or next I know, you'll be giving me a nickname."

"Not until you're one of the family … I mean, uh, we just give these silly nicknames to family members. So you don't have to worry."

"But anyone can have a nickname. Actually, Jim is my nickname; my real name is James. Look at our presidents. Eisenhower was Ike. Kennedy was Jack. Nixon was Dick. Clinton is just plain old Bill. People who are important have nicknames.

"By the way," Jim asked, "is King here this morning? I suppose his nickname has some meaning also. I hope it doesn't have anything to do with dogs. Wasn't it Sergeant Preston who had a dog named King?"

"King will be here later. He is our resident Klingon. He goes to *Star Trek* conventions and even dresses the part. As big as he is, he's very convincing. He's been studying the Klingon language and can carry on a halfway decent conversation in it. He even taught me some of it. There are an awful lot of Klingon names that start with 'K,' so we nicked him 'King' because it sounded Klingon and it makes him feel good. King of the Hills. He is also quite good at chess, and that has a king. In the original series, there was a Klingon captain named Kang."

Jim thought that King would make a very good Klingon, even without a costume. He had a certain fierce look about him that even a real Klingon would respect. Yet, he seemed gentle enough last night.

"How is it that a Christian would like *Star Trek* anyway? I thought Trekkies were mostly atheists or agnostics. I think Gene Roddenberry was agnostic."

"I know lots of Christians who like *Star Trek*. A lot of shows make the preacher sound like the village idiot or a bad guy, but *Star Trek* doesn't do that. God usually isn't mentioned at all, and a person's religion is respected. On the other hand, *Star Trek* spurs one's imagination, and it does teach good moral values, something a lot of other shows don't have. You learn to respect other people, to be dependable, to stick up for that which is right, even if it could cost you your life, to be loyal and responsible, to respect life, and to talk, not shoot, first. And *Star Trek* isn't just sci-fi. It also examines the human soul. It's really a top-notch show. I've seen all the movies myself. And I love the humor. Just because we're Christians doesn't mean we have to stop thinking."

Jim had to agree with her.

They went in and sat down. Jim fidgeted and squirmed; he wasn't prepared for this. His back hurt. He just couldn't get comfortable on the hard seats. The teacher spoke about something from the book of Romans and justification by faith, not works. Jim really didn't understand what he was talking about. The teacher read from Ephesians 2:8–9. "For by grace are ye saved through faith, and that not of yourselves, it is the gift of God. Not of works, lest any man should boast." Sandy shared her Bible with him, but he just didn't get it. He couldn't concentrate with his back hurting.

Finally, Sunday school was over. *Only one hour to go,* Jim thought. *I'll make it.*

A few songs were sung, and the offering taken. When the plate came to Jim, Sandy shook her head and whispered, "I put some in for you. Win your bet."

"Thanks," he whispered.

The song leader announced special music for the morning. Sandy Hill would sing and play the piano. She got up and went to the front. And she was wearing bike clothes! Jim felt awful that she wore them for him. He wished now that she had worn a dress. He realized he had never seen her in a dress. He tried to imagine her in one. It made his heart pound. Not many women would even dare to wear bike clothes to church, but she was performing in them. And she did it for him. Jim admired her all the more. She wore a pink sock and a purple sock, and they still looked like they matched! He was surprised that she played the piano. She didn't mention that to him at the river a couple of days ago. He loved a good piano player. How often he wished Linda could play.

She sat at the piano and started playing. He was mesmerized by the beauty of her playing; it seemed like a concert, a whole orchestra. He heard her rich alto voice. "Does Jesus care? Oh yes, He cares …" Jim thought of Roman soldiers putting up crosses, crucifying three people. The one in the middle, Jesus, said, "Father, forgive them." It was as if Jesus was speaking to him. It broke Jim's heart to see the man suffer so. Jim wondered why. Then he remembered one of the verses he'd heard at Cornerstone Baptist Church the previous Sunday: "For he has made him who knew no sin (Jesus), to be sin for us, that we might be made the righteousness God in him." *He was my substitute,* Jim thought. *I am the sinner, the one who has offended God, the one who deserved to die. I'm not a bad person, but I don't meet God's standards, and He's the one I'm ultimately accountable to, not other people. It's like Sandy said, God loves us, even though we're not pure of heart. I think I understand now.*

He felt something on his hand, and it broke his thoughts. Sandy was done playing and came back to sit with him. She put her hand on his as she sat down.

Bob Goode, the pastor, got up to speak. "This morning, I felt led of the Spirit to speak on something in such a way as I've never done before. Those of you who like science fiction may really like this, so listen up. I'm going to talk about the greatness of God."

Jim was wide awake now. A preacher going to talk about sci-fi? *Finally, something I can really get into,* he thought.

"I want to play a little mind game with you. Let's have some audience participation today. Here's a series: two, four, six, eight. What is the next item in the series? You over there."

"Ten."

"That's right. That was just a warm-up, just so you know what I'm doing. We're going to look at some series. Now for the real thing. The first series is: a point, a line, a plane. What's next. Anyone?"

"A solid."

"Very good."

Jim was wondering, *What does this have to do with God?*

"And after a solid, or three-dimensional object, then what?"

Someone said, "Time."

"Very good. The four dimensions of our known universe, also known as the space-time continuum. Now think once more. What comes after that? What is the next item in the series? Anyone?"

Jim thought. *Sci-fi. Space-time continuum. What's the connection? Parallel universes. You hear about that in* Star Trek *a lot.* He raised his hand.

"You." The preacher pointed at him.

"Other universes?" he said meekly.

"Right. We have a sharp congregation this morning. Other universes. Another way to think of this is that a line is made up of multiple points, a plane is made up of multiple lines, a solid is made up of multiple planes, the universe is made up of multiple solids in time, and multiple universes make up a higher universe, or a super universe. God is in that super universe and supervises not only our universe but any other universes there may be.

"And according to our Bible, God lives in a higher universe, or super universe, that includes our own universe and possibly others. The Bible starts out, 'In the beginning, God created the heavens and the earth.' The very fact that God existed before our universe was created shows that He exists in another, a higher universe than ours, a super universe. It's only because He is outside our little universe that He was able to create it. If God was only part of our universe, He couldn't have made it. It is only because He can be outside of our universe looking in that He can see everything that has happened and will happen. Solomon recognized this in 1 Kings 8:27 when he said of God, 'The heaven and heaven of heavens cannot contain thee.' If God existed only within our universe, He would not be omniscient. He is not a part of it in the same sense that we are part of it. He is beyond it and more. Much more. Think about it. He's not just the man upstairs. He is an intelligent being beyond upstairs and with more knowledge and wisdom than any human ever had.

"It's time to start another series: rock, plant, animal. What's next? Do I have an answer?"

Someone in the back said, "Man."

"Correct. The series has to do with personality, or life. Essentially, a rock has no personality. No life. It has zero dimensions; just like in the first series, a point has no dimensions. The second item, a plant, has one dimension, life. It grows. But it has no thought pattern, no mind of its own. It corresponds to a line in the other series. The third item, an animal, take a dog for example, has a life and it also exhibits a soul, that which feels and thinks to a certain extent. The dog has two dimensions and corresponds to a plane in the other series. The fourth item, man, has yet a higher dimension. Man exhibits a spirit. It is obvious that man has a body and soul. Man thinks and feels. But man also has self-awareness, and not only self-awareness, but God awareness. Did you ever see a dog go on a diet, change its hair color, or worship God? And man also has a will. He can decide if he is going to be a burger flipper or an astronaut, or at least he can choose to try those professions. He can decide to be good or bad or just go along with the crowd. There are certain things in a man's life that he can change. Dogs essentially don't change. Sometimes, we, the dog owner, can get them to change, but it was our decision, our will, not the dog's will, that made the difference.

"We see these three parts of man in 2 Thessalonians 5:23, where Paul says, 'And I pray God your whole spirit, and soul, and body, be preserved blameless unto the coming of our Lord Jesus Christ.' Again, in Hebrews 4:12, it says, 'The Word of God is quick and powerful and mightier than a two-edged sword, piercing even to the dividing asunder of soul and spirit, and of the joints and marrow, and is a discerner of the thoughts and intents of the heart.' Together, these three items, a body, a soul, and a spirit, make up what we call collectively a person.

"I know it is not always obvious what the difference between a soul and spirit is. A soul deals more with feelings, emotions, and instincts. A spirit deals more with intellect, will, and awareness of self and of God. Those who are not aware of God are simply spiritually dead.

"Some people can't or don't accept that there is both a soul and a spirit, but perhaps believe in one or the other or that they are the same. That's okay. The point is these things—the body, soul, and spirit—make up a person. They all contribute to our personality, just like space and time make up our universe.

"We have rock, plant, animal, and man. Would anyone like to take a stab at what comes next in our series?"

Jim was thinking. The body, soul, and spirit were all different dimensions of a personality, like time and space were different dimensions of the universe. And if multiple universes made up a super universe where God dwelled, then multiple personalities would make up a higher being, a super being, like God. It seemed logical that God must be the next step up from human, and it must be because He has multiple personalities. "Would it be God?" he mumbled. "Because He has multiple personalities?"

"I heard someone. What did you say?"

"God?" Jim spoke up, squirming in his seat. "Because He has multiple personalities." He was certainly feeling self-aware right then; every eye was on him. Had he blown it?

"Well, yes. That's exactly it. Multiple persons form a higher being than man. Just as in the first series, a super universe is a collection of multiple universes, so a higher being is a collection of multiple personalities, or a super being. God is a set of persons. If God just had super powers, He would be a different kind of person than us, like an angel, but not a higher person. He would be a different species but not a higher species."

Jim was all ears. *God has, rather is, multiple persons?* He sat on the edge of the pew. *This does sound like sci-fi. Why not a being with multiple persons? It could be sort of like the Q continuum in the* Star Trek *universe but not exactly. Q had godlike powers, but he didn't know everything. Picard had proven him wrong several times. And although there were multiple Q's, they were not one person. They disagreed, even fought one another. And one of them died once. And even with their powers, it wasn't shown that the Q ever went into a higher dimension than our universe. So God is obviously even greater.*

Pastor Bob continued, "The Bible tells us that, to be exact, God is three persons: the Father, the Son, and the Holy Spirit. As we examine scripture, we find that each has its own intellect, emotion, and will. And yet the Bible teaches us over and over again that God is one God. All three persons together are God. We have a theological name for it. It's not found in the Bible. It's called the Trinity. The three-in-one. Tri-unity, or Trinity.

"So we are created in the image of God. We, like God, have an emotion, intellect, and will. However, we are not exact copies of God any more than an image in a mirror is an exact copy of the person looking into it. But we are a mirror that reflects God's glory.

"We humans tend to make God a human. We tend to think of Him as an old man in the sky, who just happens to run things. But when we get the right perspective on God, we see that He is much, much more than that. He is as much greater than us as a dog is greater than a tree or a tree than a rock. He's at least a whole dimension above us. While we might get a glimpse of God intellectually or feel His power or see His working in our lives, we can never experience what it is like to be God."

That makes sense, thought Jim. *I guess I would expect God to be more than just a man upstairs, someone like us with super powers.*

The preacher went on, "Because God has multiple personalities, one of them could become a man to experience our life, and to share His forgiveness with us.

"The whole point is that God loves each of us so much that He wanted us to spend eternity in heaven with Him. But God is holy and just and we are all sinners. None of us measures up to God's standards. Therefore, we are all destined to perish, to spend eternity in hell, unless God Himself can find a way to forgive us and yet still satisfy His justice. God did find a way. He sent His Son, Jesus, to die on the cross for our sins. If Jesus was only a man, He could die for one other man. But Jesus was also God, making His sacrifice infinite and beneficial to *all* people. There is no discrimination there. God loves us *all*, each and every person. And yet God loves us enough, that if only one person in all eternity was to accept Christ as Savior, He still would have gone to the cross for that one person.

"I want every head bowed, eyes closed, no one looking around. If you are here today and you know beyond a shadow of a doubt that you're saved and on your way to heaven, raise your hand. Thank you. Hands all over the room."

"If you didn't raise your hand a minute ago, thank you for your honesty. I would like to take a minute and pray for you now. If you didn't raise your hand a minute ago, would you raise it now?" Jim raised his hand. "Thank you. I see one. Are there others?"

Preacher Goode prayed, and the congregation stood to sing, "Love Found a Way."

Between verses, Pastor Goode invited people to come forward for salvation, church membership, baptism, whatever. "If you have any need at all, come forward now."

Sandy touched Jim's hand and whispered, "Would you like to go forward?"

Jim nodded, and Sandy gently led him down to the front where he admitted to God that he was a sinner and accepted the gift of eternal life because of the death of Jesus Christ. He couldn't believe he was doing this, but it just seemed so right, and afterward, it felt so good. It had to be true! And for once, it all made sense. He was totally awed by the greatness of God.

After the service, he said to Sandy, "My neighbor told me this was God's country up here because it was so beautiful. And I joked about finding God up here. But it happened. I'm amazed. I think I've found a good part of what's been missing in my life. Thank you for asking me to come to church today. Somehow, I connected with God." He was thinking about what Chris had told him about connecting.

Sandy smiled and gave him a hug. "I suppose you have to get going now," she said.

"Yes, but first I'm going to stop at the restaurant south of town and have lunch. Would you like to have lunch with me?"

"You bet!"

They rode their bikes down the road a little way and went in. Jim ordered a chicken dinner, since that was the Sunday special. Sandy did the same.

"I have a feeling I'm going to be seeing more of you, Sandy. Maybe not on this trip, but when I get back home, I'm going to call you." This time, he wasn't just being nice. He really was going to call her.

Jim didn't talk. He was too happy. He was overwhelmed by love. God's love.

Finally, he spoke. "You play the piano beautifully. And you sing so well. I love your rich alto voice."

"Thanks." She smiled. She sensed he was going to share something with her and waited.

"You didn't tell me you played the piano, but now that I know, I'm excited."

"Why's that?"

"I think I'd like to sing a duet with you in church. I love to sing, and you have a great voice to harmonize with. And now I have something to really sing about. That was a great song this morning."

"I like the old ones."

"I bet you know a lot of them."

"Do you really mean what you did this morning? Or did you just get caught up in the emotion?"

"No, I meant it. What Pastor Goode said this morning really made sense to me. I've probably heard it all a hundred times before, but he put it in terms I understand. Well, not that I understand everything."

"No one," Sandy added, "really understands all that happens when they first accept Christ's forgiveness. But it's like a birth. You'll grow. You'll understand it better as you grow in your faith. The important thing is that it was real."

"It was real, all right!"

"Write this date down somewhere. August 4, 1996. Someday, it will be as real to you as your own birthday. In fact, it is your spiritual birthday. Isn't it amazing? GRACE is an acronym for God's riches at

Christ's expense. "Amazing Grace" is a well-known hymn. I'd like to sing it with you sometime."

"I'd love that. Everyone knows that song, but now it has a whole new meaning to me."

They continued eating in silence for a while, and then Jim said, "I want to share a dream with you."

"Okay."

"I had it last night. I'm not sure I can remember everything, but I was on a spaceship and Klingons were chasing me. I was having an awful time with the controls; I couldn't get away from them, and the ship wouldn't do what I wanted it to do. I was so frustrated."

"I can imagine."

"Then you came over and put your hand on mine. Suddenly, I had control of the ship. Somehow, you knew just where we had to go to escape, and we made it. We didn't get blown up."

"And?"

"That's it, or at least all I remember."

"So what do you think it means?"

"I'm not sure. But I'm glad I met you and I think you're good for me."

"Thanks," she said.

They finished the meal in silence, just enjoying being with one another. Sandy was thinking about what he had said. Jim was grateful that she didn't laugh at him for his dream. He felt like he could share with her without fear of being laughed at. Maybe he would even tell her about Chris but not now.

They went outside, and Jim stepped over his bike. "Before I go, I just want to thank you again for being a friend. I realize it was quite a sacrifice for you to come to church this morning in bike clothes, and I really appreciate it. I know I've been aloof with you and always thinking of myself, and I'm sorry. I'm not usually like that, and I'm going to make it up to you somehow. I could give you a Vulcan good-bye, but may I do something a little more … human?" Jim held out his arms, and Sandy fell into a hug. She felt warm and soft; it was as though she was filling an empty place in his life. Jim hated to let her go, but after a minute, he turned and got on his bike. He wanted to say, "I love you," but the words just wouldn't come. "See ya," was all he could say.

"See ya," she whispered. His arms around her felt so good, she hated to see him leave. She wanted to ride with him, but it just wasn't going to work. She knew he wanted to be alone, and her kinfolk were expecting her back. She sighed.

Jim headed south out of Paradise while Sandy stood and watched until he was out of sight.

Jim's plan was to ride around the shoreline of Whitefish Bay and head to Drummond Island. He wished Sandy was with him, but it didn't look like it was going to work out that day. He hated leaving her. That hug was heartfelt. Sandy had hugged him back just as hard as he'd hugged her.

It was another beautiful, warm, sunny day, and he met a group of bikers passing him on the other side of the road. It was a tour of some kind. He wondered who they were so he stopped and found out that about thirty-five men and women were headed to Cleveland by way of St. Ignace and Paradise, obviously taking a roundabout way to get there. They were foresters, raising money for a charity by riding seven hundred miles in seven days. He wasn't sure what route they were taking, but he figured there had to be a ferry trip in there somewhere.

Jim was pedaling up a hill when he suddenly realized why his back hurt; he hadn't been sitting on the bike right. After a week of riding with poor posture, no wonder his back hurt. Biking was generally very good for a back, if one sat right. He had gotten lazy, especially when using the aerobars, and let his lower back slump down into a greater-than-normal arch. His spine, misaligned like a swayback horse's, hurt. He had to start using the same muscles on the bike that he used during the exercise when he lay on the ground and pressed his lower back down to the ground. While riding, he pulled his lower back up, to make the arch in his lower back straight. He started straightening his back and immediately felt better and rode faster, especially going up hills.

Jim rode to Iroquois Point and visited the lighthouse. He counted seventy-six steps to the top and got a great view of the bay. He could even see Canada.

After leaving the lighthouse, there were two deer by the road looking at him, almost close enough to touch. Jim spoke to them gently, "It's okay; I won't hurt you." They didn't bolt, and Jim rode by wondering at them. *I wish Sandy was here to see them,* he thought. Her eyes were just as deep and brown as the deer's eyes. He was surprised the deer let him get so close.

The scenery was beautiful along the shoreline, and all the wildflowers were out. He rode by the Bay Mills Indian Reservation and, of course, a casino gambling establishment, and came to Brimley. He continued east across I-75 to M-129. Then he turned south and started looking for a place to pitch his tent. Alas, it was all farmland, no forests. He couldn't find anyplace where he could put a tent up out of sight. Maybe he'd have to ride until dark.

By the time he got to Pickford, he was pretty tired. There had been a lot of headwind that day. It was starting to get dark, and Jim would have to use his light, which, so far, he hadn't needed. He stopped at the Mobil gas station in town and got a big Baby Ruth candy bar to eat. He rested on the bench outside. A couple of boys in a beat-up brown pickup truck with oversize tires pulled up and started asking him the usual questions. "Where're ya from? Where're ya going? Where're ya staying?"

To the last question, Jim said, "The rule is—if there's no fence and it's not posted, and no one's looking … well, in I go. But I can't find any forests around here. It's all farmland. You boys know of anyplace I can camp?" Jim noticed a vacant lot across the street with a bunch of shrubs and stuff. He was thinking of hiding in there, possibly. The boys didn't know of anyplace. Jim just sat there and munched on the candy, trying to gather enough strength to go riding again. He had gone seventy-five miles and almost all of it since lunch. It was his longest day, and a lot of it, at least the part heading south, had been against a light headwind. He didn't look forward to riding any more today.

He was just about ready to start out again when the boys rumbled back in the pickup. "I forgot," said the driver, "but there's a township park just down the street. You can camp in there. It's free, too. No problem."

Just like God's grace, he thought. *Free.*

Jim thanked the boys and then said, "Thank you, Lord."

It was the first time he had talked to God in a long time. Well, not counting this morning. Suddenly, he just felt extremely elated. Joyous. He felt like singing, but he didn't know any songs that fit how he felt. He wanted to praise God for looking over him, keeping him safe, showing him the way. There were hundreds of blessings to count. Linda didn't matter anymore. His job and house didn't matter. Sandy didn't matter. Well, Sandy mattered, but he was happy beyond belief. Like a man from Mars, he had come out of his cave and had seen the sunlight. The closest song he could think of was "On Top of the World," the one by the Carpenters. Only he sung about God, not a girlfriend, not his bicycle. He realized he didn't have all the answers and never would. But he felt God's love, as sung in church this morning, "Does Jesus care? Oh yes He cares" and "Love Found a Way," and it seemed nothing else really mattered.

Jim went to the park and put up his tent in the back under some tall trees. He felt like he was in a beautiful outdoor cathedral, a leafy canopy high above, blue sky filtering through as if through stained-glass windows, each tree a steeple as if pointing upward to God. Except for one other tenter and a couple of motor homes way in the front of the park, he had it all to himself. He felt safe, secure, and peaceful in this natural haven.

"Isn't this beautiful, Chris?" He got out his water bottle and started washing up.

"Yes. But it would be even more beautiful if I didn't have this rainbow on my back."

Jim laughed. "Get used to it. It's going to stay for a while. Besides, a beautiful rainbow has just got to cheer you up." He remembered what Sandy had said. Jim was careful to avoid rubbing the rainbow on his leg when he cleaned up. It just didn't seem right to take it off after such a good day. What did Sandy say? It was a symbol of hope—of promise.

"Come on, Jim. Take if off. You said you would tonight."

"I said that I'd take yours off when I took mine off, and I've decided to keep mine at least another day. I had such a good day; it just doesn't seem right to take it off now. Besides, if Sandy owns me, she owns you too. You know we made some more connections today."

"You connected with God. And the tiny threads that connected you with Sandy have become bigger, like strings. Next thing you know, she'll have you all roped up."

"Good night, Chris. God loves you, too."

Before Jim fell asleep, one of the things he wrote in his diary was, "I met God today." He dreamed peacefully.

* * *

After Jim was out of sight, Sandy rode the short distance to the gas station in Paradise where King was working. The afternoon shift was already there, so they loaded up the bike and drove to her uncle George's.

"How was church this morning?" he asked. "Did Jim come?"

"He came. During Sunday School, Jim seemed … preoccupied. I don't think he was paying attention. But during the worship service afterward, I played the piano and sang 'Does Jesus Care.' Jim loved it. In fact, he told me later he imagined Jesus dying on the cross for his sins. And Pastor Goode spoke about the greatness of God, and Jim really got into it. I don't know exactly what he got out of the message, and maybe Pastor Goode lost a lot of the regular attendees, but after …"

"Yes?"

Sandy had tears in her eyes. "When the invitation was given … I asked him if he wanted to go forward, and he said yes … I went up front with him, and he asked Christ to forgive him of his sins. It was wonderful."

"Then what?"

"When it was all over, Jim looked so happy. He asked me to have lunch with him. We ate at the little restaurant on the south side of town, and I asked him if he really meant what he did or if he just got caught up in the excitement. He said he really meant it. We had a really good time together. After lunch, we hugged, and then he rode south out of town. Where do you think he's going?"

King thought for a moment and said, "Around Whitefish Bay. He wouldn't be going back to St. Ignace yet; there are too many days left in his vacation. If he was going to Newberry, he probably would have headed out by way of the Falls. Sandy, are you all right?" He noticed that Sandy was crying.

"Yes. I'm fine. I've never been happier. I'm sorry. I just can't help myself."

"There's something more, isn't there?"

"Oh, King! You always see right through me. I'm starting to fall in love with him. I've had such a good time biking with him these few days, when he rode off without me, I wanted to go with him so bad. I'm so attracted to him. I feel like we belong together, and he's still got a score well above 80 percent on both my lists. But it's … silly. I've only known him five days."

King reached over and touched her shoulder. "It's okay. It's never silly to love someone. It'll work out."

When they got to George's house, Judy was waiting. They transferred the Trek to the bike rack on Judy's car.

"What's my next step?" Sandy asked. "What do I do now?"

"Let's call the lighthouse at Iroquois Point. Maybe our cousin Jane has seen him," Judy said.

They made the call. Jane had seen him; he was looking at some books on Michigan wildflowers that were sold there and had continued on.

"Do you think he went to Sault Ste. Marie?" Sandy asked.

"No," Judy said. "If I were a biker, I'd want to avoid big cities. Besides, he's staying in a tent, not a motel. One night in a motel and he'll lose his bet. Unless, of course, he was going into Canada."

"Canada?" Sandy said. "Somehow, I think he means to stay in Michigan. He never told me where he's going, but I get the impression that he really likes Michigan and means to explore it."

"Well, what is there to see up here?" King asked.

"I know," Sandy replied. "He was originally going to Ironwood. That's all the way west in Michigan. Since he changed his plans, maybe he decided to go all the way east instead. Drummond Island."

"But that's too far to make tonight. He didn't leave until almost two o'clock."

"I'll tell you what," Judy said. "Let's drive over to Aunt Marie's and spend the night there. We haven't seen her for a while, and I know she'd be happy to see us. She probably will have some ideas. Maybe we'll even see him on the way."

After calling Aunt Marie and finding out that she'd be delighted to have them visit, Judy and Sandy drove off and headed south to M-28. Then they headed east and made the connection to M-129 and then south again to Pickford. They didn't see Jim along the way, but it would have been easy to miss him, so they stopped at the Mobil station and went in. The lady at the counter, Shelly, turned out to be one of Aunt Marie's friends. "Did a biker with a red Schwinn all loaded down stop here?" Sandy asked.

"Not that I know."

"If he comes here, give me a call at Aunt Marie's. I need to know. But don't tell him about it. Wait until he's gone." They drove on to a little town called Raber, where Aunt Marie lived. She greeted them with fresh cinnamon rolls.

After the usual greetings and eating a cinnamon roll, Sandy asked Marie about Jim. Of course, Marie made Sandy tell her all about him before answering.

"My guess is," Aunt Marie said, "that if he's going to Drummond Island, he'll come down M-129, just like you two did. It's the only practical way to get there. I know a Mr. Campbell who lives in Donaldson. Let me call him and see if he's seen him."

Marie called her friend and reported back. "He's seen Jim heading south on M-129, just like we thought. If Jim doesn't stop somewhere, he estimates he will be in Pickford around sundown. If

Jim does stop somewhere, my guess is he'll have to stop in Pickford anyway for breakfast tomorrow. There's no other place to eat for miles. I have another friend, Ralph, who has breakfast at the little restaurant there every morning. He's retired. I'll give him a call to keep an eye out for him."

A short time later, Mary from the Mobil station called. "He was here," she said.

Sandy went to bed thinking about Jim. It had been a perfect day, and Jim had even trusted in Christ. Suddenly, he was not just a fellow biker and an interesting person but also a brother in Christ. He was sharing with her, and she was connecting with him. She thought of her confession to King and remembered his reply. "It's not silly to love someone." *Yes, I do love him,* she thought. *But he doesn't know that I'm spying on him. How would he feel about that? Would he forgive me?* Could she forgive herself?

12

Sixteen Tons

When Jim woke up in the morning, he just lay in his tent and stared up at the netting under the rain fly. Every morning, there had been two or three spiders, daddy longlegs, between the netting and the rain fly. This morning was no exception. He noticed there were also mosquitoes up there. Not surprising. He hoped that one of the daddy longlegs would catch a mosquito and eat it. He would like to see that. No such luck. A mosquito flying around inadvertently bumped one of the spiders, and it just retracted its legs, as if it were scared. He looked up again and saw a whole bunch of legs and a large body. No wait. It was two spiders. They were mating. *Now maybe I'll see one spider devour the other. Wrong. After a couple of minutes, they just separated and each went its own way.*

Jim was in no hurry to go anywhere, so he dozed off again and woke up a little later thinking about Sandy. *She's following me.* The realization hit him. *I bumped into her on Wednesday in the park near Cheboygan. Then again on Thursday on Mackinac Island at the airport. Friday, we rode to Paradise together. Then she found me Saturday at the Falls. Sunday, we went to church together. I'd almost bet she bumps into me again today. I wonder how many relatives and friends she has up here. Are they all spying on me? But why would she do that?* He felt certain that she liked him now, but that wouldn't explain the first two or three days, would it? *I didn't tell her where I'm going today. If she finds me again today, I'd say it's a little more than an accident. Well, no matter. I'm really glad I met her, and she is fun to ride with. Even though I've changed my plans twice for her, once in going to Paradise and again in going to church, I think it worked out for the best, and I'm still setting my own course, staying where I want and doing what I want. In fact, I hope she does find me today; it would be nice to ride with her again.*

He got out the silver shoe and held it while thinking about her. It felt good to hold it and admire its beauty. *Was this shoe a magnet, drawing her to him? Was that how she found him every day?* No, he rode the first few days without her.

He started to get dressed. *Darn. Where is that T-shirt, the white one with "Texas" written on it? Oh, no. I bet it fell out of my pannier yesterday before the rain jacket fell out.* Jim had heard the rain jacket fall out yesterday. When it hit the pavement, it slid for a bit, making a hissing sound, which had fooled him into thinking he had a flat tire. *I better make sure I'm zipping up my panniers better; that's the third thing I've lost this trip. The tights, the washcloth, and now the T-shirt. Now I've only got two T-shirts to wear, the dark-blue one I've got on and the yellow one.* He stowed the silver shoe safely in his fanny pack and finished packing.

It was a short ride back into Pickford to get a good breakfast. He stopped in at a little restaurant and ordered the scrambled-egg special. He studied his map while he ate. *You know,* he thought, *I bet this road is paved, even if it doesn't show it that way on the map. Instead of taking the state highway, I could just head out east of town and go to Raber first and then to DeTour.*

When he got done eating, he went to another table where two older men sat, probably retirees, and asked them, "Do you know if the road east of here is paved all the way to Raber? I'm heading to Drummond Island, and I prefer to take the back roads rather than the state highway."

"Sure, just head east on the road you're on now. It's paved the whole way. Just go to Raber, and then the road swings around to Goetzville. That way, you don't have to go all the way to M-134. Take the back road around Caribou Lake to DeTour Village."

The man talked on and on, telling all about the deer hunting in the area and criticizing the Department of Natural Resources for all the seagulls that populated the area; there were so many of them they totally defoliated a couple of small islands nearby that used to have a nice forest on them. Then he told about the dragonfly hatch.

"Those little buggers are huge. You gotta be careful of them. I hit one of them with my car and thought it was going to bust my windshield. It was like hitting a small bird or something." Then he started telling some of his deer-hunting stories.

There was no ending to it. Finally, Jim said, "Thanks. I must get going, but I sure appreciate the advice. And if I see any of those giant dragonflies, I'll see if I just can't tie a couple to my bike. I could use an extra pull in the headwind."

They laughed.

Jim went to the little store first and loaded up on Gatorade and peanut butter and crackers. While he was looking around, he saw a purple T-shirt that matched the color Sandy wore. Hmm. He checked the price tag. Ten dollars. *I really don't need another shirt; I have lots at home. Still … I really could use another one on this trip now that I've only got two.*

The clerk saw him looking at the shirt and said, "If you're thinking about buying the shirt, I can let you have it for half price, just to get rid of it. It's been in the store for several years. It's starting to fade."

"I haven't got much money left. Just enough for food this trip."

"I'll tell you what. There's a truck parked out back that has fifty bags of salt for my water softener. Unload the truck, and the shirt's yours."

"Okay. Deal."

Jim spent the next forty-five minutes unloading and stacking the salt. Afterward, he changed shirts in the restroom.

Moving all that salt seemed like a lot of work for a shirt, but it was purple. Sandy would like it. Besides, he liked purple. *Eighty-pound bags times fifty bags is four thousand pounds. That's two tons. No wonder I'm tired. Good thing I had a good breakfast. I probably burned off most of it already.*

He left wearing the purple shirt. It felt good to be back on the bike. It was restful in a way, even in spite of the stiff headwind coming in off the lake. It was especially restful after carrying all that salt. He felt good. "Sixteen tons, and what do you get? Another day older and deeper in debt." It was an old Tennessee Ernie Ford song with a good pedaling beat. He imagined Chris chirping along with him. *That's the song today,* he thought, thinking of the salt he unloaded. *So what if I didn't actually move a whole sixteen tons? It sure felt like it!*

Remembering to keep his back straight, he stayed low on his aerobars. The aerobars allowed him to support the weight of his body on his forearms instead of his hands. Continual riding with weight on the hands eventually caused numbness in the fingers, so aerobars were good. And since a person using aerobars was down lower, the wind didn't cause as much resistance. He'd read in a *Scientific American* magazine once, that if it weren't for wind resistance, a biker could easily go two hundred fifty miles per hour if the road was smooth enough. Of course, no road was. If one was riding on the moon at that speed and hit a bump on the road, one might go into orbit. Maybe. He wondered what the escape velocity on the moon was. He could look it up when he got back.

He wondered when he'd see Sandy.

*   *   *

"Marie, this is Ralph."

"Did you see him?"

"Yes, he stopped here for breakfast, just like you said. I sent him out on the road east of town. He'll be going right by your house. He said he's going to Drummond Island. I told him about all the dragonflies."

"If he's smart, he'll catch a couple and tie them to his bike. It'll save a lot of pedaling."

They laughed.

"That's what he said. I think that kid is smart."

*   *   *

The road turned south, and a group of houses loomed ahead. Leaning against a big old oak tree on one of the lawns was a purple

Trek. *I knew it,* Jim thought. He looked toward the house and saw Sandy on the porch.

She waved. "Jim. Come here."

Jim leaned his bike next to Sandy's and walked up to the old white clapboard, two-story, square farmhouse. The porch was one of those old-fashioned ones that went all the way around the house and had a roof over it. It made the house look twice as big as it really was.

When he got there, Sandy held out her arms. Jim fell into her hug and returned it.

"I love your shirt, Jim. It's my favorite color. Look. It matches mine. We'll be two of a kind today. And you still have your tattoo. I kept mine last night. See? Wouldn't we look good on a tandem?"

"Thanks." Suddenly, it felt worth it to move all that salt. *Vulcan and Klingon greetings are fun. But these human greetings are much nicer,* he thought.

"I want you to meet my aunt Marie."

Marie came out and said, "So you're Jim. Sandy has been telling me a lot about you." Marie looked to be in her sixties but seemed spry enough—slim and full of energy and not one to take any lip. She had gray hair, and glasses hung from her neck on a cord. She looked quite nice with her bright-red lipstick.

"Telling you what? I hope it's been good."

"Good enough. In fact, I've decided to let Sandy go with you to Drummond Island today. You are going there, aren't you?"

"Yes, how did you know?"

"I could tell you I'm psychic, but I don't believe in that mumbo-jumbo. Let's just say I have my ways. But come in and fill your Camelbak first. Sandy told me about your bet, but that doesn't mean you can't take water, does it?"

"Water would be fine. That's not really food. Thanks."

Jim followed Sandy into the house and noticed a delicious aroma of fresh bread. On the way to the kitchen, he noticed a chessboard set up to play on a coffee table in the living room. *Is Sandy playing chess with Aunt Marie? What was it Sandy said to me in Trout Lake? Something about playing chess sometimes, but liking other games?*

He wondered if she was playing a game with him. Why else would she show up every day? Did she have a bet with someone? *Maybe I'm like a pawn in one of her games. Maybe part of her game is that she can't ask me where I'm going. Maybe she has to surprise me. But no, we arranged to meet in Moran for the trip to Paradise. Maybe it's because after we got to Paradise, I told her that we were on our own and she agreed, so now she won't ask. Well, it seems to be part of the deal now. I'll play her game with her. I can't believe there's any harm in it. I have her phone number, so I can contact her when I get back.* He resolved to continue not telling her his plans unless asked—at least until he got back.

Jim went into the kitchen to fill his Camelbak. Judy was sitting at the table eating a fresh baked cinnamon roll. Aunt Marie offered them some. Sandy took two. "Mmmm. Thanks, Aunt Marie. You make the best."

Jim declined, but his stomach was growling. *You fool,* he thought, *it's bad enough you turned down those chocolate-chip cookies, though in truth, I really was thinking fish at the time. Still, I could have taken a couple for later. And these rolls look good enough to kill for. I've learned my lesson. I'm never going to make another bet where I have to turn down food! I feel like I've already burned off my breakfast, and I'm starving. It must have been all that salt I hauled. Well, it won't be long until I get to DeTour. I can stop there and eat. I should be able to make it that far.*

"You two have a good time now. That's an order!" Aunt Marie smiled.

"Yes, sir." Sandy stood straight and saluted. Then she elbowed Jim.

Jim stood and saluted too, and then he started to go.

"Wait a minute," Sandy said with her mouth full, grabbing his shirttail. She swallowed and looked at Aunt Marie. "I want to show Jim the dogs. Don't chase us out yet." She took him to the backyard where three of the cutest little brown cocker spaniels jumped up on him, wagging their tails. Sandy reached down, picked one up, and gave it to Jim. "Isn't she adorable?" The dog squirmed out of Jim's arms, jumped down, and started running around in circles in the yard.

They laughed.

"I have something else to show you." She led him around to a small barn, and there, inside, was a gray momma cat with some kittens. The momma cat let her pick one up. It was a little black-and-white one, and its eyes weren't even open yet. Momma cat purred and rubbed against Sandy's legs. "Isn't she cute?"

"It looks like you have a way with animals," Jim said, stroking the kitten. "They trust you."

She put it back down.

They headed out, and since Jim was all loaded down and Sandy wasn't, she went first so he could catch her draft in the wind. Still, he had to keep begging her to slow down. *I'm sure glad I'm loaded down,* he thought. *At least I have a good excuse for not being able to keep up with her.* He wondered if he could keep up even without the load.

Sandy said, "My aunt Marie is sort of bossy. I stayed with her last night, and one night is about all I can take. But her heart is good. We have all kinds in my family, and sometimes, we get on each other's nerves. But we've also learned to stick together in spite of our differences, and Aunt Marie has been a real … help, at times."

They came to Raber, and Jim looked at his map. "We have to make a left turn. I think this is it."

Sandy turned left, and Jim followed her down a long hill. It ended up a dead end with a lot of cottages, a landing on the lake, very scenic. Jim thought of the "Sixteen Tons" he was pedaling to while mind-singing. *Well, here's another ton, getting back up this hill.* They turned around, rode back up, and then found the left turn he thought he was making earlier.

"Say, don't you know your way around here?" Jim asked. "Didn't you know that this road was a dead end?"

"Yes."

Jim was shocked. "You let me turn on the wrong road? Why?"

"It's your vacation, Jim. You can go wherever you want. I'm with you. Besides, I thought maybe you had a reason for coming down here. It is scenic." She thought of that old song by Wanda Jackson, "Right or Wrong." She wasn't going to tell Jim yet, but she had a feeling that she belonged by his side, right or wrong.

Jim thought about that. He was glad that she hadn't tried to correct him but accepted his decision and let him explore. He had a new appreciation for her.

They rode through Raber and Goetzville and passed Caribou Lake. There were a couple of young women on the road jogging, and they flagged Jim and Sandy down. "Is there a place to go swimming around here?"

"I don't think so," Sandy answered. "It looked to me like the lake back there is pretty well surrounded by private homes. Well, maybe several miles back there is a rest area, but I didn't see a beach."

Sandy and Jim continued on. The headwind was stronger now, and they weren't able to go very fast. They came to a steep hill, and Jim shifted to his lowest gear and crept up. *Here goes another one of those sixteen tons.* In the meantime, the joggers had apparently decided it was too far to go for a swim, so they turned around and now were running past Jim on the uphill. Jim thought it was funny that they could run up the hill faster than he could bike up it, but he would pass them again on the way down. *The women are in real good shape to run that fast,* he thought.

"Can you run as fast as them?" he asked Sandy.

"Of course," she said. "Do you run?"

"No."

"It's real good cross training for biking."

"Maybe I'll start when I get back. It would do me good."

Sandy was a good biking partner. Maybe she'd make a good running partner—but not if they lived in different cities. How would they get together?

They finally came to DeTour Village, and Jim was exhausted. *I feel like I've already done the whole sixteen tons for today,* he thought. *And I'm getting older and deeper in debt, too.* They found the ferry and bought tickets. It cost two dollars each to go across with a bike. That morning, Jim counted his money and discovered he had only sixty dollars and a little change left. He had six days left on his trip, counting that day. *That's only ten dollars a day,* he thought, *and I just spent two besides breakfast. I'm really going to have to watch it.* The ferry ride took about fifteen minutes, and he used it to eat some peanut butter and crackers from his stash. He thoroughly enjoyed resting on the ferry. Sandy pulled a banana out of her fanny pack and ate it.

Jim had never been on Drummond Island before. A man on the ferry had told him about a township park where he could spend the night if he wanted. Huge dump trucks rumbled up and down a special road alongside the main road carrying huge chunks of limestone from a quarry. Jim passed the township park and made a note of its location. He would stop there on the way back. They kept riding until they saw a sign that said M-134 ended. There were a bunch of restaurants and gift shops there, but with his limited resources, he decided to just turn around and go back. They came to the park and went in. Unfortunately, the road was rough gravel and they had to be careful and go slow lest a sharp rock puncture a tire or dent a rim. At least there was shelter from the wind with all the trees around, and when they got to the end, they occupied a campsite but didn't set up a tent. A lady told them they could visit for free, but it would cost six dollars to spend the night. "I'm not using electricity. I'm not even building a fire or doing any cooking. And you want to charge me six dollars?"

Jim got his dirty clothes out of his pannier and went to the water to wash them. He thought about going for a swim, but the water was too cold, so he settled for splashing the salt off his arms and legs and face. When he came back, he laid out his ground pad on the picnic table and lay down. Sandy took his Camelbak and her water bottles and filled them with water and then sat down on the bench.

"You've been following me," Jim said. "Why?"

Sandy thought about it. *Because I love you?* she thought. *Because you're the only one in the UP I can bike with? Because I'm your guardian angel?* "Why, Jim, I think you're mixed up," she joked. "You've been following me all day, just like the other days we rode together." She smiled sweetly.

Jim laughed. "I didn't mean on the bike, Sandy. I mean, ever since the first day at the park, you have managed to find me and ride with me. It's got to be a little more than coincidence. Why? Is this a game? Are you trying to win a bet?"

"The real reason?"

"Yes."

"I … You weren't supposed to know. I can't tell you now. Maybe later. Trust me on this, okay. I promise, I'm not going to hurt you. I wouldn't do that to you or anyone else."

"Okay. I appreciate your honesty, and I do believe you. I'll let it go for now. The truth is—I'm glad you're here. I can't believe you mean me any harm by it, and I've really enjoyed your company."

"Thanks. I've enjoyed being with you, too. I'm … going to walk back down to the beach now."

Jim watched her leave, and the exhaustion of unloading the salt, the ride, the whole sixteen tons, and the warmth of the day closed his eyes. In seconds, he was asleep.

* * *

She sat on a big white rock and watched the boats and gulls. She glanced back at Jim, and seeing him asleep, she sighed. *Well, I haven't ridden as many miles as him,* she thought. *And I haven't been all loaded down either.* She didn't even know about the tons of salt. *I guess he needs his rest.* While the waves gently lapped the shore, she closed her eyes and prayed. "Thank you for letting me ride with Jim. Thank you for saving his soul. Thank you for letting me have a part in it. Watch over him, us, on this trip. What would you have me do for him?" She started getting ideas, and she smiled.

* * *

When Jim woke up, it was almost five o'clock. "Sandy, we have to get going. Look how late it is. We should've left an hour ago. We … I can't stay here. I don't have the money."

They rode their bikes back to the highway, and this time, with a brisk tailwind, they flew down the road to the ferry. What fun! They were averaging over twenty miles per hour and got to the ferry in time for the five thirty crossing. But the ferry had already filled up and left early. So they sat on some of the big limestone boulders to wait for the next ferry. Jim ate some more peanut butter and crackers.

Sandy had an apple. Jim wondered how she could eat so little and still ride so well. She must have had a really good breakfast.

He watched her eat. The apple looked good, but Sandy didn't seem happy. "Is something wrong?" he asked.

"No. Why?"

"You don't look happy right now. Is something troubling you? Did you get enough to eat? I have some more peanut butter and crackers." He pulled a package out of his pack and offered it to her.

"Thanks." She finished her apple and opened the package. "I just have a lot on my mind right now."

"I'll listen if you want to talk about it."

Sandy smiled. "Those puppies Aunt Marie has are so cute, but she can't keep them. I'm afraid they'll end up at the animal shelter. They need a new home. And the kittens, I wish I could keep one of them, but cats aren't allowed in my apartment. Besides, I'm gone so much, it wouldn't be fair to it. I'm running out of clean clothes, and Aunt Marie's washing machine is broken. My bike needs a new chain, and of course, there are no bike shops up here. If it breaks, I don't have anything to fix it with. Back home, my bills are piling up. I just hope I'm not late on any of them. Late fees are awful. I'm going to be awfully busy catching up when I get back. And there is no one to fill in for me where I work, so all that work is piling up, too. Judy's car had an unexpected breakdown; the transmission had to be repaired, and she wants me to help pay for it. It's probably only fair that I do. After all, she's been driving me all over for the past week. It's just that I'm a little short right now, as my own car is being repaired and my car insurance is coming due. And I keep wondering what's going to happen next. And here I am out having a good time riding with you when maybe I should be back home taking care of some of these things."

She can't be blaming me for these things, Jim thought, *nor does she expect me to help. I'm sure she'll get these things sorted out herself. She's just venting. After all, I invited her to share. It sounds to me like she's stressed out. Tired. I can't disagree with how she feels. So I guess I should say something sympathetic.*

He said, "Yeah, I know the feeling. Things are piling up on me, too. But you know what? I have all confidence in you that you'll get them sorted out."

Sandy smiled. He understood. She said, "Thanks. I guess I'm just a little stressed right now, and I've ridden pretty hard today and am tired. I'll probably feel a lot better after a good night's sleep."

Jim smiled, put his arm around her, and gave her a little hug. "It's all right," he said. "You can share with me anytime. I know you'll work it out. If there's something I can do, let me know. Okay?"

Sandy put her arm around him and leaned her head on his shoulder. "Thanks. It's good to have a friend like you."

It made Jim feel good that she called him a friend. Would their friendship continue when they went back to their own towns?

Sandy felt good that Jim had listened to her, and she felt safe next to him. Somehow, all her problems didn't seem so bad with him next to her. He put his arm around her, and she rested against him while waiting for the ferry.

It was only about fifteen minutes before the next ferry finally arrived, but they both felt better after the rest. Sometimes, a fifteen-minute rest could do a world of good.

They boarded the ferry, and a big, fully loaded garbage truck followed them aboard. The ferry sank deeper into the water from the weight of the truck as it drove aboard, and the operator had to adjust the angle of the ramp so the next vehicle could get on.

"This is not very romantic," Jim said and smiled. "I don't think it was supposed to be in the script."

"What?" Sandy asked.

"The garbage truck. Whew. Let's see if we can get upwind of it. This has got to be the worst ferry ride I've ever been on. Certainly the smelliest!"

Sandy laughed. "Maybe the garbage truck driver thinks that about us. He wants to be upwind of a couple of dirty, smelly, sweaty bikers."

They laughed and moved to the other side of the ferry.

By six thirty, they were back on M-134 heading west. With the nice tailwind, they were able to make good time, and by eight o'clock, they were in Cedarville.

"I think this is the end of the line today, Jim. I have to go north on M-129 here." They stopped their bikes to say good-bye.

"Thanks for riding with me today. You've been a great help, pulling me all that way," Jim said, using a biker's term for the person in front doing the work of breaking the wind. "You've been good company too. It's fun to go alone, but it's a lot more fun to be with someone." Jim wondered if he should or could kiss her. Would she object? He wanted to.

"I had a good time, too," she said. "See ya." She stepped down on the pedal to take off. He heard a click, and her foot went down suddenly. She lost her balance and fell into Jim's arms as he caught her. He wondered if she'd done that on purpose. "Oh no! My chain just broke. Do you have a chain tool?"

I guess she does need a new chain, he thought.

Jim took advantage of the moment and held her just a little longer than he needed to before he released her. She didn't seem to mind.

"Sure, I can fix it. Are you all right?" he asked.

"I am thanks to you. Thanks for catching me."

He laid his bike on the ground, got out his tool kit out, and found his chain tool. She held her bike up so he could work on it. In a few minutes, the links were reconnected. "Try that," he said, standing up.

She stood over her bike and tried it. "Thanks, Jim. It's fine. I knew it was a good idea to ride together. We help each other." Still standing over her bike, she reached over, slipped her arms under his, and gave him a hug, pressing her cheek to his chest. Jim reached around and held her close, enjoying the warmth and softness of her body.

"It's been a long day, Jim. I better go now." She relaxed her hold on him, stretched up, and gave him a kiss on his cheek. Jim returned it. "Bye," she said, staring into his eyes with a look that disagreed with her words.

In the lengthening shadows, Jim thought she wanted more. He wanted more. Their eyes sparkled, caressed, and danced with each other. Slowly, as if their eyes were projecting tractor beams, their heads pulled together. He moved closer to hold her better. Their knees bumped, rainbow to rainbow. They gently kissed on the mouth and held it for a minute—not a passionate kiss, a treasuring kiss, a gentle, loving kiss. It made them feel like they had found the most important thing on earth. It was a kiss that told of future passion and possibilities. It spoke of acceptance, of appreciation, and affection. When they finally broke it, they held each other a little longer as they stood over their bikes. Slowly, they released each other.

"God bless you," he whispered, avoiding those three little words that were so hard for men to say. He felt that he loved her; he just couldn't say it. *Human farewells may be better,* he thought, *but they're also harder.* He hated to see her leave.

"God bless you," Sandy echoed his words, her love also unspoken. She started pedaling north on M-129.

Jim watched her until she was out of sight and then rode to a nearby grocery store and bought some food and Gatorade, spending another six dollars before continuing west. A mile or so out of town, he found a place in some woods to put up his tent. It was his longest day so far, eighty miles.

Safely in his tent, he said, "Chris, we had another good day."

"What about my rainbow, Jim? Are you going to take it off now?"

"I kissed her tonight. I better leave it on another day. I'll probably see her tomorrow."

"But you can't leave it on forever."

"Maybe not. But it seems good to have it. What do you think, Chris? Do you like her?"

"Me?"

"Well, yeah. She's nice, for a human. Sandy made out a list of ten 'must haves' and another list of ten 'must not haves.' And she's rating me. I guess I'm passing so far, or else she's not being honest with herself. What if you and I made out a list? Would she pass?"

"Probably."

"How does she rate compared to Linda? Linda is a good woman; she has a lot going for her. I was even engaged to her for a while. Would Sandy be as good for me as Linda, or should I hold out for someone better?"

"A lot of this has to do with personal tastes. I wouldn't say Sandy has Linda beat in every area, but I would say that I think she's a better match for you."

"And why is that?"

"You're definitely better connected. You have a lot more in common with her. For starters, biking is a big part of your life, and Linda never biked with you. Sandy has been out with you a lot, and you've had a good—no, a *great* time together. You also connect through *Star Trek*, probably chess, through God, and music. Linda never connected with you through any of those things."

"Yeah," Jim said and grinned, "and we're also connected through rainbows."

"Get off my back," Chris said.

Jim laughed and gave Chris a mischievous smile. As he was making himself comfortable on the ground, the silver shoe fell out of his fanny pack. He'd forgotten about it. He picked it up and held it for a while. Somehow, this shoe was connected with Sandy, but he didn't know how. He would show it to her when the time was right.

He went to sleep thinking about Sandy, the kittens, the puppies, the dead end where they had to turn around, the ferry ride, and the kiss. He had no doubt that Sandy would somehow, somewhere, find him again tomorrow. He would play her game. Before he fell asleep, he said a little prayer for her.

During the night, it rained softly, soothingly, for a while.

* * *

When Jim was out of sight, Sandy stopped and used her cell phone to call Aunt Marie. "Tell Judy to pick me up on M-129 north of Cedarville."

Sandy was glad to see the big red Olds. She loaded her bike on the rack and got in. "It's been a long day," she said. "I'm tired, and I didn't want to ride all the way back."

"I'm tired too," Judy said. "I think I'll go to bed early tonight."

Sandy told her all about the ride, the wrong turn, the garbage truck on the ferry, his asking about why she was following him, and the chain breaking.

"So he knows you're following him. Does he know why?"

"No. I didn't tell him, but he said he'd trust me on this. He told me he doesn't mind and that he enjoys my company. In fact, he kissed me before we parted tonight."

"You let him do that? Sandy, you better be careful. This is *not* good. You don't even know who Chris is yet. Jim's probably two-timing you. You know how men are; they'll say whatever they think you want to hear. Use your head, Sandy."

"I am using my head. He still has a grade well above 80 percent on both my lists. I know he's not perfect, but he's still in the running, and besides, I think when it comes to love, you have to use your heart, too."

She continued, "I don't know who Chris it yet. But I'll find out. Just because a man hurt you, doesn't mean all men are that way. Look at Dad. He's been faithful to Mom for forty years now. Just because you were burned doesn't mean Jim will hurt me. I think Jim is honest. Besides, with all the time I've spent with him, I haven't seen anything that would indicate there's another woman involved."

"And you're naive. You've only seen him five, no six days now, and you think you know him? If I'd known you were going to fall for him, I wouldn't've agreed to help you. But tomorrow is the last day for a while. If you can make it through tomorrow, you still have time to come to your senses."

"So how do we find him tomorrow?"

"I'd guess he's heading back to the bridge," Judy replied. "Where else could he go now without retracing his steps somewhere? He's only got a few days left, and he'll use them to go back to Lansing."

"That makes sense, so what should I do?" Sandy asked.

"We don't know how much money he has left," Judy said, "probably not much. It costs more to take the ferry, so I bet he takes the bridge. We could wait for him in St. Ignace; he'll most surely come down Mackinac Trail. But let's wait for him in Mackinaw City. It's smaller, so it will be easier to watch, and it will give me a chance to visit Fort Michilimackinac. I'll drive you across the bridge first thing in the morning, and you can wait for him there. When he shows up, you can ride to the park with him where you first met him. I'll pick you up at the park at five o'clock. That way, I can have time to visit the fort."

"That sounds like a good plan. Let's do it."

When Sandy went to bed, she said a little prayer for Jim. That night, she dreamed she was on a starship with Jim. She heard a chirping sound coming from somewhere in the ship, like a cricket. Did something need oiling? A starship like the *Enterprise* needed over four hundred people to run it. Was there someone on board named Chris?

Before she could find the noise or check the crew list for a Chris, Klingons came out of nowhere and started chasing them. Jim (*My Jim,* she thought, *not Kirk*) was having trouble with the controls of the ship. Would they die out there in the coldness of space, shot down by the enemy? She went over to help. She didn't know exactly how to run the controls, but she put her hand on Jim's hand and started praying. She saw a rainbow on the view screen—not a real rainbow, it couldn't be. But something that looked like a rainbow. Maybe it was a reflection or a space anomaly of some kind, but it seemed to be their only hope. She helped Jim steer toward it, and as they went in, the Klingons disappeared. It was a miracle. She awoke with a sense of wonder and awe. What was her subconscious trying to tell her? God was in control? She would have adventure with Jim? She could help? Whatever it was, it seemed a good sign.

13
King of the Road

Jim slept late again. When he woke up, he just lay there for a while, staring up at the daddy longlegs under the rain fly. What day was it? Oh yeah. Tuesday. Four more days after today on the road. He checked his pulse. Sixty. He checked it again. Fifty-four. Before he started this trip, it was around seventy, and after the first day, because he was stressed out, it had gone up to ninety. Here was physical evidence that the bike trip had done him good. He felt good, but he didn't really need a heart rate to tell him that.

He didn't just feel good; he felt great! His depression was gone, his back didn't hurt, and his butt wasn't tender anymore. Little by little, he'd gotten well, physically, emotionally, and even spiritually. He bowed his head and gave a silent prayer of thanks. He felt like he was really in charge of his life again. He was back to his old self again, in some ways better. He was sorry his vacation was going to end so soon; there were only four nights left, only four more days to ride with Sandy.

Jim put on his yellow T-shirt, made sure the silver shoe was in his fanny pack, and finished packing and loading his bike. He whistled a little tune, nothing in particular; he just made one up while he was loading. When he finally got on the road, his whistling evolved into "King of the Road," an old Roger Miller tune. Soon, he was cruising down the highway, and he had to stop whistling. He needed his breath for pedaling, but he kept on mind-singing. He was king of the road that day, and he felt great. Even Chris with his rainbowed back was happily keeping time with the music.

It wasn't long before he came to Mackinac Trail and headed south again to St. Ignace. By noon, he had stopped at Bessie's Pasty

House and had a pasty for lunch, a meal fit for a king—especially a king of the road. Even King Arthur would have appreciated it.

After lunch, he decided to stop in one of the many souvenir shops in St. Ignace. He was low on funds, but he thought maybe he could buy something inexpensive, a trinket, something that would remind him of this trip when he got back home.

Maybe he could get something to share with Sandy. *Where is she? She should've found me by now. He glanced at the rainbow above his knee. Sandy.* Her name kept going through his mind. Her face kept flashing before him. She understood him. She didn't laugh at his secrets or quirks. She accepted his wanting to be alone and his desire for adventure. She also made him feel needed, appreciated.

Sandy. The one with the purple trek. The piano player. The one with the golden voice. The one with a kind word. The one with a pretty smile. The one who could share Star Trek. *The one who could share King Arthur. The one he could harmonize with. The one who wore mismatched socks. She said she plays chess. Is she any good?*

Sandy. The one with the soft kiss. The one with the soft touch. The one who can make me laugh. The one who could make me forget my troubles. The one who is driving me out of my mind. The one who branded me. He looked at the tattoo on his knee again.

Sandy. The one I'm falling in love … no, that's not right. The one I'm already in love with. How did this happen so quickly? I'm not ready yet. And yet, well, maybe I am ready. I've even stopped thinking about Linda. He thought about what Chris had said last night. Linda, he realized, as nice as she was, was a mistake. Was Sandy a mistake? His heart told him no.

He stopped in a little store and after looking around, found a music box display. *Wow! Here's one with a bike on top, a tandem.* He wound it up and watched the wheels turn. The figurines, a man and a woman, pedaled the bike around in circles. Tears came to his eyes as it played a rendition of "Daisy, Daisy, give me your answer do. I'm half crazy all for the love of you. It won't be a stylish marriage. I can't afford a carriage, but you'll look sweet, upon the seat, of a bicycle built for two …" an old song. Perfect. Sandy said she wanted a tandem. Sunlight came in through the store window and sparkled on the turning metal and decorative rhinestones. Little rainbows danced around the room. It was beautiful.

The store clerk came up to him and asked, "Can I help you, sir?"

"Uh ... yes. How ... uh ... how much is the music box?" he stammered.

She picked up the music box and looked on the bottom. A label said $94.99.

"Thanks," he said. He felt like a dummy. He could have picked it up and looked on the bottom himself.

Jim thought about the price. With tax, it would be a hundred dollars. Steep. He'd expected it to cost may twenty-five dollars. *But where else could I find a music box like this? If I get it, I'll certainly lose my bet. I can't do that. I wonder if they will hold it for me a week. I could drive up here and get it after my vacation. But they'd probably want a deposit to hold it. Even if the deposit is only ten dollars, it would be too much.* On the other hand, he wouldn't mind spending that much for one he loved. Loved? *Yes, I do love her.* He couldn't imagine life without her. The words in the tune the music box played, "It won't be a stylish marriage," came to mind. *Am I thinking about marriage? What's come over me?*

Maybe a ring would be better. He began looking around for a ring. *What size is her finger?* This was not a jewelry store, and Jim couldn't find what he was really looking for, a diamond ring. But he remembered someone telling him once, "If the woman really loves you, it won't matter what kind of ring you get her." *But does she love me? Her kiss said so. But does she love me enough to marry me? Only one way to find out.* He thought that since St. Ignace was a small town, there probably wasn't a good jewelry store there; he might have to go to Cheboygan for that. Better yet, he'd wait until he got home. After all, St. Ignace didn't even have a movie theater. It was a tourist town, like one gigantic gift shop.

This isn't a good idea, he thought. *I've only known her for six days, or is it seven now? If she's really the right one for me, she'll wait a little longer. Besides, she hasn't told me why she's following me. I probably should at least wait until I find out the answer to that question.*

He continued to look around and found a small metallic chessboard about eight inches on a side with silver and gold squares. It was small enough and looked durable enough that he could carry it on his bike. But where were the pieces? He thought Sandy might like that, and even if she didn't, it was something he would like. But it needed some playing pieces. He looked around but didn't find any. He looked on the bottom of the board, and a price tag said, "$5.00." That was reasonable.

He looked around some more and saw some charms for a charm bracelet. There was a whole box of them with hundreds of charms of all kinds. The sign said, "$3.00 each or two for $5.00." There were hearts, diamonds, clubs, spades, horses, unicorns, cats, dogs, birds, dragons, spaceships, rainbows, moons, stars, shamrocks, and shoes. All kinds. And shoes. Sandy liked shoes. There were several different kinds of shoes. *Maybe I could use these for chessmen,* he thought.

After much looking, he thought he could make a set out of shoes. He remembered that Sandy said she had over a hundred pairs and really liked shoes. She had also talked about making chess a more feminine game. She'd really go for this.

There were different kinds of shoe charms and in different colors. But none of them matched the silver shoe in his fanny pack. That shoe was unique and probably cost a lot more than the prices posted there.

He finally chose a color scheme of gold and silver, like the board. He picked out flip-flops for pawns, mules for horses/knights, platform pumps for rooks, and high-heeled sandals for bishops. He found a stiletto pump for the queen and a stiletto ankle boot for the king. His imagination was working overtime. He decided to change the names of the pieces also. The pawns would be called maids. The rooks would be doyennes. The knights or horses would be ladies. The bishops would be princesses. The queen would be the queen, and the king would become a domme. The game of chess was now totally feminized. Sandy would love it. As a matter of fact, he loved it.

Now, he thought, *I need something to put the charms in.* He looked around until he found a small cloth bag with a shoe embroidered on it. It would hold all the charms easily and only cost a dollar. *Let's see,* he thought. *There are thirty-two shoes; that would be sixteen times five or eighty dollars, plus the board would make eighty-five and the bag eighty-six. Add 6 percent sales tax; that would be $4.80 plus $0.36 or $5.16. It would cost $91.16 in all.*

Wow! That's a lot more than I thought it would be when I first came up with this idea. With all those empty squares on the chessboard at the beginning of the game, it doesn't seem like half the squares on the board actually have a piece on them. But they do. And now that I've gone to all the trouble to make this set, and I just love the idea, I hate to put them back.

He took the board and charms to the checkout, and the woman rang it up. It came out to exactly what Jim had figured, but he was so excited about this, he didn't care if he lost the bet. He was sure it would make Sandy happy. Why not? It made him happy.

Perhaps he'd lost his bet with Dave by using his charge card, but the chess set was not really part of the bike trip, he told himself. *I can still try to see if I can make the trip on what I have left in my fanny pack and at least win the bet in my own mind, even if I lose to Dave.*

The clerk put the chess set in a small paper bag, and he left with a happy heart. He still had no doubt that Sandy would show up today.

Life is strange, he thought. *I've lost my bet, and I've lost my heart again (or am I giving my heart?), but I feel so good.*

Jim left the gift shop and started pedaling up the long hill to I-75. He was going to take the bridge back across since it only cost a dollar and the ferry was sixteen. He got on the entrance ramp and pedaled down to the Bridge Authority house, which was on the northbound side of the freeway. Inside it, the air conditioning felt good. He went up to the window.

"That will be two bucks," the man said.

"But my state map says it's only one," Jim replied.

"It used to be one, but they just raised it." It was still a lot less than the ferry.

Jim gave him a five.

"Can I keep your change?" the man joked.

"Next time," Jim said, "I'm in danger of losing my bet. I've barely got enough left for food." Jim told the man about the bet and then sat down.

A couple of minutes later, a state pickup truck came and Jim went outside and helped the driver load the bike in the back. Bikers and walkers were not allowed on the bridge except on special occasions, like the Labor Day Bridge Walk or the DALMAC bicycle ride. They got in the truck cab, and the driver took him across. On the way across, the driver told him that construction was started on the bridge in 1952 and it opened in 1957. It was almost exactly five miles across the water and the road bed rose to two hundred fifty feet while the towers rose to five hundred fifty feet. In short, it was one of the world's largest bridges. And even more amazing was that it went from nowhere to nowhere, Mackinaw City with a population of eight hundred to St. Ignace with a population of 2,600, hardly what you'd expect for a bridge of this size. But it did unite the two peninsulas of the state.

The driver stopped, and they got out and unloaded his bike. Jim promptly rode to his favorite store and bought some more caramel corn. *For breakfast tomorrow,* he thought.

When he came out, he saw the purple Trek with the rainbow. He sat down on a bench, and after a short wait, Sandy came up to him. She was still wearing the rainbow just above her knee. "Sandy," he said, giving her a quick hug, "let's ride out to the park. Then we can talk."

"Great! I'd like that."

They hopped on their bikes and sped out of town. Jim could hardly wait to get there; it was almost like they were racing. In fact, this time, Jim rode in front most of the way, and it didn't take them long to get to the park on US 23 about seven miles out of town. Jim thought she was being nice to him by letting him lead for a change.

On the way, they passed a whole bunch of riders going to Mackinaw City. When they got to the roadside park, Jim talked to some of the bikers in the other group who were getting water at the pump. They were from the Shoreline Bicycle Tour, East Route, and had started in Oscoda and were going through Alpena, Rogers City, Mackinaw City, Gaylord, and back to Oscoda.

It was early afternoon when Jim walked his bike over to a grassy area in the sun and laid it down. Sandy followed and laid her bike down next to his. He took his blanket off the back of his bike and spread it on the grass, and they sat down shoulder to shoulder and watched the boats go by. She leaned against his left side, and he took her right hand and held it lightly in his left. He kissed the index finger on his right hand and gently placed it on her mouth. She kissed it back, and he touched it to his own mouth. She pulled her hand out of his and placed it around his back. He pulled her closer. They didn't talk. The warmth of the sun, the gentle breeze, the white gulls flapping and skreeing, and the lapping of the waves did all the necessary talking. There were two ore freighters on the horizon, one following the other. It seemed a good sign.

Jim reached over to his bike and pulled the bag of caramel corn off the top of the rack where it was attached with an elastic cord. "Want some?"

"Sure."

They shared some caramel corn for a few minutes, and he put the rest back. Jim said, "Sandy, I've had a number of dogs in the past; in fact, I still have two. I want to share with you about two of them, not the two I have now. Once I had a little white dog that barked at everyone and got into things, and at times, he really annoyed me. There were times I could have killed him. He used to jump up on my bed at night, but every night before he jumped up, he would scratch on the side as if asking permission to jump up and be with me. He always did that, every night. I thought he would eventually learn to come up on his own, without asking, but he never did. Every night before I went to bed, I would put him out the front door and then let him in the back door; that way, he had to at least walk around the house and hopefully do his duty so I didn't have any surprises on the floor in the morning. I had the dog since he was a puppy, and when he was about fourteen, I put him outside one warm summer night, but he just didn't come back. I found him the next day, cold and stiff. I buried him in the backyard. It was the hardest thing I ever did.

I cried. I was the only friend he had in the whole world. Everyone else hated the mutt, and I don't blame them; at times, I did, too. The night after I buried him, I lay in bed and I swear I heard him scratch the side of the bed. I told him to come on up, but of course, he didn't. I never realized how much I loved him until that day, when I heard the ghost scratch. But it took me years to love him that much.

"Later on, I got another dog, a little brown mutt with fur as soft as silk. He had quite a nice personality, and everyone liked him. I don't know what there was about him, but he won my heart very quickly. In fact, I even kissed him once—a dog kiss. He went to kiss me with his tongue, and I stuck my tongue out at the same time and touched. I know it sounds awful, but for whatever reason, I did do it. Funny. I'd never done that before and probably never will again. It was only a couple of months after I got him that he got hit by a car. I was devastated. I think I cried more for him than my first dog, even though I had him for such a short time. He was so easy to love.

"I've had a number of dogs, but never one I liked as much as those two. Duffy, my little black dog is mostly Scottie. He's okay. At least he's faithful. He follows me around wherever I go. Won't let me out of his sight. He's probably waiting at the door for me to come home right now. My other dog, Booty, the little white one, I could care less about her. But she used to be someone else's favorite pet before I got stuck with her."

Sandy reached over and touched her left hand to Jim's cheek but said nothing. She sensed this was one of the moments of male sharing.

"The reason I'm telling you this …" Jim looked her in the eyes. "… is because I … I … you're … like that little brown dog with the silky fur—easy to love. I've only known you for what? Six, seven days now? I met you last Wednesday, and today is Tuesday. It's true that there are a lot of things I don't know about you, and you barely know me, but I already do know that you're someone I'd want to be with the rest of my life. I … do love … you." There! He said it. Finally. He closed his eyes for a moment. It was hard for him to say.

She snuggled closer. "I love you, too," she whispered. She wanted to say more but just waited. This was his time to share.

Jim's heart was pounding. *So far so good,* he thought.

After a couple of minutes, he continued, "I stopped at a gift shop earlier today. I bought you a present." He got up, opened up his pannier, and dug out the package with his homemade chess set in it. "I want you to have this. Here."

She took it from his hand and opened the bag. "A chessboard and a cute little bag. It's even got a shoe embroidered on it. What's in it?" She bounced it up and down in her hand.

Jim said nothing but watched her face as she opened it.

"Look at all the little shoes." She had a puzzled look on her face. "What am I going to do with all these charms?"

He sat back down with her. "Remember when you told me you'd like chess more if it was a little more feminine. This is my solution for you." He set the board down and started pulling out the shoes. He placed the flip-flops where the pawns would go. "These are maids," he said. He pulled out a platform shoe and placed it where the rook would go. "This is a doyenne."

"What's a doyenne?"

"That's a female senior member of a group who is quite knowledgeable and experienced and who others look up to. The group leader. I thought it was appropriate for that board position."

Next, he pulled out a high-heeled sandal and placed it where the bishop would go. "Behold a princess."

Sandy laughed. "This is good!"

He pulled out a mule and placed it where the knight would go. "This is a lady."

"I see that," Sandy said, "a mule for a horse. Cute. A lady for a knight. That makes sense."

He kept setting pieces up on the board until he had pulled out a stiletto pump with an ankle strap and put it where the queen would go. "Bow down to the queen."

"What? You didn't change the name?" She laughed.

"No need." He pulled out the last piece, the stiletto ankle boot, and placed it where the king would go. "The domme," he said.

"The what?"

"Domme. It's a woman with a lot of power, someone who has authority over all decisions and even people, sometimes treating them as property rather than a person. She could even have power over the queen. In the bondage scene, she would be called a dominatrix.

"The point is," he continued, "all the pieces on the board are now women. And what better way to represent femininity than with shoes?"

"I love it. Do you want to play a game now?" she asked.

"No, not tonight. We'll have plenty of time for that later, I hope. I just wanted to give this to you because I've been such a jerk these last few days and because I wanted you to be happy. I just wanted you to know I'm not always so cold. I was just really caught off guard when I was expecting to be alone for two weeks. And now you have a completely feminized chess set. Chess is no longer just a man's game; it's a woman's game too. And besides, I think this set is more for display than to actually play a game on. We would probably lose a piece in the grass if we played here."

"Oh, Jim, that's so thoughtful. This is one of the nicest gifts I've ever had." She wrapped her arms around him and kissed him on the mouth. Hard. Passionately.

Jim had to catch his breath when she broke it off. She picked up the charms and put them back in the cloth bag. She got the paper bag and started to put the board in when she saw a piece of paper in it. "What's this?" She pulled out the paper and looked at the sales receipt.

Jim saw the receipt. "Oops. You weren't supposed to see that," he said. "I put the charge slip in my wallet, but I didn't realize that there was a receipt in the bag." He took it from her and put it in his wallet.

Sandy looked shocked. "You can't have spent that much money on me. You'd lose your bet."

"I did," he said. "But if the chess set makes you happy, I don't care. It was worth it. Personally, I don't think this charge was actually part of my trip. It was more along the lines of a personal expenditure, not a travel expense. But if Dave sees it differently, I've lost. Anyway, I plan on seeing if I can finish the trip within the allotted amount. I haven't got much left, but I think I can do it. I don't need much for the next four days."

Sandy was surprised. He'd cared more about her than about his bet, and the bet was really important to him. It made her feel loved. "Oh, Jim," she said. "Thank you, thank you, thank you." She imagined setting the game up on the coffee table in her apartment. She could hardly wait to show her friends back home.

They sat together for a few moments, Sandy leaning her head against him. Jim put his arm around her.

After Sandy had a chance to collect her thoughts, she said, "I had a dream last night."

"Oh?"

"I can't remember all the details. I was on a spaceship. I kept hearing this chirping noise, like there was something on the ship that needed oiling. And then I was looking for a Christine. I don't remember why, maybe I thought she knew how to fix the chirp. But before I could find her, Klingons attacked. I saw you trying to steer the ship, but you were having trouble, so I went over and prayed for you. Suddenly, I saw a rainbow on the navigation screen and helped steer you toward it. As soon as we flew into it, the Klingons disappeared. Then I woke up."

"You really do like rainbows, don't you?" He looked at his knee.

"My heart was pounding when I woke up, but it seemed to be a good sign. I mean, that you were in it, and we got away. I don't have a clue about the noise or Christine or the rainbow. I mean, imagine that, in space, a rainbow. How could that be? I thought it must be an illusion or something."

"Sometimes we know things in our subconscious that haven't hit our conscious state yet."

"Do you know who Christine is?"

"Nurse Chapel?"

"No. It wasn't her. Besides, you were the captain. It was your spaceship, not Kirk's." Suddenly, it occurred to her that it was Chris, not Christine, and Jim didn't want her asking about Chris. "Well never mind. It was just a dream, after all."

"It sounds to me like I keep getting into trouble and you keep bailing me out. You must be good for me."

"Oh, Jim." She chuckled. "I hope I'm good for you. In fact, I know I'm good for you."

She opened her fanny pack and pulled out a package. "I have a gift for you, too. It's not as fancy as the one you got me, but I think you'll like it." She handed him the package.

Jim opened it and pulled out a small Bible, a New Testament with Psalms and Proverbs. "Oh good. The last couple of nights when I was alone in my tent, I was wishing I had one of these. I probably won't read much until I get home, but even a little would be nice. And this is small enough to carry conveniently on my bike."

Inside was written:

To Jim
From Sandy
Tuesday, August 6, 1996

There was a place to enter a name and birthday for the owner. Sandy gave him a pen so he could fill it out. "You can also enter you spiritual birthday on this page to help you remember your decision."

Jim wrote "August 4, 1996," under his birth date.

"Just a suggestion. You could read a chapter out of Proverbs every day. Today is the sixth, so you could read the sixth chapter. Tomorrow, read the seventh chapter. Every month, you can read through the book of Proverbs once. There's a lot of wisdom in that book."

"Thanks. I'll try that."

Sandy pulled another small package out and held it out.

Jim took it and opened it. "Foot and hand warmers. I've been wanting to try these out. These are the kind that, when exposed to air, give off heat, and they work for hours. All I have to do is seal them up when I'm done. Right?"

"Right. King said they work good. Also, I have another gift." She pulled a third package out for him."

Jim opened it and said, "What's this? A beach ball?"

"No, it's a blow-up pillow. I remember you saying that you really missed having a pillow."

"Oh bless you! I really have missed a pillow. This has got to be better than using my helmet stuffed with clothes. And it's small enough and light enough to carry on my bike. I should have sweet dreams of you now." He pulled her closed and kissed her.

"Wait," she said, pushing off him. "I have something else."

"Four? Aren't you getting a little carried away?"

"Maybe. But this is for both of us." She took a little disposable camera out of her pack and gave it to him. "I think I remember you saying you wished you had a camera. I want you to get double prints made so I can have a copy too." She started posing, hands behind her head, chest out. "You can start using it now."

Click. "Show off." Click. "Hey, I got an idea."

He went up to a couple who were picnicking and asked if one of them would take their picture. The guy took the camera and starting giving them directions.

"Stand over here, facing the sun. You don't want your faces in the shadows. Good. That's it. Now stand next to one another. Closer. Come on, this isn't a police lineup. Smile. Pretend that you actually like one another."

By then, both Jim and Sandy were laughing. They stood face-to-face, holding hands, and kissed. Click. They turned their heads to look at the camera, still holding hands. Click.

Jim said, "Let's get our bikes for a shot." So they stood between the bikes facing the camera. Click. Then they got on their bikes and faced the camera. Click. Then Jim had the guy stand back for a wider shot with the bikes lined up, Sandy in front and Jim behind, like he was drafting. Click. Jim said, "That one will help me remember how I saw you most of the week. One more." This time, he posed the bikes so that Sandy's front wheel was hidden behind his rear wheel. It looked like a tandem but with three wheels. Click. Jim thanked the guy, who said he was happy to help and then went back to his picnic.

"That three-wheel tandem will look sort of dumb, but it's the best I can do for now. Someday, I'll get a real tandem. I got another idea," he said. "Let's set up your chess set, and I'll take a picture of it, too." After they set it up, Jim had Sandy hold it up by her face and look at it as if she were studying a position in a game. Then he took her picture with the set.

They sat back down on the blanket and stared off into the lake again, just enjoying one another's company but each lost is his or her own thoughts. Sandy felt like Jim really loved her, but she was still uncertain about Chris. Jim felt Sandy really cared too, but he didn't understand what game she was playing. They both felt that they should wait before taking the relationship further. The shadows lengthened, and a red Oldsmobile pulled into the parking lot and tooted. Sandy looked back and saw Judy waiting for her.

"Jim, I have to go now. Judy's here, I forgot to tell you she was going to pick me up at five." They got up, and she got her bike. They walked to Judy's car together and loaded her bike in, and Sandy gave him a hug. They kissed and said their good-byes. Sandy got in the car, and Judy drove off. Jim stood and watched her go.

Jim got his own bike and loaded up the gifts and his blanket, walked the parking lot, got on, and took off toward Cheboygan.

When Jim got to Cheboygan, he had a flat tire, the first one this trip. He stopped to fix it and used one of those new glueless patches. The tube had two little holes in it side by side, a snakebite, caused by low tire pressure when the tube got pinched between the tire and the rim when hitting a bump, probably a little stone. After reassembling the tire, Jim used his frame pump to inflate his tire as hard as he could and then used it to bump up the pressure in the other tire also. He didn't want any more flats.

Just before sundown, he reached that Christmas tree farm where he'd slept before. He went in and found the exact place he'd camped before and set his tent up there, but the missing tights were not there.

"Well, Chris. What do you think now?"

"I think she's on to me. You heard her dream. Chirping. Rainbow. Christine. I think she thinks I'm a woman."

"In that case, she's not onto you yet. Only hints of you. She didn't find the chirping noise. She didn't find Christine. And she has always liked rainbows; it probably has nothing to do with you. After all, they're a sign of hope or promise."

"Maybe, but I doubt it. Wasn't it amazing how much she loved that chess set? I thought she was going to smother you with that kiss."

"That was good. But I felt like it was Christmas. Four gifts! One would have been plenty, not that I don't like them. I think I'm going to like this pillow the best. I hope it doesn't leak."

He blew up the pillow Sandy gave him and then laid down to read Proverbs chapter 6 before falling asleep for the night. He slept soundly. The pillow worked wonderfully.

* * *

As soon as they were out of sight of Jim, Judy asked, "How'd it go?"

"Better than I expected. He was fantastic on the bike today. It was all I could do to stay with him. It's a good thing he was all loaded down."

"He's that good? Sounds like you found a good training partner for your next triathlon. At least for the biking part. Do you think he'd go for the running and swimming too?"

"Maybe. I'm just real happy he bikes. That was one of the things on my 'must have' list, that he exercises and takes care of himself. I don't want to marry some guy who has a big beer belly and lies around on the couch watching football games all day. I want someone who I can train with at least part of the time."

"Knowing how important it is to you, I think that's wise. Did anything else happen?"

"He gave me a wonderful gift."

"Really?"

"Maybe not everyone would like it, but it means a lot to me. It's a chess set."

"Okay. Clue me in. What's so special about it?"

"I could tell you, but I think I'd rather show you. When we get to Aunt Dora's, I'll set it up for you."

"What? Is it made out of gold or something?"

"No, but I saw the receipt for it, and I think he's going to lose his bet because of it. He's over budget now."

"He'd lose the bet for you? My, you are special to him. Or perhaps he's just setting you up. Did you find out who Chris is?"

"No. But don't worry. I'm not taking the relationship any further until I do. Although he's passed most of the items on my two lists, there are a couple of things I'm not sure about yet. This Chris thing is one of them. Until I know for sure he doesn't have a wife somewhere or another girlfriend, I'm in a holding pattern."

"What about you? If he has a list, are you passing it?"

"I'm worried about that, too. He knows I've been following him, but he doesn't know why. I'm not sure what he'll think when he finds out or what he thinks now for that matter. Perhaps he's in a holding pattern also."

"It's best to be cautious. I know too many people, myself included, who got married in a rush only to find out too late that they weren't right for one another."

"Yeah. Too true."

"He'll've probably forgotten about you by the time we get back home on Saturday."

"Dang! I forgot to tell him that I won't be able to see him again until Saturday when we go home. I don't have any way to contact him. I guess it'll be our first test. Will we still care for each other after being apart for four days?"

They drove back across the bridge to Aunt Dora's to spend the night. Sandy set up the chess set for them and explained the new names for the pieces. Aunt Dora loved it. Even Judy was impressed with it.

Sandy went to bed after asking God to direct her and give her wisdom in this matter. She asked for Jim's safety on his trip and wondered where he was that night. She wasn't worried about him; either he could take care of himself or God would. She was sad that she wouldn't be seeing him the next day or for two days after that. She hoped he wouldn't worry too much about her. Judy had the car, and she wasn't leaving the UP until Saturday. Saturday could be a big day. Perhaps she could share her secret with him then. Perhaps he would share his. There was nothing more she could do but trust God until then. During the night, a big storm woke her. But she knew Jim would be safe, just as she was.

14
And Then I Kissed Her

It was Wednesday, August 7. Jim noticed that during the night, there was a lot of thunder and lightning going on north of him, across the lake. Someone in the UP really got pounded. He figured Sandy was in it, but it probably didn't matter, since she wasn't in a tent.

There was a lot of humidity in the air and a good stiff south wind. Jim figured for a hard day on the bike. With the silver shoe in his fanny pack, he hopped on his bike and headed for Onaway, humming, at least in his mind, "And Then I Kissed Her," a tune sung by a number of different singers. It had a good beat for pedaling and just seemed so appropriate after the previous day. He thought about Sandy as he rode by Black Lake and then across the little bridge where he had heard that funny man singing "The sands of time are running out on me." He wondered where Sandy would meet him that day. He hoped she wasn't running out on him. He didn't remember telling anyone his route, and as to where he was staying, he didn't even know that himself until he chose it. He could be staying anywhere, depending on the weather, among other things. The night at Cornerstone Baptist Church proved that. And yet Sandy kept finding him every day. What was her game?

It didn't matter. Jim was finally over the depression that had been plaguing him. He was done grieving for Linda. That a new relationship with Sandy was budding made things that much better. Like Chris said, he would always love Linda in some small way, but she was not a part of his life anymore. He was over her. Would Sandy be his life now?

In Onaway, he rode around the town looking for a place to eat and finally decided on Jan's restaurant for breakfast. He ordered an omelet. The waitress there was really cute, he thought, with a reddish-brown ponytail and sparkly eyes. She was joking with the regulars and seemed to enjoy her job. She reminded him of Sandy. Sandy could have made a good waitress.

He went south and discovered that while he was in the UP the highway department had put fresh pea gravel on the shoulder, and it was rough going. Loose gravel was only a little better than riding on ball bearings, and he had to be careful. Finally, he reached the county line and the loose gravel stopped.

He came to the Jackson Lake State Forest campground and went in. The south wind, the heat, and the humidity were making things tough, and it was the warmest day of his ride so far. He figured it must be in the nineties. The lake didn't have any beach, and when he tried to go in, he found it had all kinds of mucky stuff on the bottom that floated up as soon as he stepped in. Otherwise, the water was clear and begging for him to come in. At least the water would be warm compared to Lake Huron. He decided to use his foam ground pad as a floatation device and go in at one spot on the lake and come out at a different spot. He could avoid most of the muck by staying on top of the water and not stepping on the bottom when coming out until the last possible moment. So he walked around, chose his spots, and then went in. Once out in the lake, the water was warm and refreshing, and as long as he stayed on top of the water, it was clear. So he kicked around for a while using his float and then headed back.

He might have stayed in longer, but the ground pad wasn't providing as much floatation as he had thought it would, and it could be dangerous out swimming alone, especially in deep water. *Best not to take chances,* he thought. He should've used the little pillow Sandy had given him. *It would have floated better,* he thought. Next time. He got a little muck on him coming out, but not much. There was no one else anywhere in the campground, so he just stripped off his clothes out in the open, dried off with his towel, and changed into clean clothes. Then he wrung out his wet clothes and hung them on his bike to dry. He spread out his ground pad, which by then had dried off, on a picnic table and lay down to rest in the gentle shade of the tall trees overhead. It was so peaceful there. He had learned from experience that if he sat on the ground, flies would bother him. But for some reason, flies didn't have enough sense to find someone on top of a picnic table. Soon, he fell asleep.

When he woke up, he felt much better, not only clean but rested. It was in early evening, and things were cooling down to a bearable temperature. Jim figured he had only about twenty miles to go before he would pick his campsite south of Atlanta. There was no hurry; he only had to go a few miles, and the further into the evening it got, the more likely the wind would die down and the cooler it would be. Finally, he packed up and headed south again. When he got to Atlanta, he stopped for a moment at a canoe rental on the Thunder Bay River. *Someday,* he thought, *I'm going to take a canoe trip instead of a bike trip. I bet Sandy would like that.*

He rode south and found a clearing where a gas well had been put in by some oil company. These gas wells were all over in Montmorency County. This particular one was far enough back from the road that Jim didn't think anyone could see his tent there, and it looked like no one had used the access road in quite a while, so he went in, pitched his tent out of sight of the road, and sat down to read Proverbs 7.

"Chris, did I outfox her today or what? Sandy didn't find me today. I missed her."

"Good question. Maybe it is just part of her game."

"I wonder who she's staying with tonight. Maybe she doesn't have any relatives in this part of the state."

"I think she could have found you if she wanted to."

"Yeah, she's pretty smart. She must've had other plans today."

He unwrapped the silver charm, held it in his hand, and stared at it. It made him feel better. "I wonder what your story is," he muttered. "How are you connected to Sandy?" After a while, he wrapped it back up and stashed it for safekeeping. He lay back down and slept.

When Jim pitched his tent, he hadn't heard anything but a slight breeze in the trees, a few crows cawing, and some insects buzzing. But late at night, the birds and the bugs were asleep and the wind had stopped, so it was deathly quiet, no leaves rustling, no birds singing or flapping—even the insects were still. He could only hear one thing, a compressor station. It woke him up. The pumps took gas from the well and other wells nearby and pressured it up to put in a high-pressure gas transmission line for processing or sale, and the pumps droned on and on, day and night. It wasn't that loud. He couldn't even hear it during the day over the other noises. But in the still of the night, something he couldn't even hear during the day somehow became unbearably loud. It even kept him awake.

"Hey, Chris."

"Huh?"

"Would you mind chirping? I need something to drown out the sound of the gas pumps."

"What? You'd keep me awake all night so you can sleep? How is that fair?"

"Okay. I just thought I'd ask. I thought you might enjoy singing a while for me. Just until I get back to sleep."

Chris started chirping anyway, and soon, Jim was sleeping again.

The next time Jim woke, just before dawn, Chris was quiet, but there was a screeching sound—or was it a hacking sound? It was the same dragon sound he had heard outside of Mackinaw City the day he met Sandy. He heard hoofbeats. *It's got to be a deer,* he thought, *or maybe an elk. There are elk in this county.* He tried to see outside his tent, but it was still too dark. The animal went away a short time later. He wondered if that was what they called a "buck snort." He thought of King Arthur. Surely Arthur had heard sounds in the night, too. He had probably heard this very sound and even knew what it was.

15

Sweet, Sweet Smile

Thursday morning brought blue skies and a promising day. It wasn't as hot, and the humidity went back down. On the way to Lewiston, Karen Carpenter's song "Sweet, Sweet Smile" kept running through his mind, along with visions of Sandy and her smile. He could even imagine Sandy singing this song about him. The fifteen miles to Lewiston went by quickly, as the song in his head had a good beat. Along the way, he saw a lot of blue phlox along the roadside.

He went to a different restaurant in Lewiston than before and ordered an Irish omelet. It had corned beef hash inside with Swiss cheese, a wonderful breakfast treat after working up an appetite and still having a long way to go.

A lady in the restaurant told him that he could go south out of Lewiston and turn right at the first light, which would take him to F-97 by way of Red Oak instead of going through Lovells. Jim, always looking for adventure, had considered this route before and decided to give it a try. He was not disappointed; the road was good and lightly traveled, and he was surprised by a golf course that had its very own beautiful wooden covered bridge crossing high above the road. He stopped to take a picture of it. When he rejoined F-97, he was almost to McMaster's Bridge, a small bridge that crossed the Au Sable River and had a canoe landing.

Jim pulled his bike in at the landing and spread his blanket out on the grass. He was considering another swim, but when he waded out into the water, brrrrr. Spring-fed rivers were not very warm; in Michigan, ground water ran around fifty-five degrees, so Jim just splashed himself clean and washed some of his clothes. Then he went back to the bike and checked the tires. The back tire was worn out and was starting to come apart. So he took the wheel off the bike and replaced the tire with a new one from his pannier. He wanted to stay longer and rest, but there was no outhouse, no store, no trees or shade, and not even a picnic table. About the only thing there was a trash barrel, where Jim put the worn-out tire and then headed out.

When he got back on his bike, he noticed the ride was smoother. It was the tire that had a hop in it, not the rim. Perhaps overinflating the tires wasn't such a good idea after all.

North winds meant easy riding and lower humidity and temperatures. It was downright pleasant after the day before. That storm really cooled things down.

Now where is Sandy? he wondered. *Is she going to find me today? It sure would be nice to have her along. I wish she could have seen that golf cart bridge back there. It was beautiful.*

He rode into St. Helen and stopped to eat for the second time that day, this time for supper. The restaurant there sold emu burgers. Unfortunately, he had already ordered a wet burrito before he noticed the burgers, or he would have tried them. He wished Sandy was there to share the meal with him.

He pulled the silver shoe out of his fanny pack and held it in his fingers for a few minutes, staring at it. It helped him picture her pretty face and reminded him of the fun he had riding with her. It made him think of her in the dream he had, clicking across the starship floor to help him. He would be seeing her again soon, even if it wasn't until his trip was over.

Jim considered staying in the township park for the night but decided to go on instead. He headed out of town, and just before he got to Cornerstone Baptist Church, he found a high spot on the east side of the road that looked like a good place to spend the night. So he climbed up there with his bike, and it turned out to be perfect. He set up his tent and sat down to read Proverbs 8. Then he checked his bike computer.

"Eighty-one miles today, Chris. Not bad, eh?"

"You weren't even riding hard today. You could have gone a lot farther than that. You probably could have doubled that if you'd wanted."

"I know. It was a really easy day. But there's no reason for me to ride hard; I still have to be on the road fourteen nights. So I'm killing time. I can't come home early."

"True, but you could have gone to Ironwood if you'd put your mind to it. Even after going to Paradise. And then you wouldn't have gotten that tattoo from Sandy, and I'd still have a black back."

Jim looked at his knee. The tattoo was still there. He wondered if Sandy still had hers. "That's true. Knowing that I could have gone to Ironwood doesn't exactly console me. I think I want to take this trip again someday. Maybe Sandy would go with me. On the other hand, I don't regret going with Sandy. It led to that fantastic tandem ride and some other pretty fantastic happenings. Maybe I should just be happy with what I did. After all, I did accomplish what I set out to do, which was to have an adventure."

"That's true. You've had an adventure."

Jim went to sleep thinking about Sandy. *I guess I outfoxed myself,* he thought. *I should've told her where I was. I should've asked her where she was staying, and then maybe I could have called her from a pay phone.* Whereas before he was sorry his trip was ending, now he wished it could end sooner so he could just see her again. But he had to make it last fourteen days.

During the night, it got cold. Jim opened up one of the foot/hand warmers Sandy had given him, stuffed it in a sock, and put it inside his T-shirt. It heated up almost immediately and felt good.

16

I'm into Something Good

In the morning, Jim poked his head out of the tent. There were three deer on the edge of the small clearing he was in. When they saw him, one of the deer made that dragon sound, the screeching, coughing sound that had scared Jim in Mackinaw City. So now he knew for sure, it was a deer. He felt like he'd bonded with King Arthur somehow, at least in this one small way.

"Chris, did you see the deer?"

"Yeah. I saw your dragon."

"Tonight will be my last night. I'll be home tomorrow. I'm glad I found out the answer to that noise."

"Such gentle, quiet creatures. Such an awful noise. Who'd'a thought?"

He unwrapped the silver shoe, held it in his hand, and thought of Sandy. "Will you bring her to me today?" he asked it. No answer. Still, it felt good to hold the shoe for a minute. Before he wrapped it up and put it back in his fanny pack, a Herman's Hermits song popped into his mind, "I'm into Something Good." It was a great song to pedal to, and he knew he'd be mind-singing it that day.

He headed south, past Cornerstone Baptist Church and into Gladwin County where he retraced his route home. There was a northwest wind helping; he could make really good time, but he was ahead of schedule, so it didn't matter. He felt a little stronger on the bike every day and believed he could do more than a hundred miles in a day now, easily, but there was no need to. He knew he was into something good when he stood on a big gear and blasted up little hills that he could only crawl up using a low gear on the first day. There was a noticeable improvement in his biking. It amazed him how much better one could ride after only two weeks on the road. He wondered how much he'd improve if he had a whole month. It felt good to be able to stand up on hills again. It wouldn't be so hard to keep up with Sandy now. If only she were there.

He stopped in Winegars again for snacks and then in Edenville. This time, the little restaurant was open so he went in. He sat down and ordered a burger. Restaurant burgers tasted much better than fast-food ones and didn't cost that much more. Right then, he needed something that didn't cost much; he was down to his last few dollars.

While he was eating, a man came in who had a limp, a regular, he judged, by the way he talked to the owner and a retiree, he guessed from the time of day and the color of the man's hair. The man wanted some company, and since Jim was the only person in the place, he asked him if he could sit down with him. Jim smiled and nodded.

The man was from Hope, a little town not too far from Edenville. The man joked, "I live in Hope, and I'll die in despair."

There was no town named Despair, Jim found out. He pointed out that if you'd trusted Christ, you didn't have to die in despair. Christians lived and died in hope.

The man asked Jim where he had been, what he was doing, and where he was going. Jim told him about his trip and about Sandy. Then Jim stated, "I feel like a new man. Sometimes a man just needs to go on a trip like this to get away from it all and do what really is important in life."

"Which is?" asked the man.

"Nothing!" Jim remembered his conversation with Chris earlier. They both laughed. He understood.

Jim rode on past Sanford to Gordonville and stopped at an ice-cream parlor for another burger. *It must be my day for burgers,* he thought. Actually, Jim knew this would be the last chance to eat something decent before he got home. There were no more restaurants from there to home. From then on, it would be whatever he carried on his bike or purchased in stores.

He rode on to the Pine River where the bridge was out and climbed over the barricades. This time, it seemed a lot easier. It felt like going home was like riding downhill. The closer you got, the faster you went. The old horse to the barn analogy. *It works for me,* he thought.

Jim thought he'd spend the night at the Pine River, but he couldn't find a place where he wanted to risk being caught. There seemed to be recent signs of people all over the place, and there were a lot of residences in the area. Besides, it was all either posted, fenced, or a big ditch filled with water separated it from the road. So Jim rode on back toward the Gratiot County State Game Area.

Before he got there, he stopped at the little store in Sickles and stocked up on Gatorade. When he left, he only had two dollars left. *It's enough,* he thought. *I have enough food and drink to make it home. I'll win my bet, maybe not with Dave, but at least with myself.* The man in the store told him about the big storm that went through during the week. A tornado!

He rode south and noticed trees uprooted all over the place and a barn blown down. *I sure am glad I wasn't camping here when that happened,* Jim thought. He found a place in the game area and pulled way back from the road and behind some bushes. There he set up his tent for the last time. *Storms behind me,* he thought, *and storms ahead of me, but I've seen nothing but good weather. Is my life charmed or what? Probably what. Blessed. God, for some reason beyond my understanding, is watching over me. Sandy's prayers maybe? Even my tent has stayed together for the trip. But I'll probably have to buy a new one before I do this again.*

He felt happy, but Sandy hadn't found him that day either.

"How do you like that, Chris? It's another no-show today."

"She was riding with Judy. Maybe Judy couldn't bring her down here for some reason."

"We'll have to ask her when we see her again."

He felt sure that Sandy could have found him if she had wanted to and would have if she were alone. *Well, I'll see her tomorrow or at least call her.*

He read Proverbs 9 before going to sleep. During the night, he heard dragon/deer snorts several times. *It must be a good game area,* Jim thought.

17

Climb Every Mountain

It was only about forty-five miles to home, and Jim thought he could make it before noon. He took a minute to hold the silver shoe in his hand before he finished packing up. It was early morning, and doves did their hoooo-he-hoo-hoo-hoo song. The goldenrod that was only a thought two weeks earlier was starting to come out.

He rode all the way home without stopping and pulled into his driveway at eleven thirty in the morning. He felt strong and happy. He had spent fourteen days on the road and fourteen nights in a tiny tent, traveled 914 miles on a bicycle, most of those with a cricket on his handlebar, and managed to spend only $199—not counting the chess set. He was sure that he could have gone farther than 914 miles, probably the whole 1,200 miles the original bet had been. He could have made it all the way to Ironwood if he hadn't been … what? Sidetracked? Detoured? Lured? Ambushed? Bushwhacked? He wasn't sure exactly what to call it. He was a only little less than three hundred miles shy of the 1,200 miles he had originally estimated. Surely he could have made that up. The last four or five days he had basically been riding easy, killing time so he wouldn't be home too soon. Normally, when he started out to do something, he finished, no matter what. And if he didn't finish, he would try again until he did. In fact, he knew already in his heart that he would try this trip again, and next time, he would make it to Ironwood. Well, maybe. If he didn't go to California. He had won the bet about the money with himself, even if not with Dave. He did use his card once to charge something. He wasn't sure how Dave would react to that.

When he rode into the driveway and opened he gate, Duffy and Booty came out wagging tails, jumping up and down on him, causing him to lose his balance and almost fall over.

"Home sweet home. It's good to be home, Chris. I'm even happy to see these dumb dogs." Jim stooped to pet the dogs for a few minutes. They didn't look any worse for him being gone. Dave must have been taking good care of them. They were jumping around until Jim got tired of petting them, and then they barked to go into the house. Jim let them in.

Jim saw his hammock in the backyard and thought how good it looked, a perfect day for it. He'd been riding hard and thought he'd rest a bit before cleaning up and unpacking. He laid the bike down on the lawn. "Are you coming up, Chris?"

"No, I think I'll stay here on the handlebars. I've been here so much; it feels like my home sweet home."

Jim lay down in the hammock and soon fell asleep. After a bit, his dogs woke him, barking through the screen door. The dogs usually barked at anyone, even someone just walking by the house on the sidewalk—sometimes even people on the other side of the street. But this time, someone was pulling into his driveway.

Chris said, "Trouble."

"It sure is hard for a guy to get some rest around here. Even if it is home. Who would be coming to see me? It looks like a woman. Linda? No, that's not her car. Or did she get a new one?"

It was a light-blue Buick Century. The woman got out, went to the side door, and knocked.

"Back here!" Jim yelled.

She opened the gate and walked toward him

She was wearing a mint-green cotton dress that had a simple, down-home effect. As plain as it was, she looked elegant. She had on strappy silver sandals with two-inch heels, and her hair was combed straight down to her shoulders, with a curl in her bangs, and a dark-green hair ribbon to offset her dress and the gold necklace with the rainbow pendant. As she drew near, he could see she was wearing little gold star earrings and a charm bracelet on her left wrist. He could see a rainbow just above her knee through her hose, but it was looking a little worn, like his. There was a fresh-looking rainbow tattoo on the back of her left hand. She was wearing makeup. Red lipstick, his favorite. Her eyes looked bigger and brighter than ever. Her eyelashes were long. She batted her eyes at him. The butterflies in his stomach awoke. She was wearing a fragrance; he wasn't sure what it was, but she smelled clean and fresh. He liked it.

"Sandy! What are you doing here?"

"Jim, you know I can always find you when I want."

"True. I'm just so surprised." Jim hugged her. "I missed you so much the last three days. That dress looks great on you. I like the green." He kissed her. "You look just awesome! When you bat your eyes at me like that, it melts me."

"Thanks."

"I barely recognized you. I've never seen you in anything other than a ponytail and bike clothes before. You really are a fashion queen! You look fantastic."

"Thanks."

"Would you like to sit on my hammock?"

Sandy had something else on her mind. Judy had been bugging her, rightly so, to find out who Chris was. She was going to ask him today but wasn't quite sure how to go about it. She thought she'd be friendly for a few minutes, make small talk, and then just be direct about it. King had told her than men never took a hint and couldn't read her mind but appreciated forthrightness. She was going to try that method and hope for the best. She sort of felt like Queen Esther, who put her life on the line to serve her people, but she was only putting the relationship on the line. Still, if there was a problem with the relationship, it was better to get it over with soon rather than getting further into the relationship or even marrying, like Judy did, before finding out.

"No, I think I'll just sit on the grass today. Did you win your bet yet?"

"No, I just got home a little while ago. I haven't seen Dave yet."

"You stayed within the two hundred dollars, though. Right?"

"Right."

"I came over to ask you something. I have to know this before we go any further with our relationship. It's been bugging the daylights out of me, but you told me not to push."

"Okay. So ask."

"I want to know …" she started. This was hard. She looked over at Jim's bike. "Oh look!" She was startled. "A rainbow." She reached over to the handlebar on Jim's bike and pulled up a cricket. "Oh, it's not a rainbow; it's a cricket." She had it in her hand. "Cute little thing," she said. It gave her an idea. She could ask if this was Chris. That way, she wouldn't sound pushy. Maybe Jim would open up. "Is this Chris?"

"She found me, Jim. I told you she would. It's been nice knowing you. Thanks for the ride."

Jim was amazed. How did she find Chris? *He went with me in all those restaurants and even to church with me, and no one ever noticed him. It wasn't really possible to notice him; he was imaginary. But Chris said she would find him. How did he know? And how did she?*

"Yes, you found Chris. I don't know how you did it; there's just no way you could've found him, but you did anyway. He's been with me since the first day of this trip, riding on my handlebars, you know. How did you find him?"

"Him? I thought I saw a rainbow and reached for it. Chris is a cricket?" Sandy was having a hard time believing this. "I thought Chris was a woman. I was just kidding when I asked if it was Chris. Oh! Where did he go? He was in my hand just a second ago."

"Christopher Cricket is definitely male. I know, it's hard to tell the sex on a cricket, but trust me; Chris is a male. He was my friend and traveling companion. He's gone now, you know." Jim sounded sad.

"Gone? I'm … sorry. I didn't mean to—"

"It's all right. He'll be fine, wherever he is." He looked at the rainbow tattoo she wore on the back of her hand. "I'm sure he's in good hands."

"So there's no other woman? It was just a cricket. And you were talking to it?" She sounded doubtful.

"Chris was not just another cricket. He was my cricket. You've heard of cowboys talking to their horse or dog owners talking to their dog? I brought him along because I didn't have anyone to talk to, and it was going to be a long trip. I didn't expect to be riding with you or anyone else for that matter. Talking with him helped me work out some problems. He was my counselor. He helped me get over Linda. He helped me understand why Linda and I broke up. He helped me see that I was connecting with you. I know it sounds crazy, but there is no other woman."

Sandy started to believe him. Her woman's intuition told her he was telling the truth but maybe not all of it. But how could this be? "How did you get him to ride on your handlebar for two weeks?"

"Okay, Sandy. I'm going to level with you on this. First of all, there is no woman named 'Chris' in my life. There never has been. There was a 'Linda.' I think I already told you about her."

Jim took a deep breath. He wondered what she would think if he told her the whole truth. "This must be what you came to ask me about, isn't it?"

"Yes."

"When I told you not to push it, I barely knew you. This is very personal, and I didn't want to share it with you at that time. I know you better now, and I think I can trust you with this. But I don't want you to share it with anyone else."

"Okay."

"The thing is—and I hope you won't laugh or think I'm too crazy—Chris was not real."

Sandy wondered about that. *If I picked him up, how could he not be real?* Remembering what King said about men having a hard time communicating, she knew he needed a lot of time to say this, since apparently it was very personal. She wanted to keep him talking. "Okay, he's not real."

"Right. Here's how he came about. On the very first day of my vacation, I realized how alone I would be. I didn't know you'd be showing up later. I thought it would be sort of fun to have an imaginary friend. You know, like kids do. But I'm not crazy, I was just pretending, and I knew it. It was fun. However, as the trip went on, and I started talking to him more and more, I realized I was talking to myself. I was looking at myself from another viewpoint. He actually became a friend and more than that, a counselor. By talking to Chris, I understood why Linda left me and why we weren't right for one another, that we just were too different. He also talked to me about you and showed me how we connect on a lot of different levels. So, of course, you couldn't see him, nor could anyone else. Even when I took him to church with me. He wasn't real. He was just my imagination. Do you see what I'm saying?"

"Yes. He was a figment of your imagination." Sandy waited. Maybe he had more to say.

"He was also me. What I know, he knew. What I don't know, he didn't know. I am male, so I made him male. When I made him, I named him Christopher. I just called him Chris for short."

"So when I came upon you on Mackinac Island, you thought it was him?"

"Bingo."

Sandy thought about this. It did all make sense—at least in a way. There was just one thing. "If he wasn't real, how did I happen to have him in my hand a few minutes ago?"

"That's a very good question, one that has me puzzled also. But you said you saw a rainbow."

"Yes. That's what I reached for."

"You remember the evening in Paradise when you put this rainbow on my knee?"

"Yes."

"At first, I was going to take it off. But then you asked me to church the next day, so I decided to leave it on for another day, just to be nice to you. When I got to my camp that night, it felt as if you had branded me. Made me your property. Chris was getting on my case about it. I got kind of peeved with him, so I blinked my eyes and imagined him with a rainbow on his back. He hated it. I told him I'd take it off him when I took mine off my knee. Guess what."

"You never took it off."

"As you can see. So he had it on until the end."

"Remember that dream you had, with the chirping noise on the starship and someone named Christine on the crew? I don't know how, but you were getting into my mind without realizing it."

"Actually, I remembered later it wasn't Christine in my dream. It was Chris."

"I don't have a logical explanation as to how you thought you saw a rainbow on my handlebar. Perhaps the sun was shining funny on my handlebar and made a rainbow, or perhaps you imagined a rainbow there. Neither do I know how you managed to pick up a cricket there. Maybe there was one there in the grass and you got it by accident. But an illogical explanation is that part of my imagination became part of your reality. A figment of my imagination became real, at least for a while."

"That's it?"

"That's the truth about Chris. The whole truth. Believe it or not, I just ask that you keep it to yourself. No one would believe it anyway. I don't even know if you'll believe it.

Sandy waited. He said nothing more, so perhaps he was done. After another minute, she said, "Well, thanks for being honest with me." She sat a minute saying nothing, just thinking. Her intuition told her that he was telling the truth, or at least thought he was. She didn't think he was lying. She didn't think he had held anything back. Was he crazy? Maybe she could get some advice from King or Dave.

While she sat, lost in thought, Jim got up and said, "I ... I guess I better go get cleaned up now." He was tired and didn't want to talk any more right then. It had been hard for him to share Chris with her. Perhaps she thought he was crazy. Perhaps this was the end of their relationship. The thought didn't make him happy, but if she couldn't accept him, it was probably better to end the relationship now than later. He hoped she would accept him.

"All right. I want to visit your neighbor anyway. Meet me next door when you're done."

"What? You know Dave, my neighbor." He held out his hand, and she grasped it so he could pull her up.

"Yes, he gets around."

Jim went inside his house, and she walked next door.

While Jim was cleaning up, she pumped Dave for information about Jim. Everything he said about him was good, and Dave didn't know anyone in Jim's life named Chris. Dave confirmed everything she thought about him. He was intelligent, thoughtful, kind, responsible, financially secure, hardworking, had a good sense of humor, and was a lousy chess player. She laughed on that last one. Dave didn't think he was crazy, just imaginative.

A girl can't be too careful, though, she thought.

Jim brought his bike into the house and started unpacking. First, he took out all his dirty bike clothes and put them in the laundry pile. Then he took out his tent and set it up so it would dry out. He rinsed out his Camelbak and hung it up to dry. Finally, he took a shower, the first one in two weeks. He was careful not to touch the rainbow; it was starting to look a little worn but not too bad. Yeah, it was looking bad. But he left it on anyway. While showering, he wondered how she knew Dave. What business would she have with him? Then he shaved. *I owe that much to Sandy,* he thought. He put on a green dress shirt, as it would look nice with Sandy's dress, and a pair of black slacks. The slacks covered the rainbow. Oh well. He slipped on some black penny loafers. *Time to face the music,* he thought.

He walked next door and knocked.

Dave opened the door. "Jim, come on in. It's good to see you back! How was your trip?" They went into the kitchen and sat at the table where they'd played many a game of chess.

"I had a wonderful adventure," Jim replied. "It was worth it. I feel like a new man."

"So you had a good time. Did I win the bet?" Dave asked.

"Maybe," Jim said. "I'll let you decide. I actually spent just over $199 for the trip, but there was one unanticipated personal expense unrelated to the trip, and I used my charge card."

"Really? And what was that?"

"A chess set," Sandy said, coming into the kitchen. When she saw Jim, she stopped for a minute to look him over. "You look fantastic. I've never seen you clean shaven and in nice clothes before. She gave him a hug and a kiss. You even smell nice. I'd love to take you to church with me tomorrow."

"Thanks, I'd love to go with you. Maybe we can go for a bike ride after."

"I think my parents will want to have you for dinner first. Then we can go for a ride." She sat down at the table with them.

"How do you know my neighbor?" Jim asked.

"He's my uncle. Well, actually, my grand-uncle, my mother's father's brother. You must know I have a lot of relatives. And, by the way, I brought some of my world-renowned chocolate-chip cookies for you two."

Dave asked, "Would you guys like something to drink. Coffee?"

"Just water for me," Jim answered.

"Same here," Sandy said.

While Jim was munching a cookie, he suddenly put his hand to his forehead. "Wait a minute. It's coming to me. I think I see it now." He looked at Sandy. "Dave had you follow me. Didn't he? Before I left, he was really worried about me biking so far by myself. He told you about me. You already knew about the bet, didn't you? And he wanted to win the bet, too. That's why you offered to have me stay at your aunt Dora's. And that's why you offered me those chocolate-chip cookies. He was using you to test me. Well, Dave never had a chance with that scheme. But he got lucky and won anyway."

"Guilty," Sandy said. "He offered to give me a hundred dollars to keep my eye on you. As long as I was in the UP anyway. Dave made me swear to secrecy. That's why I couldn't tell you. But you figured it out on your own. I kept up my part of the bargain, so I expect him to keep his."

Dave pulled a brand-new hundred-dollar bill out of his wallet and gave it to Sandy. "This is one of the new bills the US government came out with this year. See, it has a bigger picture of Ben Franklin on it. I'm happy to give it to you," he said with a smile. "I slept a lot better at night knowing that neither of you would be riding alone as much. Besides, it helped you with your vacation, and I also slept better knowing you were riding with someone who would keep you safe."

Sandy took the bill and gave it to Jim. "At first, I was doing it for Dave. But it wasn't very long before I was doing it for myself. I feel so guilty about spying on you; I just don't feel right about keeping it. I really do love you," she whispered. She kissed him.

So that was her game, Jim thought. He took the bill and put it on the table. He wasn't sure he wanted to take the bill from Sandy, but he didn't want to argue about it in front of Dave, either. There would be plenty of time to give it back to her later. He looked at Dave. "That wasn't playing fair. I lost the bet because of your interference."

"Now wait a minute. I was just concerned about your safety and well-being and hers too. As long as you were both going biking anyway, I thought you might as well ride together. I told her about the bet and to let me know if you cheated, but I didn't tell her to tempt you. Anyone could have offered you a place to stay or a meal. If you were tempted, I had nothing to do with it."

"But I'm going to be thirty next month. Don't you think I can take care of myself?"

"Of course you can. And I'm sixty-six already, but do you think I can stop worrying? I did this for my own peace of mind. It's my nature, I guess. I hope you'll forgive me for caring."

"I guess I don't mind that you care, but I've lost the bet because of your 'caring.'"

"How could that be, since you didn't take up Sandy on her offers?"

"Because I used my VISA to buy her the chess set. Except for that, I stayed within the two hundred. I still had thirty-seven cents when I got home. I thought I was prepared for anything on this bike trip. But I wasn't prepared for her."

"Well, tell me about it. How did you lose the bet?"

Jim pulled out his wallet again. He took out the visa slip and showed it to Dave. "See? I spent ninety dollars on the chess set. And here's the money I came back with." He emptied thirty-seven cents out of his fanny pack. "If I hadn't made that charge, I would have won."

Sandy looked at the table. "But, Jim, there's a hundred dollars and thirty-seven cents here. I think that's enough to cover the VISA charge."

"What?"

Sandy said, "You have enough money to cover your VISA charge. I think you won."

"Now wait a minute," Jim said looking at the money, "that hundred-dollar bill there was just given to me by you. It doesn't count."

"And why not?" Sandy demanded. "You had it in your possession before you settled up. Besides, I don't think the chess set should count against the bet anyway. It wasn't a travel expense. It was a personal expense, like you said. You could have easily waited until we got back to buy it."

"I hate to admit it," Dave nodded his head in agreement, "but I think Sandy's right."

"You mean … so … I really did win." Jim grinned. He took Sandy's hand and kissed it. "Thank you. But there's one thing I still don't understand. "Why didn't you ride with me the last three days? I missed you so much."

"My sister Judy had the car. I really couldn't follow you below the bridge without her. It was her vacation too. I'm sorry. I meant to tell you, but you didn't ask and I had so much on my mind, I just forgot to tell you. Until it was too late, that is. I just didn't have any way of contacting you."

Dave spoke up. "Let's go out on my porch, and we can talk."

They went out, and Sandy saw the new porch swing. "What a gorgeous piece of workmanship." She sat down on it. "Where did you get it?"

"I made it myself," Dave said. "I do a lot of my thinking out here. I have this theory that swinging keeps the blood circulating; the brain gets more oxygen and thinks better. I have some of my best ideas here, some of my wildest schemes. I love this swing. I even had special cushions made for it. Next, I'm going to make a rocking chair because it's too cold to sit on the porch in the winter, but I can rock indoors this winter. You won't catch me in a recliner where the blood just drains out of the old head and pools in the feet. Rocking helps pump blood up to the brain."

"There may be something to your theory," Sandy said as she rocked. "I'm getting ideas already." She had a grin on her face that spelled trouble. Jim wondered exactly what she was thinking up next. He sat down next to her, and Dave sat in a chair across from them.

"Why did you buy her a chess set?" Dave asked.

"I've been dying to show it to you," Sandy said. "You'll understand when you see it." She pulled it out of her purse and set up the pieces, explaining the new names as she went.

"That's incredible," Dave said. "Have you been using a porch swing, Jim, or a rocking chair?"

"No, it's the biking. Pedaling pumps blood to the old brain, too."

Jim and Sandy spent the next half hour telling Dave about the trip, all the fun things they'd done. They were all laughing, and even Dave had tears in his eyes, especially when Jim told him about what he had thought *Q'plah* meant when he'd first heard it.

"You two really connected," Dave said. "You especially enjoyed riding the tandem together."

Jim said, "That's very true. Riding the tandem was one of the most fun things I ever did."

"The tandem was great," Sandy said.

"Well, bless my soul!" Dave said. "I'm so happy for both of you."

"I'd like to show Sandy my house," Jim said. "Do you mind?"

"Not at all," Dave said.

"I'd love to see it," Sandy said.

"I'll see you later, Dave. Thanks for taking care of my pets and other things. It looks like you did a great job."

"Thanks."

Jim and Sandy walked over to his house. "I love this kitchen," Sandy said. "The yellow scheme is really cheery. It makes me feel like cooking."

"Thanks. But let's go in the living room." They went in and sat down on the sofa.

Sandy looked at Jim's chess set on the coffee table. "Oh my word!" she exclaimed. "That's the same game that's on the chess set at Dave's house."

"So?"

"I have one set up in my apartment just like it."

"Why would you have a game set up like this?"

"Because I was making a move a day against Dave in this game."

The realization came to Jim slowly. "You mean … let me guess. You're playing black? You move on Tuesdays, Thursdays, and Saturdays?"

"Yes! Exactly."

"That old fox. He's been setting us up. He's not only been having us play a chess game against each other, but this thing about paying you to ride with me was a pretense. He was really setting us up. He wanted us to fall in love."

"It worked, didn't it?" Sandy said.

"Well, yes. I don't know if I should beat him or thank him."

"I think we should thank him. Think about it. If he had been open about it and said, 'Jim, I know a beautiful, intelligent girl who I think you'd like and I want you to come over to my house on Sunday and have dinner with me so you can meet her,' would you have gone?"

"Certainly not. I was in no mood for a new relationship."

"And if he had said the same thing to me, I would've declined. But even if somehow we both accepted or were cajoled into meeting each other, what are the chances we would have hit it off? I'll tell you, slim to none. Remember what I said about meeting under pretenses?"

"I do. Everything is set up, the roses, the candles, the clothes. Nothing is like that in real life, just the dating scene."

"What he did do was bring us together without us knowing it and without the pretenses."

"And if it hadn't worked, no one would have known or been embarrassed," Jim said.

"Right. We met in bike clothes, and we had a good time together. Even so, you didn't want to have anything to do with me. But

217

because Dave paid me to spy on you, I had to keep meeting up with you. With a little advice from King and help from my relatives in the UP, I was successful, and you warmed up to me. Actually, we warmed up to each other. Do you see what Dave did?"

"I do. He's a genius."

"He's the Dolly Levi of the twenty-first century. You know, like in the musical *Hello, Dolly!*"

"Well," Jim said, "now that we know about the chess game, do you want to finish it?"

"Not now. We'll have plenty of time for that later, I suppose."

Just then, there was a knock at the door. "Yoohoo. Anyone home?"

"I wonder who that could be," Jim said, but he thought he recognized the voice. He just couldn't believe it. He got up to answer the door, and Sandy followed. There was a woman at the door. She was tall, Jim's height, and had dark, somewhat curly, shoulder-length tresses. Her face was immaculate, perfectly made up, and she wore emerald pumps, white hose, a matching shimmering green silk dress with white trim, little gold hoop earrings, and a green crystal-studded hair clip. She oozed style, class, and beauty.

Jim opened the door. "Come in. Let's go sit down." Jim was always the gentleman. They walked back to the living room, and Jim sat in a chair while the two women shared the sofa.

The visitor was stunning, and Jim was stunned. Even Sandy was stunned. Her perfume was a heavier scent than Sandy's, but he liked it a lot, like Opium or Tabu. It was one of those scents that if a woman walked by his office wearing it, he would want to get up and follow her. Was it a pheromone? Was he a moth? She was a knockout. Jim was knocked down but not out.

Sandy was alarmed. Was this Linda? Was she about to have her heart broken? What would Jim do? She decided to wait and see what Jim did before she did or said anything rash.

"Jim," the woman said, "you look wonderful. And we're both wearing green. I've been trying to reach you for two weeks. You haven't returned my calls. You haven't been home. Where have you been? What's going on?"

"Linda," he answered, "I … uh … what a surprise. I haven't seen you for months. I … I … you … you shut me out. I thought you left me … I've been on vacation and … and …"

"Well, never mind. I'm glad to see you now. And you look so delicious. I came back to apologize. I realized I haven't treated you right, and I've been beside myself. I did leave you, but I was a fool. I was confused and uncertain and … and—"

"Scared," Jim said.

"Yes. Scared. I just didn't know what I wanted. My life was falling apart, and I finally got professional help, a counselor; she helped me see this. Now that my life is coming together again, I just wanted you to know I appreciate all that you did … tried to do, for me. This house we selected, it's coming along nicely. I see you finished the kitchen. It looks great. The yellow color scheme makes it feel warm and sunny, the way a kitchen should. The fireplace, the love seat, and coffee table, they look nice. And the chess set is a nice touch. It adds class."

"I … I'd … uh … like you to meet Sandy Hill, my girlfriend. Sandy, this is Linda Fenton, my ex-fiancée."

"Good to meet you, Sandy," she said without any real feeling. She continued, "Jim, I know you like to bicycle. I've taken up aerobic exercise myself. It's been helping me get my life back together. I even bought a bicycle. I was wondering if you'd go riding with me tomorrow."

"No, I don't think that would be a good idea. Besides, I'm going to church tomorrow morning."

"Church? You never went to church. And I didn't either. But three weeks ago, I watched an evangelist on TV and I trusted Christ as my savior. Now my sins are forgiven, and I'm on my way to heaven. God is helping me get my life back together."

"That's wonderful, Linda. I trusted Christ as my savior just last Sunday."

"Really, Jim?"

"Yes. My life was sort of falling apart, so I went on a vacation to get it straightened out, and I met Sandy, who helped me find the love I needed, which is God's love. I've been born again, and the last two weeks have been the best two weeks of my life. I don't have all the answers, and I probably never will, but I am happy again. It sounds like you had a similar experience, and I'm happy for you."

"Jim, I know I'm not a very good rider yet, and I'd have a hard time keeping up with you, but I was really looking forward to a ride with you tomorrow. How about in the afternoon? After church. Say one o'clock? Or maybe two?"

"It's good of you to ask, Linda, but I'm going to have dinner with Sandy tomorrow and we're going for a bike ride after dinner. Besides, I don't think it would work out for us. My counselor has helped me see that we're just not a good match. But if you're really getting your life back together, as you say, you should have no trouble finding someone else to ride with. There must be a club ride you can do. Maybe you'd like to join the club."

Linda thought for a moment. "I suppose you're right. Now that I think about it, we did have to work awful hard to be together even when we were getting along. There was an awful lot of compromising."

Jim got up and offered Linda his hand. "Thanks for stopping by. It's been really good to see you again. I hope things work out for you."

Linda took his hand, and he pulled her up. "Well, I guess that's that then," she said. "Good luck to you. Both of you." She smiled at Sandy.

Jim walked her to the door. Just before going through the door, Linda nodded at Sandy and whispered, "She's a very pretty girl. Lucky you."

Jim closed the door softly behind her and sat back down with Sandy on the sofa.

Sandy and Jim looked at one another and gave a sigh of relief. They fell into each other's arms and just held one another for a couple of minutes, saying nothing. Finally, Sandy said, "She is a dream girl. You gave her up for me?" She was so happy there were tears in her eyes.

"Not really. I gave her up for me. She's just not right for me."

"She has me way outclassed."

"Like most women, you way underestimate yourself. You're my dream girl."

"Thanks. Linda actually seemed pretty nice."

"She is nice."

"She said she left messages. Have you checked your answering machine?"

"No, let's do it." The phone was on an end table next to the sofa. Jim reached over and pushed the message button on the machine. There were four messages from Linda, the first one time-stamped July 27 at two in the afternoon. "Oh, wow. I was just leaving then. I was already so late getting out of here that when I heard the phone ring, I decided to let the machine take it."

"What if you had answered it? Do you think it would have made any difference?"

Jim thought for a moment. "Nah. I would have gone on my bike trip anyway. I had a bet to win. And I learned something on this trip. Although Linda and I were strongly attracted to one another physically, we weren't really connected. She never did anything with me like singing or biking, and I guess I didn't listen to her very much. She wasn't into *Star Trek* or chess. We had sort of a common dream but little else in common. She'll always be someone I love in a way, but I could just never go back to her."

Sandy thought about this. It was clear from what had just happened that Jim was over Linda.

"You know," Jim said, "I'm getting hungry. I don't remember having lunch today, and it's getting near suppertime. What would you think if I ordered pizza?"

"I'd love some."

They talked it over and decided to order a medium pizza with pepperoni and ham. Jim called in the order.

Jim said, "I think I'll build a little fire in the fireplace. I know it's a warm day, but the atmosphere would be nice." In a few minutes, he had a small fire going. "This is the first time I've had a chance to use the fireplace."

The pizza man came to the door, and Jim paid him. Jim went into the kitchen and got some napkins and paper plates. "Would you like something to drink?"

"Diet Coke, if you have it."

Jim came out with the drinks and pizza and set them on the coffee table. "We need one more thing." He went back into the kitchen and brought out some candles, which he set in various places around the room and proceeded to light.

Sandy smiled and said, "So, we're being pretentious now?"

Jim laughed. "Sure. Now if I only had some roses. Actually, I don't think I'm being pretentious. I'd like to do this for the woman I marry someday. I'd go draw her a warm bubble bath and put flowers and candles around and let her soak. And when she got all done, she'd put on some sexy clothes."

Sandy was all ears. "Okay, what next? Keep going."

"Oh, well, isn't it obvious? We'd go get our bicycles and go for a ride."

Sandy laughed. "Silly me. I should've seen that coming."

Jim turned the radio on softly, and it was playing, "Climb every mountain, ford every stream, follow every rainbow, till you find your dream."

Sandy started humming along without thinking about it. Finally, she said, "I always liked this song—especially the follow every rainbow part."

"Of course." Jim wondered about Sandy. She was sort of like a rainbow to him with all her tattoos and the necklace. She was like his dream.

Just then, the phone rang. "Excuse me a moment," he said as he picked up the phone. "This is Jim."

"Oh good! I caught you home." Jim recognized Loretta's voice.

"Yes, I just got back today. Are you in town again?"

"No. I was calling about the offer I made you before you left two weeks ago. What do you say?"

"I was going to take you up on it, but now I'm not so sure. A lot has changed since then. Can I have a little more time?"

"Okay, but we need you. What's going on, anyway?"

"Actually, there were some things I wanted to talk with you about; some sports equipment I made myself. I was wondering if you would be interested in marketing it for me."

"I'll take a look at it. I can't promise you anything until I've seen it."

"Fair enough."

"One other thing. There's a woman I know who seems to be knowledgeable about clothes and just loves shoes. I think she could be a real asset to your company. Are you interested in interviewing her?"

"Is she a friend of yours?"

"Definitely. I'm sticking my neck out by asking for her, since I haven't had a chance to talk with her about it yet. I know I'd like to come out for the interview. Maybe she'd be willing to fly out with me. Can I call you back Monday? I did just get back from my vacation, and I could really use a couple of days to recuperate."

"All right. I expect to hear from you then."

"By the way, I know LA is in a different time zone. Is it still Friday there?"

"No, silly. We're not that far behind. Can't a girl work on Saturday if she wants?" She laughed.

Jim laughed too. "Talk to ya Monday then."

"Okay. See ya." Click.

"Uh, bye?"

He turned to Sandy. "One thing I like about my cousin Loretta from Los Angeles is that she doesn't waste time or words. Sorry about the interruption, though."

"Did you say you wanted to go there for an interview?" Sandy was alarmed. She'd just fallen in love with him, and now he was talking about leaving.

"A job interview. Yes. I was wondering if you'd like to come and interview with me. Didn't you tell me you'd like to live in California, that it's a great place to run and bike?"

"Yes. I'd love to live out there. Anything to avoid our nasty cold winters. Are you thinking about moving out there?"

"I am. Thinking that is. I've made up my mind to go for the interview anyway. There's no harm in that."

"Tell me about the job. What would I be interviewing for if I went with you?"

Jim shared with her what Loretta had told him earlier.

When he got all done, Sandy said, "I'll go with you. Like you said, there's no harm in interviewing."

After the pizza was all gone, Jim took the empty box out to the trash. When he got back, he asked, "Where's your church? And what time is the service? Would you like me to meet you there or at your apartment tomorrow?"

"It starts at ten, but pick me up at my apartment at nine thirty. That should give us enough time to get there. I'll show you the way then." She gave him the directions to her apartment. "I really should be going now," Sandy said. "I've got some catching up to do at home."

Jim walked her to the door and opened it for her. She turned and put her arms around him. "Thanks for the pizza and the good time. And just for the record, I do believe you about Christopher Cricket."

"Thanks for coming. And thanks for believing me about Chris. It's really better that couples say what's bothering them at the beginning, even at the risk of a little spat, than to keep it inside in the name of 'getting along' and then totally explode at a later time." They kissed, and Jim didn't want to let her go, she felt so soft and warm. Sandy didn't want to let him go; he felt big, strong, and safe. She felt loved. He felt accepted. The kiss seemed to last forever. They finally broke it, and Sandy went to her car and drove away.

Jim felt alone after she left. He got his silver shoe and held it for a minute, admiring the craftsmanship, the delicacy of work in this beautiful charm. It looked like it was handmade, not stamped out or molded like things were today. *It must be very old,* he thought. Tomorrow, he would show it to her. He remembered she was wearing a charm bracelet.

He went next door to see Dave, and they played a game of chess. While they were playing, Jim pumped him for information about Sandy. He had a lot of nice things to say about her, which wasn't surprising, since he'd set them up and also she was his niece.

$*$ $*$ $*$

When Sandy got home, she called her sister Judy.

"Hey," Judy said.

"Hey, yourself. I just wanted you to know I found out who Chris is. I even met him."

"Him?"

"Chris is short for Christopher, not Christine. I also checked with Uncle Dave about him. He's okay. Uncle Dave really likes him; in fact, he actually set us up, can you believe?" Sandy shared with her about the chess game.

When Sandy was all done, Judy seemed mollified and said, "Okay, but let's see him at church tomorrow, and what Mom and Dad say about him. A girl can't be too careful, you know."

"I know," she agreed, but her intuition told her she was into something good.

18
And I Love Her

When Jim woke early Sunday morning, the first thing he did was unwrap his silver shoe and hold it for a couple of minutes. He would offer it to her today. Maybe there was a place for it on her charm bracelet. All he could think of was Sandy. He had it bad. The title words to the Beatles' song "And I Love Her" and the tune that went with them kept going through his head. He was mind-singing again, a four-word song. Even when he was thinking of other things, those four words were playing in the background of his head. He'd never had it this bad with Linda. How could he have been engaged to her? In comparison to the love he felt for Sandy, with Linda, it was only like.

As he showered, he wondered how he could live life apart from Sandy. "And I Love Her." *I do love her,* he thought. *I really, really do.* He wasn't trying to convince himself. He was just trying to understand how he felt. It was hard for men to get in touch with their feelings sometimes, he knew. Before, when he had told her he loved her, on a scale of one to ten, it was an eight or nine. That day, it was a fourteen, at least. His heart was ready to burst. "And I Love Her."

"So you're thinking of proposing?" he asked himself. Chris was no longer around, but he could still hold conversations with himself.

"I suppose I've been thinking about it ever since I saw that music box in St. Ignace."

"But you don't know her very well. There must be a ton of things you don't know about her."

"True. But I got a very good recommendation from Dave, and he's known her a long time. Also, I think I've been with her enough myself to get some insight into her character, and I think it's good.

Besides, look how we connected. And I've heard married folks say that they still don't know everything about their spouse after years of marriage. I don't think I have to know everything, but I know a lot about her character and her personality. I believe I can trust her. I get along with her easily. She is easy for me to love. She appreciates and accepts me. And I love her."

"But she lives in a different city."

"One of us will have to move. I sure wouldn't mind quitting my job for her. She might have a better job than me anyway. Maybe we'll both go to LA."

"What about your chances in LA? What about your house? Where will you live?"

"Everything is negotiable. We'll talk about the wedding date and what we're going to do and make decisions later. We'll just have to work things out."

"What if she says no?"

"Yikes. It would kill me. Maybe I should wait until I'm more sure of her. I don't want to scare her off."

The arguments stopped. He continued to get ready for church. When he was all done, he was wearing his black pants and shoes with a white shirt and navy suit coat. He decided to wear a red tie with little American flags on it. He thought he looked rather patriotic in red, white, and blue. He took one last look at himself in the mirror and was satisfied he was ready. He put the silver stiletto in his back pocket.

About an hour later, he pulled up to Sandy's apartment in his black Ford Escort and walked to the door. It was nine thirty, right on time. He knocked, and Sandy invited him in. She had on a navy skirt and white blouse with a red silk scarf. A necklace with a rainbow pendant matched her earrings and her charm bracelet adorned her wrist. The silver stilettos on her feet made him think of the little shoe in his pocket.

"I see you got the memo," he said.

"Memo?"

"Yeah. The one that said today everyone was to wear red, white, and blue. You look fabulous! Patriotic even."

"Thank you. You look pretty spiffy yourself. Have a seat. I'll be ready in a couple of minutes."

Jim sat down on a two-cushion sofa in her small living room. He could see a small kitchen with a little table to eat on and a small vase on the table with a single yellow daisy in it. The apartment was small. There looked to be a small bathroom and one bedroom in the back. It looked clean and organized. The plastered walls were a light blue and the curtains a darker blue. In the window were some sun catchers. Rainbows, of course. There was a computer on a small table that also appeared to serve as a desk. He was tempted to go turn it on but resisted. In a moment, Sandy came out of the bedroom, softly closing the door. A fragrance came with her. "I love your perfume," he said.

"Thanks. It's my favorite. Tabu. Let's go." She held the door for him and locked up.

He held the car door for her while she got in. He got in and asked, "Where to?"

She directed him to Riverdale Baptist Church, a rather large church on Flushing Road on the west side of town. In a few minutes, they were there, and she directed him to a room of single adults for Sunday School. She was busy introducing him to everyone, and Jim, while happy to be there, was a little disappointed that he couldn't spend any quality time with her. He wanted to ask her about the bracelet. The lesson started, and they studied from the book of Ephesians, which said that salvation was free, not something you could earn. After the lesson, he was hoping to have a word with her, but no, she was busy introducing him to all her friends.

"This is Jim," she said. "He rode his bicycle up to the UP on a two-week trip and camped out in the woods alone at night. He's a really good biker, and he protected me from a big dog up there and fixed my chain for me when it broke. He also went to church with me in Paradise and trusted Christ there." She was beaming at him, as though he was some kind of hero. But Jim didn't think of himself as a hero. He was just being himself. *Anyone could do it,* he thought. *But then, why aren't there more people doing it?*

"Jim," she said. "I want you to meet my parents, Henry and Helen. We'll sit with them during the service this morning."

Henry was a little taller than Jim and had a shock of white hair. He was dressed in a good-looking dark-blue suit and had a nice tan and Sandy's dark-brown eyes. Sandy had told him he worked for Buick. He looked more like a manager than a line worker. "It's nice to meet you," Jim said. "I can see Sandy gets some of her good looks from you."

Helen was a third-grade teacher. She looked good in a red dress with a gold necklace and matching red shoes with a medium heel. She was a little shorter than Sandy and a little rounder. She had the same sweet melodic alto voice that Sandy had. Her hair was the same color as Sandy's and while not long was stylishly chic. A little twinkle in her eyes made her seem wise, and Jim liked her immediately.

"I love your dress," he said. "That red color is very cheerful."

"Thank you. We'd like you to come to our house after church for dinner," Helen said. "It would be so nice to have you. Both Sandy and her uncle Dave have said a lot of nice things about you. It was nice of you to look after Sandy while she was biking up north."

Jim accepted the invitation, and they all went to a pew and sat down just before the service started. It was a good service, and when the invitation was given at the end, a couple of people went forward. Jim thought of how he had done that himself only a week ago.

After the service, Jim and Sandy, in his little Escort, followed Henry and Helen in their Buick Riviera to their house, which was a couple of miles further west in the country. It was a modern house, white, with a two-car attached garage. Jim parked out front, and they went in. The house was clean and tastefully decorated. The living room was fairly large with a big sofa and a couple of recliner chairs. Jim sat down on the sofa, hoping that Sandy would sit next to him, and Henry sat in one of the recliners. Sandy and Helen went into the kitchen to get the food ready and set the table in the dining room. The TV was off, and Jim felt ill at ease.

Henry seemed to sense Jim's discomfort. "Tell me about the bike trip," he said. "Why did you decide to go?"

Jim told him about reading the story of King Arthur and his desire for adventure. As Henry asked more questions, Jim felt more at ease and eventually told him all about it, omitting Chris. So Jim said, "Sandy told me you work at Buick. What do you do there?"

Henry was telling about managing one of the departments when Helen called them to eat.

Jim and Henry went into the dining room and sat down. Sandy sat next to Jim on his right and Helen sat next to Henry on his left, so the two men were together and the two women were together. There were three lit candles in a beautiful glass candelabra. The dishes and silverware were elegant. The smell of roast beef and potatoes made Jim's stomach growl. Henry said grace, and soon, they were passing dishes and talking. Jim had a moderate portion, trying hard not to overeat. It was such a temptation.

Everyone was relaxed and happy, and it seemed a good time to ask about the bracelet. "That's a nice-looking bracelet, Sandy. You have some interesting charms on it."

"Thanks. Let me tell you about them. There's the rainbow. You know all about that by now. The star is me. My middle name is Star. My parents were sort of flower children of the era. Judy's middle name is Sun, hence the sun charm. Lisa's middle name is Moon, and that's this charm. The flame is my brother Bob—he's in the heating business—and the wind is Bill, who's in the cooling business. Actually, they're both in the heating and air-conditioning business together. This empty place is where I had a stiletto shoe charm, because I just love shoes, but I lost it. Then I have the running shoe because I like to run, and the bicycle because I like to bike, and the dolphin because I like to swim. There's the cross; I think that's obvious. That would be eleven charms if I had the shoe."

"You're getting quite a collection."

"I know. I didn't get any for my parents yet, and what if I have children someday? I'm thinking about getting a spaceship. That would be you, because of the dreams we both had and because I like *Star Trek*. There's just too many things I like; I could never get a charm for everything."

Golly, Jim thought, *I must be pretty important to her if she's thinking about putting a charm on for me.* The thought made him feel appreciated and accepted.

"You know, Sandy, I have a shoe charm for you if you'd like it."

Helen and Henry, who were having their own conversation, suddenly shut up and looked at him. Sandy said nothing. The silence was unnerving.

Yikes, he thought. *What did I do? Somebody say something.*

After a moment, Sandy said, "You've already given me thirty-two in the form of a chess set."

"I did, but I have another one. It's different. I think it's special. Would you like to see it? I mean, if you don't like it, you don't have to take it. I'm not pressuring you. I just thought you might like it."

Silence.

Jim didn't know what he said or what was going on. He decided to say nothing more and just wait. Sooner or later, someone would have to say something. He put his fork down and stared back at them. Both parents and his girlfriend, frozen in time, he thought. *What is this? The Twilight Zone?*

Finally, Sandy spoke. "May I see it?"

Jim reached into his back pocket and took out the silver shoe. He unwrapped it and gave it to her.

"That's the one I lost. Oh, thank you, Jim!" A tear of happiness ran down her cheek. She leaned over and kissed him.

Wow, he thought. *I wish I'd given it to her sooner.* The smell of Tabu was driving him crazy. Sandy's charms, or was it charm, was overpowering. Finally, he said, "If you get me some pliers, I'll reattach it."

Henry said, "I'll get some." He got up and left.

Sandy said, "I need to get something, too." She left.

Helen said, "The silver shoe charm has been in my family for many years, maybe centuries. No one knows who made it or when. But when I lost the charm, Henry found it and brought it to me. Later, we were married."

"That's quite a coincidence."

"Maybe not. Before I had the charm, my mother had it. She lost the charm once, and a guy brought it back to her. She became his wife. And my mother told me the same thing happened to her mother, and that it's been happening in the family like that for generations, as it was handed down from mother to daughter."

"So you're saying it's magic? The charm is, uh, charmed?"

"I don't know anything about magic. I'm just telling you facts as I know them."

Jim thought about that.

Henry came back with the pliers and handed them to Jim. Sandy came back, sat down, and stuck her wrist out so he could attach it. Jim attached it and said, "There you are."

Jim thought about how when he found the charm, the image of Sandy came to mind before he had even met her. He remembered how every time he held it, he felt happy, and how he often thought of Sandy. Finally, he said, "So the charm seems to bring two people together. Does it keep them together?"

"No," Helen answered. "That takes work, compromise, and relationship skills. I've heard there was a divorce or two and maybe even a murder in my family history. Henry and I believe that the two people it brings together are right for one another so there is an excellent chance the marriage will work. But there are no guarantees."

Jim looked at Sandy's parents and asked, "I know you don't know me very well, and I don't want to put you on the spot, but how would you feel if I married Sandy? I mean, just theoretically?"

Helen and Henry looked at each other, as if communicating through eye contact alone. Finally, Helen spoke. "I liked you when I first met you in church this morning. Dave and Sandy have had nothing but nice things to say about you. If anything, I like you even better after having dinner with you. If Sandy loves you and wants to marry you, I have no objections." She looked at Henry.

"I agree with my wife. She has always had good sense."

Wow, Jim thought. *Wow!* What could he say? He looked at Sandy. Would she say no?

Sandy opened her hand. In it was a spaceship charm. He understood. She wanted him to put the charm on her bracelet, but he would have to ask first.

He thought for a moment and said, "Sandy, remember how I said you were like the little tan puppy dog I had, easy to love? And I said you were one I'd like to live with for the rest of my life? I really do love you. You know that." Jim knelt down before her. "I don't have a ring to offer you, but if you say yes, I'll take you shopping and buy you one right now or whenever you're ready. Will you marry me?"

Sandy whispered, "Yes. Please." She looked at her hand. "Put this charm on my bracelet. Be the captain of my—make that of *our*—spaceship."

Jim attached it, and then they got up, hugged one another, and kissed. Jim looked over and saw Helen and Henry hugging and kissing also.

When they sat back down again, Sandy asked, "Where did you find it? I have no idea where I lost it."

"In the grass by the sidewalk in front of my house. I found it the day I left for my vacation and have been carrying it with me ever since. It looked too valuable to throw away, and I always sensed it was somehow connected to you. I just didn't know how."

"The day before you left, I was at Dave's house. I brought him some chocolate-chip cookies. So that's when I must have lost it."

"So you're the one who made those cookies that Dave gave me to take on my trip. They were good!"

"Thanks." Sandy smiled.

Helen asked, "You two lovebirds want ice cream for dessert?"

Jim said, "I think our engagement calls for some sort of celebration. May we eat it in the living room?"

"Sure," Helen said.

Sandy said, "But we just want one dish and spoon. We're going to share."

"Okay," Helen said. "Here you go."

Jim and Sandy went into the living room and sat on the sofa together. Then Sandy scooted up tight next to Jim, and they took turns feeding one another.

Before they were done, Dave walked in. "Congratulations, you two," he said. "I just heard the news."

"Thank you," they said together.

"What brings you here?" Jim asked.

"Henry invited me over for ice cream earlier today. I ate mine in the kitchen with him and Helen. I have to go now. See ya later."

"But you just got here. Where are you going?"

"Well, as someone once told me, there are two rules you need to know to be successful in life, and the first one is 'Don't tell people everything you know.'" Dave opened the door and left.

"What was that all about?" Sandy asked.

"It's a joke. I told it to Dave about a month ago, and now he's getting even."

"So what is the second thing?" She grinned.

"I don't know. No one ever told me." Too late, Jim saw that Sandy was teasing him. "Oh you … you … come here and tease me."

She got up, sat back down across his lap, and put her arms around his neck. "Tell me more."

Jim explained, "I told him that joke back when we made the bet. What I didn't tell him was that I was taking my vacation by bicycle. That was the only way I could do it so cheaply and win the bet. He thought I was taking the car. Later when he found out, he was worried about me." He kissed her and continued, "You know, the really funny thing is—the joke is true. What if you had told me what you were up to when we first met? What if Dave had told me about you before I left? I guess we all have things we don't or shouldn't tell."

"Right, but what do you think he's not telling us now?"

"Heaven knows. But did I ever tell you I love you?" he asked.

"Never," she teased. "Tell me. And then tell me again and again and again. Don't ever stop telling me."

"I love you," Jim said. "Do you think the silver shoe is really charmed? I have a hard time believing in magic. Besides, Dave is the one who set us up; he started doing that before I even found the shoe. Perhaps some of it is just coincidence. God probably had His hand in it, don't you think?"

"Magic is what we use to describe things we don't understand or can't explain. What makes you think science knows everything? There was a time when science didn't know about electricity or radio waves or gamma radiation. Once science didn't know about relativity or subatomic particles or even DNA. I think there is probably a scientific explanation for the effects of the silver shoe, but we just haven't discovered that knowledge yet. Besides, isn't falling in love itself sort of magical? Perhaps this was all from God, so He could bring you to Himself through Jesus Christ."

"After that sermon in Paradise, I don't think I'm going to try to second-guess God. I suppose He doesn't tell people everything He knows either. No wonder He's so successful."

"That's right, Jim. When the Bible talks about the wisdom of God, it says in Corinthians 2:8, 'Which none of the princes of this world knew: for had they known it, they would not have crucified the Lord of glory,' and if they hadn't crucified Him—"

"None of us would have had our sins forgiven," Jim interrupted. "It's like the song says, 'Love Found a Way.'"

"And our love has just begun," Sandy said. "But our problems are not over. One thing I've learned is that as we grow older, we just keep changing problems. Our problems are never truly over on this side of heaven. And we still have a lot of decisions to make."

"So what are we going to do, sell or keep the house? Live in Lansing, Flint, or Los Angeles? Any ideas about our wedding date?"

"We'll just take it one day at a time. But we can discuss possibilities," she said.

"Are you going to take my name or keep your own?"

"Take yours. Definitely. If one of our brothers or sisters has children, do you think I want to be known as Aunt Hill? Yech. It's bad enough being called Dune."

Jim laughed. "Good point."

"You know what? I've got something for you. I'll be right back." She got off his lap and went to her old bedroom, where she still had a few things she hadn't taken to her apartment yet. She came back with a small silver decal that was striated so that it changed colors depending upon the angle it was viewed at. The decal said, "Enterprise." "King gave this to me a while back, and I just never made use of it. When you get home, I want you to put this on your bicycle, which, in effect, was your starship for the last two weeks. You deserve it!"

"Wow! I was trying to come up with a name for my bike the very first day of the trip, but nothing sounded right, and I gave up. Now you've gone and done it for me. What a great idea. Thanks. And it even changes colors, like a rainbow. It's so like you!"

She sat back down on his lap, and they spent the rest of the evening hugging, discussing future possibilities, and kissing. "And I Love Her" was still running through Jim's mind.